Advanced Praise *for* Rov

G000166159

"Bittersweet, engrossing, richly textured ar harrowing but incredibly rewarding read."

—S. Bear Bergman
The Nearest Exit May Be Behind You • *Butch is a Noun*

"Remember that time in your life when you had just escaped the terror of childhood to create your own path in the world, maybe a queer path of chosen family, desire and love and lust and intimacy on your own terms, remember all the joyful pains and painful joys you were discovering? Roving Pack nails that bold and precarious time with a precision so rare it's almost claustrophobic in its intimacy. It's about a specific culture and place and moment – transmasculine queer punk kids in Portland in the early-2000s – but it's also about the transition to self-actualization in all of our lives, and the scary and heartbreaking reality that often the pack mentality required for belonging in our new communities leaves us stranded. I'm not sure that I've ever seen a book that explores the intoxication and viciousness of peer pressure in queer lives with such candor. Goddamn this book is brave — I can't wait to see the havoc it wreaks."

—Mattilda Bernstein Sycamore
Why Are Faggots So Afraid of Faggots? • *That's Revolting!* • *Nobody Passes*

"Sassafras Lowrey is so much more than one or the other anything. Ze is for sure a vital voice of hir generation, expressing as ze does, many mutually exclusive points of view on politically and emotionally live wire subjects. So, much to my delight, I find hir work filled with mischief, mayhem, and multiple meanings."

—Kate Bornstein
My Gender Workbook • *101 Alternatives To Suicide for Teens Freaks and Other Outlaws* • *Gender Outlaws: The Next Generation*

"Fucking A. Sassafras Lowrey takes 'queer punk' to a whole new level of insidious drama. Roving Pack cracks out the microscope to examine this Portland-based scene circa 2002 – whether or not the rest of the world can take it. My guess? Hella no!"

—Kristyn Dunnion
The Dirt Chronicles • *Mosh Pit*

"Roving Pack is a rough and tumble, tender-hearted novel that grips you in its teeth and won't let go. A satisfying debut by a writer to watch."

—Zoe Whittall
Holding Still For As Long As Possible • *Bottle Rocket Hearts*

Roving Pack
Sassafras Lowrey

Published in 2012 by PoMo Freakshow Press
Brooklyn, New York, USA

www.PoMoFreakshow.com

Printed in the United States of America

ISBN: 978-0-9857009-0-4

Cover Design: KD Diamond

Editing: Toni Amato

Copy Editing: Gabrielle Harbowy

Book Design: Red Durkin

To the ghosts of who we were, may our worlds never be forgotten. In memory of those we lost, and for the future of queer punks as you create your homes and families.

Packs are formed with raised hackles, gnawing teeth, and pricked ears...

~~Granddaughter~~ ~~Natalie~~ ~~Skyler~~ Zander ~~Nate~~ Click
Birthday: May 16, 1984

~~3258 St. Jude St. Clackamas, Oregon~~
~~c/o Cindi 123523 rural road 5 Oregon City, Oregon~~
~~c/o Frank 1345 highway 8 Molalla, Oregon~~
~~2344 9th ave, basement SE Portland, Oregon~~
~~c/o James 2345 Heart St. Jacksonville, Florida~~
~~974 apt 60 35th ave Jacksonville, Florida~~
~~c/o Mrs. Jann 2345 Beach Drive Jacksonville Flaa~~
~~c/o Buck 1469 apt 5 NW Portland, Oregon~~
133 Hawthorne Blvd Apt 3 Portland, Oregon

Date: September 5, 2002

I can't believe I'm back here. Buck rode the max train to meet me at the airport this morning. It's weird to think that last night I was down south. James drove me around one last time past the barn where hys sister's horses are boarded. We parked on a dirt road and I thought hy was going to lean over the center console in his mamma's car and fuck me like hy used to, but instead hy just said hy would miss me. I had to pull really hard on the barbell in my tongue to keep from crying. I think that was the nicest thing hy had said to me in a while.

It was already after midnight when we got back to hys mamma's place and I had to be at the airport at five this morning. I thought hy was just heading to the bathroom before coming to bed with me, but then I heard the front door close and the car engine start. My last damn night in the south, and hy couldn't be bothered to stay away from that stupid femme. Hy didn't get back until right when it was time to leave. I was sitting out on the front steps waiting and trying to figure out how much it would cost to get a cab if hy didn't show up pretty soon.

Hy didn't even get out of the car, just popped the trunk so I could get my luggage out. Getting through security was a damn hassle. I didn't have suitcases or anything and didn't have the money to buy any, which was how I got the bright idea to use these giant Tupperware tubs. I shoved everything I was bringing back to Portland inside, wrapped them with duct tape and then wrote my name and Buck's address in permanent marker. I guess the airline security thought all this looked pretty suspicious. They slit open the tape with box cutters, and reached in. The first tub was just my dirty laundry. The second tub had the plastic plates, cups and bowls and the rubber ducky shower curtain James and I had got together. Then the security guard had my cock in his hand. I didn't know what to say. He got all red and flustered and waved me through to the ticket counter. I set off the metal detector with the damn safety pins I've been using to hold my bandage binder together.

Once I found my gate I shoved the boarding pass into my backpack and headed to the nearest bathroom. I almost just walked right into the men's bathroom but then I saw another security guard looking at me. In Portland you have a right to be anywhere that corresponds to your gender identity, but it ain't that way down south. James and I would always have fun getting into trouble over that, freaking out old dudes, picking fights with hicks and arguing with security guards, but this morning I was alone. I locked myself in a stall in the women's bathroom for a while. I'd planned on just taking a piss but then I started crying. I punched the Formica that separated the stalls. I was trying to calm myself down, but nothing helped. I didn't come out of the bathroom until I heard the announcement that my flight was boarding over the loudspeaker. Thankfully nobody sat next to me. I stretched out, but couldn't sleep. The transfer in Atlanta was uneventful, and again I had the whole row to myself for the five-hour flight.

Buck was at the airport just like he said he would be. I was pulling the Tupperware tubs off the baggage claim when I saw his little red head weaving through the crowd. He was just as cute as I remembered. Seriously, if we weren't family I'd have been all over him. He stood there in his boots, ripped up jeans, thermal shirt and hoodie, but when he saw me he started jogging over through the crowd. His ears were bigger than they were before I left. The stupid restaurant he worked at had this rule in the dress code that you couldn't wear earrings bigger than a quarter. It had been written a million years ago to keep ladies from wearing crazy dangly shit, but Buck used it to keep them from firing him over stretching his ears real big. Right then he was working on getting them to the right size where he could actually wear quarters in his ears just to piss off this stuck up manager he had. Buck helped me carry the big tubs out of the airport and onto the train back to his place.

Date: September 6, 2002

I can't believe it's over. Three months ago I got a scholarship to go with QYRC, the Queer Youth Resource Center, to this big national queer youth conference in DC and had no idea that I was going to meet someone worth running away for. I'd never even dated anyone before. James and I met the first night I was wandering around the lobby, pretending like I was looking for someone I knew. Hy swaggered up to me, dark blue jeans sagged low around his hips held in place with a

thick black leather belt, a clean white
t-shirt tucked in. Hy was really little,
not even five feet tall, and the cuffs of
hys jeans were rolled to show the gouges
in the toes of hys black boots. James
was sharing a hotel room with hys wife,
this weird fat activist high femme, but
I had my own room and we were inseparable
the whole conference! James is seriously
the hottest butch I've ever met. I was
leading a workshop about incorporating
queer youth into nonprofits, and hy was
running some leather programming. We went
to every workshop session together, and
I kneeled on the floor right at his feet
on that ugly hotel carpet.

James collared me that first weekend, not
for play but for keeps, right before
hy had to leave for the airport. I was
crying so hard. That night I wandered up
to Union Station, which wasn't too far
from the hotel. I ate in the food court,
and then went and bought train tickets.
Nothing was keeping me here in Portland.
When I called Buck three months ago and
told him I'd moved to the South instead
of getting on the plane back to Portland
he'd been so mad and worried. James and
I were crashing at hys mom's house since
once I got there hy obviously couldn't

stay with hys wife. Buck had been pissed
I up and ran off, but he's been collared
before too, and he knew how important it
was to me to have this. It scared James
a lot. Hy'd never dated another butch,
thought that was crazy shit we do out
here in the West.

We caught a lot of flack from the folks at
his queer youth center who thought it was
hella unnatural for us to be together.
I always say that James saved me, but
that's not quite right. James made me. Hy
bought me my first binder, a thick elastic
back brace from the drugstore, took me
to get my first cock. James was the first
person to tie me up, beat me, and hold me
while I cried. James taught me how to be
a good boy for Daddy.

I guess I'm an orphan now.

Date: September 7, 2002

Buck had to work first thing this morning.
It's so weird to be back. I'm just glad
that I can crash with him. I don't know
where I'd be without my brother. Anyway,
Buck had to work so I decided to stay
here at his place. I wasn't much in the
mood to wander downtown all day, I'm

not really ready to go to QYRC yet even though it's pretty much the best place in the whole world. Gus is the main staff person but pretty much the place is youth run, and it's mostly all punk kids that created the space so bike tires hang from the ceiling and there is dumpstered furniture, and spray paint all over the walls. Before I went to be with James, QYRC was my home, and I'm nervous about going back. I mean, I had been invited to join the steering committee, which is the group of youth that make all the important decisions about what the space looks like and how it runs. I was supposed to get to be part of that! But, then I became James' boy. I didn't have the guts to call QYRC myself to say I wasn't coming back from the conference they paid to send me to. I just let my brother tell them.

I did all the dishes stacked on the counter. The kitchen sink doesn't work so I had to carry everything to the bathtub. I couldn't find a towel so I used one of my clean undershirts to dry everything. Until I get my own place I'm on the couch but I don't think Buck's girlfriend likes me much so I'm trying to get on her good side. Last night I heard them arguing. I couldn't hear what she said, but I'm sure it was about me. I heard Buck whisper, "We're family," and then it got quiet. I thought doing the dishes and stuff might help.

Buck lives in this old apartment building in NW. I've never really spent much time up in this neighborhood. None of the punk houses are here anymore since everyone got kicked out of the warehouse squats about five years ago. Gus from QYRC sometimes talks about what it was like back then. Now the neighborhood is filling up with galleries and condos. Buck lives here because his girlfriend has had this apartment forever. It's a pretty good place other than the sink, and how the electricity in the hallways is all busted. At night if you don't have a flashlight you can't see shit, but their place is only on the second floor so it's not too bad. My favorite part of the apartment is the huge purple unicorn painted onto the living room wall. It's right across from the couch so it's also kind creepy to wake up to.

Date: September 8, 2002

I've been needing a new name for a while now. As James' boy, I was Zander. He gave me the name right when I moved down there. Getting back to Portland I switched to Nate, mostly to have something different to use so I wouldn't think about James every time someone asked what my name was now. I don't really like Nate. I went with it because it reminds me a little of my birth name, which is both good and bad. I like it because it seems on the more masculine side of gender-neutral. The problem is that I didn't realize that Nate was short for Nathan, and once someone pointed that out, it messed up all my thoughts of genderqueerness. I've been trying to come up with a new name, a good one that I can keep for a while. Tonight Buck's girlfriend was out so we decided to have some brother time, and figure out what my new name is going to be. I wanted to be sure to have it settled before going back to QYRC tomorrow night for the first time. I mean, everyone changes their name all the time, but I want a fresh start for when I go back.

I'd been thinking of names all day while Buck was at work and came up with something. He said that he'd been thinking of names too, but hadn't been able to come with anything that seemed really right for his little brother, and he was really curious to see what I'd come up with. I was nervous so Buck had to drag the name out of me. I was worried that he'd think it was too unusual even for a boy like me. I started talking about dogs, my dogs, in more detail than I've ever given anyone. Growing up, dogs were kinda the only things that mattered to me. They were my best friends, and the only family I trusted. It sounds hella dorky, but I used to actually compete in dog sports. That stuff where dogs run over obstacles and everything. It was the only thing that kept me from going crazy all through high school.

My mom was really fucked up. I pretty much never was allowed to do anything without her, except for when I was at dog trials. When she hit me the last time and it was so bad I had to go to the cops, I even took my dogs with me and went to live with my dog agility coach. My grandma wanted me, but she's just been a spy for my mom forever so I knew I couldn't do

that. I was out before I went to live
with my coach, but I had to go back in
the closet when we went to stay with her.

She's totally a dyke, I fucking know she
is, but she's so homophobic she'd never
ever admit it. Anyway, four months later
she read my journal and BOOM! I was on
my own. She didn't even have the balls
to tell me to my face. She called the
office at my high school and had them
page me over the intercom. When I got
there she said she'd decided it was best
if I didn't come back to her place, and
said I had forty-eight hours to find a
home for my dogs. She kept my youngest
dog, Flash, because she thought he'd be a
national star if he kept competing, and
my older dog, Roo, went to my grandma's
house because she liked him.

It's almost harder having Roo be so close.
Grandma's always calling me or asking to
see me, but it's not real. It's a setup
to get me and my birth mom in a room so
she can try to get me back under her
control. Like last Christmas, Grandma
kept talking about how she was going to
invite me over and how it would be a
good holiday, and then on Christmas Eve
she let slip that my mom was going to be

there. I told her there was a restraining order and my birth mother couldn't come close to me. Grandma said that she didn't give a damn about a restraining order and that no law could control family. I was so upset I didn't talk to her for about two months. I can't trust my grandma, but at least I know she'll take care of Roo.

Buck told me if I changed my name to either Roo or Flash he'd beat me in ways I wouldn't enjoy. I started laughing really hard and told him that I definitely wasn't thinking about either of those names. I was a little worried that he'd think the name I wanted was even weirder, though. Buck doesn't really know anything about dogs or dog training so I started telling him about positive reinforcement and about the way you can shape an animal's behavior through rewarding positive behavior and that there's this cool method for doing it called clicker training where you have this little plastic box with a metal strip inside that makes a clicking sound when you press it. Essentially it's a signal to the dog or whatever animal you're working with that they have done something good. You use a metal box that makes a clicking sound when you press it and then at the same time you offer a treat.

```
I told Buck that I wanted a name that
every time it was spoken would honor the
canine pack that I lost, and would also
be this subtle leather thing about how
I'm looking for someone to take me down
and train me and keep me. I told him that
I thought my new name was "Click."

I still thought Buck was going to make
fun of me, but he didn't at all. He said
that Click was the perfect name for me.
```

Date: September 9, 2002
Security: Friends
Subject: <3

I was nervous about coming back to QYRC tonight. I mean word travels fast so I knew everyone already knew shit with James didn't go well and I was back in town and crashing with Buck. I'd told him back then to tell them all that I wasn't going to come back to QYRC ever, because I moved away to have this awesome Daddy. Now, here I am, a failed boy.

I was so anxious about seeing people but I shouldn't have been. Everyone was so nice to me. I told them right away that Click was my new name and wrote it on the big white board that lives in the kitchen. It has three separate columns "old name" "new name" and "pronoun." Folks are good about checking it every day so we know what's going on with folks. I wanted to make sure Click was on the board so folks wouldn't get confused, and so that people would know I was back.

Gus gave me a big hug as soon as I walked in the door. I think that Buck had been talking to them about everything going on with me. They asked if I wanted to get the first haircut of the night and I said yes. They are my favorite staff person ever. It gave me a little bit of time just to sit and look at everything going on, and meant that my poor overgrown mohawk is back in shape. Gus is so hot. They were flagging red, left out of these old work pants rolled up into shorts and skater shoes and binding completely flat under a t-shirt from a concert like ten years ago. Gus uses "they" pronouns. They have this really sexy stringy androgynous hair and are always wearing cool old faded t-shirts from queer Europe punk bands (Gus grew up in London). Gus has such a sexy accent and their arms are covered in tattoos of bike parts. They aren't like other adults, I mean they are barely a grownup, but they don't say stupid shit. I know it sounds dumb, but I want to be just like them someday, and if they weren't staff I would seriously try to bone them.

Billy and Grace came up to me right when Gus was done with me and took me over to the couch next to the pool table. Billy settled in on the floor at her feet and Grace pulled me next to her and told me that there were lots of other Daddy's in the world and that someday I'd find one who would really take care of me. Then, Sean ran in from the smoking area and pounced on me! He's my favorite fag ever!

Oh, and I'm still using gender-neutral pronouns ze/hir.

Date: September 10, 2002

It was good to see that the GSA kids haven't taken over while I was away. QYRC doesn't even really have that many GSA kids, and the ones that do come mostly stick to themselves and street punks do the same. Sometimes the volunteers try to get us to include them in decisions about the space, but they don't push that too hard. After all, for the GSA kids, QYRC is just a place to hang out, and for us it's home. I'm not really a street punk but, close enough.

The GSA kids never have enough respect for anything important. Their parents always drive them to and from QYRC so they don't have to take the bus. They show up with these big steaming takeout boxes with noodles and tofu. The rest of us are usually in the kitchen eating store brand mac & cheese that someone donated. Ok, to be honest, all my friends are the ones eating it. The GSA kids mostly don't have much respect for the space. They come and make a mess and fucking leave it like their mother is here and is gonna follow them around cleaning up like I guess she does at home. The rest of us don't have mothers, so we know we have to clean up our own shit. They are just pretty useless, and not very political. They come to hang out and dance and always want to play pool with us but the pool table is our turf so when they come over we just finish the game and go outside to smoke. Ok, I don't smoke obviously, but I always go out with everyone else.

Date: September 12, 2002

Buck and his girlfriend were both out this afternoon and I was hella lonely. I went out this morning and put in job applications for a bunch of places, bookshops and grocery stores mostly, but also this new dog spa that just opened not too far from QYRC. Hopefully someone will get back to me soon. Buck's girlfriend works both her jobs today, but came and let me in after getting off from the bookstore and before heading to the bar. Buck won't be home until late and I've been keeping everything clean so really there's been nothing to do all day. Finally, I decided to call this dyke named Kristin I'm sorta friends with to see if she wanted to come over and keep me company.

I called QYRC, and luckily Gus was around the office to give me Kristin's phone number. I got all nervous before I called her and dragged the phone around the kitchen door and sat in the middle of the living room floor because the cord doesn't reach all the way to the couch. Kristin's older like twenty-two or something and has been dating Saucer whose a street punk junkie whose been around QYRC a long time. Kristin's girlfriend Saucer is in jail for a parole violation and is way old, like twenty-four. After this year she won't even be able to come to QYRC anymore.

Saucer's been on the streets since she was little, twelve or some shit. I don't know what happened with her family, that's not the kinda shit you ask someone and it's not exactly like we're all that close. Mostly she sleeps in Paranoia Park with the het punks. I know she fights a lot too. I think it's mostly to protect folks like her street sister, Hope, who catches a lot of shit from the skinheads.

Saucer always keeps her hair dyed black, and she's covered in tattoos, even her face and hands. It's mostly all stick and poke stuff-she's got a bunch of ex-girlfriends names up and down her arms separated by track marks, lots of stars, some cartoon characters and XXX from when she was really young.

I think Saucer is hot. If she weren't with Kristin I'd totally try to get with her. She and Kristin have been together a while now, kinda a weird couple but what do I know. Kristin says Saucer had told her she could fuck whoever she wanted while Saucer was locked up. It was going to be at least a couple of weeks, and she'd planned on getting some action from her cellmate. Kristin is sorta this grungy butch, and not really all that hot but still, cute enough.

She picked up after a couple rings, and seemed surprised it was me calling, but remembered who I was. I told her I was crashing at my brother's place and that it would be great to see her. She said she had to stop by her work later, but if I wanted she could come visit me first. I had the place to myself so I gave her the address and waited.

The apartment door locks automatically when it closes so when Kristin buzzed the door I had to prop it open with a phone book to run downstairs and let her into the building. She walked around the apartment for a while, looking at Buck's girlfriend's paintings. They are mostly half-finished images of babies sinking into fire, stuff like that. She said it was really good. I came up behind her while she was looking closely at one of the paintings and started to play with the short hairs at the base of her neck. She was wearing an a-shirt with some ratty jeans and I could see all the muscles in her back ripple when I touched her. She turned around and pushed me up against the wall with the purple unicorn and started kissing me hard. I wanted to actually fuck her, but I started getting worried that Buck was gonna get back, and I'm not supposed to have folks over without them knowing so I told Kristin she should probably go. She was all hot and bothered and started whining because I wasn't going to fuck her. I twisted her nipple hard as I kissed her one last time at the door. I don't know what I'm doing with her. It's probably not the best decision I've ever made. She hangs around all the gutter punks but goes home every night to her damn parents in the suburbs.

Date: September 13, 2002
Security: Private
Subject: @ QYRC

Came to QYRC to give Buck and his girlfriend some private time. Their bedroom is really just a dining room with only a painting drop cloth hung with tacks to separate my couch from their bed. It's been a little awkward because I mean my brother has to fuck like two feet from me, and it's not like they aren't getting it on or anything. I really don't want to overstay my welcome.

Date: September 14, 2002
Security: Public
Subject: work

I had to work today. I got that stupid job at the dog wash near QYRC. Today was my first day. At the interview the owner who is this total dyke but then talked a lot about her husband made the work sound very complicated. It seems like most of the time all I'll be doing there is folding towels and filling shampoo bottles while I'm waiting for people to come in and wash their dogs. All day I was really bored. I don't understand why people are so against getting their bathtubs dirty and actually pay money to go wash their own dogs. The owner was at the shop all day training me (because filling shampoo bottles is so difficult). She said after a few months if I'm trustworthy enough maybe I'll get a key and can work on my own.

Date: September 16, 2002

I had a nightmare about James last night. The whole dream was just reliving a bunch of our fights, like the last big one where hy told me how I was ugly and a bad boy and no one would ever want me. It pissed me off. I lied and said there were lots of folks in Portland who wanted to fuck me. Hy told me I was full of shit, because I'd told him all about QYRC and my friends and hy knew that hy was my first Daddy. We'd been standing in his mamma's kitchen waiting for some grilled cheese to finish cooking. I remember trying to think of anyone who I hadn't told hym too much about so I could pretend they had the hots for me. The first person I thought of was Kristin. We would say "hi" to each other at QYRC before I went down south, but we'd never hung out or anything. I told James that when I got back to PDX we were going to hook up.

Kristin is really in love with Saucer and is convinced if Saucer could stay clean and finish the gang tattoo removal program, they can get away from all the drama and drugs and get a place together up in the Vancouver suburb. I can't believe I'm helping her cheat on someone she cares about. When I told James that Kristin was going to be the next person I fucked I figured that she would have broken up with Saucer by the time I got back to Portland. But she hadn't. Hy told me that I was full of shit thinking I had someone who wanted to fuck me waiting. Guess I proved hym wrong! I think I'm just as bad as James.

Date: September 17, 2002
Security: Private
Subject: Family

I agreed at the last minute to do a QYRC organized community education training. Basically it's a bunch of us who go into schools or jails or offices and tell folks about what it's like to be young and queer. We do some activities to teach folks basic 101 kinda stuff, but mostly we just answer fucked up questions in order to show these people how to not be assholes. I get asked to do them a lot because the staff say my story "helps people to understand how homophobia is still working in our culture." I don't know about all that, I just know it makes all these people cry. I wasn't supposed to be doing this one, but I got a call at the dog wash from QYRC telling me that a bunch of folks were sick and couldn't make it. They knew I was at work but said if there was any way I could do the workshop, it would mean a lot to them. I told my boss I was sick and hopped on the bus.

I should have stayed at work, but it's hard to say no to the QYRC staff. I mean they always say that I don't have to do everything they ask of me, but I really want to. I took the bus to QYRC where I had to wait like twenty minutes to get picked up in the vagina mobile. It's a big pink van that belongs to this dyke who volunteers in the community education program. She used to live in it when she was up in Alaska, but here in Portland she mostly lives in some big house in South East with a bunch of other artists, but I guess it's not a punk house. The van is really really pink, and last year when she drove to Mich Fest a whole group of lesbians painted a big clit onto the hood as part of some sacred women's ritual. Now she lets QYRC use it to get us to different trainings. I'm always embarrassed every time I have to get into it, because it just doesn't work with my gender.

Usually there are four or five of us that lead trainings so that we can take turns with the different activities, but when everyone called out sick it was just me and Buck. He wore these dark blue work pants and a thermal shirt and looked so hot. I hadn't known I was doing the training so I was wearing a dirty undershirt and my overalls. We got stuck in bunches of traffic getting over the interstate bridge and didn't get to the school until five minutes before the training was supposed to start. Buck and I had to promise the volunteer we wouldn't tell QYRC staff how we were almost late. The training room didn't have any windows. Old plastic chairs were set up for us at the front of the room. Everyone who came for the training was already sitting down. There were probably thirty or forty folks. They looked bored. Buck and I sat down while the volunteer quieted the room and started giving an introduction about who we are and what QYRC is. Everyone stared at me. I mean we were sitting in the front of the room so of course folks would be looking, but this was different. Folks were doing that "what the hell are you" sort of stare. I don't have much patience for that, and started staring back at people one by one until they looked away.

We opened with this definitions game where they had to work together to match words like sexual orientation, drag king/ queen, transsexual, transgender, genderqueer with little cards that have definitions on them. For a bunch of social work students, these people were pretty fucking dumb. They also were super uncomfortable with everything and kept trying to get out of participating. After definitions, Buck led the Gender Gummy activity. Pretty much that's all about helping these folks to realize that gender is complicated, and that no one has perfect gender. If you're facilitating you have to start by drawing a big gummy bear on poster paper. Then you draw four lines across the gummy bear and label them: Assigned sex, gender identity, gender presentation, attraction and label one side of the paper male/masculine and the other female/feminine. The activity is supposed to show people that there is a spectrum and that the different spectrums aren't connected to each other. You could be assigned male but identify as female and dress in clothes that make people think you're a boy, or you could be trans and identify as straight, that last one always confuses people at trainings. After drawing the poster Buck defined everything like how assigned sex is what the doctors said when you were born, gender identity is how you feel inside, gender presentation is what other folks think about your gender, and orientation is obviously about who you like.

To get things started everyone who's presenting has to go up and plot themselves on the Gender Gummy so that the folks we're teaching get an idea. You have to put a dot on each of the four lines for where on the spectrum you are today. It's important to try to help the group understand that this stuff can change all the time and that where we plot our gender today might not be where our gender is tomorrow. For mine I tell folks, when I was born, the doctor said "it's a girl!" so I put a dot all the way over on the female side. For the gender identity line I say that I'm not so sure that doctor was right and put a dot right in the middle of the spectrum between male and female. I don't wear any girls' clothes so for gender presentation I put my dot all the way on the male side. Orientation is a little tricker to plot for audiences like this. I always put my dot all the way over female side because I'm completely queer and I want these people to know that, but it also makes me look like I'm into girls which obviously isn't true, there just isn't time to try to get them to really understand complicated gender.

Buck did a great job facilitating, but some dude in the back got all pissed off. He tried to mess with Buck, asking all kinds of fucked up questions like if he was really a boy, and if he had a dick. Buck fielded the questions pretty well on his own, but I was pissed! I wanted to cuss the fucker out, but we're not supposed to do that. Buck started ignoring the guy, so he grabbed his coat and left. He let the door slam really loudly. Shit like this happens a lot, so I try to not let it bother me.

The last thing we do is storytelling. Pretty much it's just all us youth telling our coming out stories. We're supposed to explain how our parents reacted, what our schools did, where we found support, how we identify, and what our lives look like now. As usual, I started talking about being kicked out and how I was on my own and shit. I had to remember to slow down and add in a bunch of details. I can tell this story pretty fast by now. Basically it goes, "Hi, my name is Click. Growing up, I didn't know my dad, my mom was an alcoholic, my stepfather was very abusive. Everything got really bad when I came out as a lesbian. My mom beat me up really badly and I had to file charges with the police. Then I went to live with some adult friends, they read my journal and found out I was gay and kicked me out." I know it's sad or whatever, but really most of the time I'm just so damn happy to have escaped. It's not like I spend a bunch of time crying about the parents I don't have anymore, even if folks think I should.

Date: September 20, 2002
Security: Friends
Subject: Need a place to crash?

Got an apartment! Have the keys and everything! Buck has been so good to let me crash with him all this time, but now that I got the job, it's time I get out on my own again.

Before I moved to the South I had that little basement room I lived in for my senior year. That place was nuts. This witchy hippy lady upstairs with her daughter and boyfriend. I should be grateful, I mean they rented me the room way before I was eighteen, so it's not like I could even legally be on my own. They were hard to live with though, cuz I wasn't supposed to be out of my room except to shower, piss and grab food. I got two little shelves—one in the fridge and another in a cabinet to store whatever food I had. When I was living there I rode the bus out to a pet store in the suburbs near my grandma's house to get a little rat to keep me company. His name was Elliot and he would chatter really loud every morning when my alarm went off at 4am so I could catch the first of four busses it took to get me to the shitty high school out in the sticks. I kept thinking of transferring but it was too damn hard with it being my senior year so I just gave up.

Elliot would ride inside my hoodie on my shoulder whenever I'd go to QYRC. I didn't bring him the first couple of times because I thought I'd get in trouble, but once I started going regularly I realized that everyone brings their critters! When I went to DC for the queer youth conference I left Elliot with this kid who was a closeted faggot at my high school except he wasn't actually out because his parents were all Born Again and he saw what happened to me. When I called him from James' place I told him I wasn't coming back and asked if he wanted to keep Elliot, and he said sure. Kinda wish I had him now, though. I left whatever stuff I hadn't taken to the conference in the basement room and used James' phone to call the landlady. She could just throw everything out.

Today when I got off work I decided I'd save the bus fare and walk all the way back to Buck's apartment. When I was walking down Hawthorne I saw this building with a sign saying "NO CREDIT CHECK! MOVE IN NOW! STUDIOS!" I grabbed a marker out of my bag, wrote the number on my hand, and jogged over to QYRC. Sean, this really cute glittery drag queen who's been my buddy forever, was on the phone with some guy and gluing plastic jewels onto heels he found in a free box. I leaned against the kitchen wall and waited. I think he got sick of me standing next to him, so he let me have the phone. I called the number and talked to this dude who told me the rent for a studio was $300 a month and asked if I wanted to go see one. I brought Billy and Sean with me to see what they thought. I think that scared the guy a little bit to have a drag queen and two butches standing in this tiny little room with him. Besides the living room/bedroom where we were standing, there was a little attached kitchen and bathroom and two windows looking out onto the walkway. I wish it wasn't on the first floor, but it's cheap and the rent includes all utilities so I told him I'd take it. I thought he was gonna want to see a pay stub (which I don't even have yet) but he said if I could give him $50 today the place was mine and I have until the rest of the month to pay him. Luckily Sean had seen a client before going to QYRC and lent me the cash to pay the guy right away! He gave me the keys and left.

Gotta get offline so I can go back to Buck's and tell him I'm moving out!

Date: September 21, 2002

I was so glad to have Billy there when I saw the apartment today. I know he's Grace's slave but he's kinda like the Daddy I don't have. When the management company guy left Billy started talking about all the places where we could put eyebolts into the molding if I wanted to be able to turn the apartment into a play space. He's so hot. He was just standing there with his hair slicked back all 50s style and jeans and a white t-shirt and these really old boots he never takes off, talking about someone tying me up.

Sean had already taken off to go back to
QYRC before seeing another client, and
I'd been seeing if the refrigerator was
plugged in. When I walked back into the
main room I saw Billy leaning against a
wall and for a second he looked just
like James. I've been fucking around with
Kristin, but it's such a waste of time.
I know after James I'll never be happy
with anything less than a Daddy for very
long.

Date: September 22, 2002
Security: Friends
Subject: Tattoo!

I got paid today. Right after work I cashed my check at the
grocery store and dropped off my rent. I'd spent my whole
shift today thinking about what I was going to do with the extra
money. At first I thought about going to get another piercing.
There's this crusty dyke who pierces for cheap at the outdoor
craft market. She started piercing me when I was underage.
I didn't even have any ID, just a photocopy of the restraining
order against my mom in my back pocket. I used that as some
kinda proof that I didn't have any parents who were going to
come sue her for putting metal in their kid's face. I kinda can't
believe she went for it. At the time I thought it was because
I was flirting hard and really wanted to hook up with her, but she
never went for it, giving some dumb excuse about being too
old to fuck me. She's only like twenty-eight.

But I couldn't really think of anything I wanted to pierce. I'm pretty happy with my tongue and my snake bites and stretching my ears, and septum. What I've really been wanting is a tattoo. Usually, whenever I have the cash I chicken out, but today I did it!

Downtown near the bus depot is a tattoo shop right next to the old strip club so I decided to head down and see if they were open. The shop was kinda sketchy and filled with gross dudes but I grew a pair and went in anyway. I said I wanted four paw prints on my right bicep (one for every dog I've ever had and lost). I expected that the guy was going to laugh at me, but he didn't! He just took my forty dollars and said to take a seat. In about ten minutes he had a drawing and we went into the back. He put the stencil on my arm, and asked if I was ready.

I've always avoided tattoos because James said he didn't think I'd be able to handle the pain, but dude it felt so good! It took the guy about an hour and I so wasn't ready for it to be over. I came right to QYRC when he finished and can't wait to show everyone. Billy knew I'd been wanting to get inked for a while now but was scared. When he saw the bandage, he grinned and punched me right in the middle of the tattoo. I didn't know I had to keep the bandage on for a while. I almost ripped it off right when I got to QYRC, but Gus said it could get infected if I did so I've been good and patient for the last couple of hours.

It's finally time to wash it off, though, so I'm going to get offline and head into the bathroom. Can't wait to see the tattoo, and can't wait to get more work done.

Date: September 23, 2002

Grace has a car, and she and Billy decided to take a big road trip down to Utah to meet Grace's parents. She was attempting some kind of "family reunification" bullshit. Five years ago they sent Grace to "straight camp." She ran away from the program, got to Portland and hid the fuck out until she turned eighteen and they couldn't touch her again. She hasn't been in the same room as her parents since they locked her up. I really don't know why Grace and Billy drove down there in the first place! They left a couple of days ago and weren't supposed to be back until next month, but tonight they squealed into the QYRC parking lot.

All of us ran outside to meet them with bowls of the soupy soy milk mac & cheese we'd been eating. I recognized the sound of Grace's car but couldn't believe they were really back. The trip hadn't gone very well in terms of reconnecting with her family, but the two of them had a great time. Billy got his eyebrow pierced twice, and Grace said she'd had her nipples done. Billy was talking about how they even fucked in truck stop bathrooms.

Everyone was freaking out, but I tried to play it cool and act like that was totally normal shit. Folks were asking if they ever got caught, and if it was full on cock fucking and fisting, or of it was just heavy making out. I couldn't help myself, and asked if it was a single stall bathroom.

Date: September 25, 2002
Security: Friends
Subject: dogs

I'm lonely. I hate not having a dog. When I'm not having nightmares about James I'm thinking about my pups and how more than anything I wish I knew where they were and if they were ok. When I do community education trainings everyone always asks dumb questions. They always ask about how hard it is not to have parents. Shit, parents are easy to live without, it's my dogs I miss the most. No one understands that.

Being at work is getting hard because I see all these dogs and none of them are mine. I'm supposed to be friendly but the whole point of the business is for people to have a place to bond with their dogs so I'm not supposed to "interfere" too much. I hate waking up early because it means there is a long time before QYRC opens. Even by the time I got off work today there were still a couple of hours before drop-in starts. I didn't want to go back to the apartment, it's too quiet there and it was a nice day so I went to the park and wandered around for a while. I ended up near the off-leash field and just sat there for a long time watching the dogs play. It sounds stupid, but that was probably the very best part of my day.

Date: September 25, 2002

It's so hard to be here all alone. Last night I woke up grabbing at the place on my wrist where James' cuff used to be. At least when I was with hym the only thing I was afraid of was what hy would do. Here, I'm afraid my mom might come for me or some queerbashers will break in. It's easiest to sleep when I have someone crashing here, but I can't just tell people that I actually need someone to stay here. I think I'm looking at another night of jacking off trying to put myself to sleep.

Date: September 27, 2002

The minute I got to QYRC tonight Billy grabbed me and dragged me into the bathroom. He said he had something to show me, and he knew I'd love it. We bolted the door and he started unbuttoning his boiscout shirt. I love that shirt, and really want one, but feel like I can't wear one until I have a Daddy again. He got down to his a-shirt and sports bra and that's when I saw it right on his chest over his heart, an oozing fresh and swollen black kanji tattoo (which explained the lack of actual binding). "It means 'slave,'" he whispered. He explained that he did it for Grace and that today is their six-month collarversary. I guess it was a special surprise and I was the only person who knew about it other than the tattoo artist, obviously. It was hard to keep the secret when we left the bathroom and Grace was watching us by the pool table. She motioned us over and asked what kind of trouble two little boys could be getting into together. I know I turned bright red.

They left early to go celebrate. They've been living with Billy's leather family, Big Billy and her slave Aurora, who have a sweet play space in their basement and are really really old, like thirty or something. I hope that Grace likes her surprise. Billy's lucky to have a Daddy like her.

Date: September 29, 2002
Security: Friends
Subject: Blah

Work sucked. Last night I tried to dye my hair blue but the dye dripped all over my face. I didn't have gloves so I was just using my bare hands. I thought the dye would wash off easily, but it didn't. I had to come to work all blue this morning. My boss was so fucking pissed about it. She gave me some long lecture about professionalism and shit. She said it better not happen again (I'm not sure if she means the blue hair, or the blue face/ hands). Whatever.

In the afternoon, these yuppie faggots came in with these little dogs that peed all over the floor of the shop. They made me mad, acting like they owned the place and ordering me around about how to do my job. They also kept acting like they had little accessories with them, not dogs. That stuff makes me so angry, because I want people to just let dog be real! They were mean, but I was still excited to see some "family" in this place. The owner might look like a dude with her t-shirts and jeans and short hair, but she's really just a homophobic bitch.

She's always saying how gross QYRC is and how she doesn't understand why I go there. The real reason I got the job in the first place is because the owner of the dog wash is a dog agility competitor, and I met her back when I was still living with my coach and competing in all kinds of dog shows. My coach didn't like her, so I don't think she knew about me getting kicked out of her house or anything.

The guys finished washing their little dogs and I kept smiling at them, but they just kept giving me these dirty looks. I was worried I was going to cuss them out, so I just went into the back and folded towels until the end of my shift.

Date: October 1, 2002

In the free box at QYRC I found this black mesh underwear shirt thing (I don't know what it's really called). I was looking at it when a couple of GSA kids walked up, so I started making fun of it. When they walked away I put it in my messenger bag under my journal. I don't even know why.

Kristin and I left QYRC together and headed over to my place. She had been out at her landscaping job earlier, and was hella dirty so she asked if she could shower. When she closed the bathroom door I yanked the underwear from my bag and ripped off my sweatshirt and sports bra. I squeezed into the mesh thing, and pulled my sweatshirt back on. It was itchy. The only mirror is in the bathroom so I couldn't even see how I looked. Kristin came out and didn't say anything. She was in sweats that I guess she'd had in her backpack, hoping I'd invite her over tonight. My bed is just a shitty mattress on the floor but she came and sat down on it, wedging herself into the corner, legs spread. I curled up on her lap.

We were kissing as I rubbed her shoulders. Then she stuck her hands into my sweatshirt. I was so into kissing her that I forgot what I was wearing. She pulled back with this nasty look on her face. "What the fuck are you wearing?!" she said. I told her that I was just fucking around. Kristin said dykes don't wear shit like that. I tried to kiss her but she pulled away and gave me some bullshit story about how she forgot her mom wanted her home tonight and she still needed to go see Saucer.

Date: October 3, 2002
Security: Friends
Subject: freaking out

This morning I woke up to the fucking Clackamas County Sheriff leaving a message on my answering machine. Fucking nasty way to start the day. The message was hella short. Some dude talking to my old name telling me that the restraining order that's been in place since my mom beat the crap out of me and I left her house has expired. They told me good luck with everything, and that if I had any problems I could contact them again.

I didn't know this was coming. When they gave me the restraining order they never told me it was gonna expire. Hopefully my mom will leave me alone, but I kinda doubt it. I think I'm gonna have to start really watching my back.

Date: October 5, 2002
Security: Friends
Subject: Puppy!

I went to the dog park again today while I was waiting for QYRC to open. It was nice out so there were a bunch of dogs. I just sat there and watched them run around until I knew it was close enough to opening time that Gus would be around and let me in. I hate not having a dog. I know it sounds crazy, but honestly I don't know how much more of it I can take. I seriously sat alone in a park, watching dogs chase tennis balls! There was a copy of the paper lying on one of the QYRC couches. I was so lonely after the park that I flipped past the funny pages to the want-ads. I was just looking, not expecting I'd see anything. I haven't really thought about what kind of dog I might get, just that it needs to be really small. I want to be able to take it everywhere with me, and that way if I go traveling or something it will be easy for me to bring it along.

Anyway so I found this ad in the paper for Chihuahua mixes, doesn't get much smaller than that! Five girls and three boys the ad said, and ready to go to their new homes. Buck was alone in the kitchen cooking a ten-pack of noodles and flavoring for everyone to eat from tonight. I told him about the puppies. I was glad he was alone because I was worried he was going to tell me that it was a bad idea. He said he thought it would be really good for me! I called the number in the paper from the youth phone by the pool table. I had to keep covering the receiver with my hand and yelling at people to be quiet! The lady who picked up the phone told me the puppies were six weeks old. She asked if I wanted a boy or a girl, and what color. It was really hard for me not to give her a lecture about how gender is socially constructed. I told her that I didn't care about all that and the only thing that matters to me is that my puppy has a really good temperament because I'm going to be taking it everywhere. She said that one of the boys sounded like exactly what I was looking for.

The ad in the paper said the puppies are down near Salem so I was freaking out trying to figure out how I was going to get my puppy. The Portland busses don't run down that far, but the big national bus does, of course. Problem is, they don't let you have animals. I remember when Billy and his ferrets went down to a squat in SF for Pride last year. They caught a ride down with some kids he met at a party, but he had to bus back to Portland. The ferrets are good at traveling in his backpack but by the time they hit the Oregon border Billy was hella lonely so he pulled them out to play and the driver got pissed and threw them off the bus. Billy had blown all his cash on the Pride play parties down in SF and on the bus ticket, so he had to hitchhike all the way back.

But then it was like magic, because the lady, she said that she was driving up towards Portland to one of the suburbs tomorrow morning to deliver a couple other puppies. She said she could temperament test the remaining puppies tonight to figure out which would be best for me, and bring it with her tomorrow morning if I wanted to meet her out in Milwaukie in the grocery store parking lot. I told her that I'd be there.

I'm getting a dog!!!!!!!!!!!! No way in hell I'm sleeping tonight!!!!!!

Date: October 6, 2002

Buck went with me to get my puppy this morning! We had to leave hella early because the breeder lady was meeting people in a parking lot way out in the suburbs. It's right by where my grandma lives and I was afraid that she'd be going grocery shopping this morning or something and see me and call my birth mom. Being out in that area really triggers me out. I was glad that Buck was with me to keep me safe. When we got off the bus we started walking around the parking lot.

The lady said she was driving a black minivan, which on the phone had seemed like it would be easy enough to find, but I forgot that everyone in the suburbs has a minivan! Then we heard dogs barking and I saw them! Buck and I started jogging towards the van. I was so excited to meet my puppy I couldn't handle the thought of waiting a second longer. I think the lady was a little scared of seeing two really pierced up obviously queer kids running at her. Other people already had puppies in their arms-some lady with a couple of kids, and a young straight couple. There were Jesus stickers all over the bumper of the van. I was fucking praying to some god that ain't hers that she was going to let me have my puppy. I was really worried that I was going to break into tears if I lost this puppy before I even had him. I caught my breath and introduced myself.

She reached into the van pulled this little yellow ball of puppy out of a crate and handed him to me. "This is the calmest one," she said before turning back to the other folks. He was sleeping but opened his little eyes as I started petting him. He's so small, probably only two pounds, and I was almost worried I was going to break him! He smelled like grass and dirt and this spicy smell that all little puppies have that I don't know how to even describe.

Buck reached over and started to pet him too. I handed him to Buck and pulled my wallet out of my back pocket and handed her the hundred dollars in crumpled twenties that I'd pulled out from my special hiding spot under the loose floorboard under where my mattress is last night. We started to walk away back towards the bus stop and I got all panicky. I remembered what it was like to lose my dogs last year. I knew it was different now, but I couldn't stop the panic. I left the puppy with Buck and walked back towards the van, pulling my notebook out of my messenger bag. I asked if she'd be willing to write up a receipt for me saying that the puppy was mine forever. I think she thought I was crazy, but I don't care. She wrote the note. Once I had that I pretty much ran back to Buck and my puppy.

When we got on the bus I ripped the page out of my notebook and put it in my wallet with the expired restraining order paperwork. I used to carry it in case my birth mom ever tried to get near me. Now it can't do shit to protect me. I just met him but

I can already tell this little puppy is going to be something special. I wasn't sure about what his name would be. I was up all night coming up with ideas but on the bus ride back to Portland I decided on Orbit because my whole world is going to revolve around making sure he's happy and healthy.

I wanted to spend the day with Buck and Orbit but I had to go into work. I hadn't told my boss I was getting a puppy, but figured she wouldn't really care if I brought him with me. Buck left me at the dog wash and said he'd meet me at QYRC tonight. Work lasted forever but at least Orbit was with me, he was so good, sleeping in his crate all day. On my breaks I took him into the parking lot out back to play. My boss was even really nice today. We have a few toys and leashes and stuff for sale in the front and when I came back from my lunch break she gave me one of the puppy toys we sell! With my employee discount I bought him a tiny collar that's blue with stars on it.

As soon as my shift was finished we rushed to QYRC so I could introduce Orbit to everyone. Gus fell in love right away and Buck had spent the day preparing a little surprise for me. He'd found all kinds of queer pride bumper stickers to decorate Orbit's little crate, and he'd gotten his girlfriend to sew a little tiny black shirt and then he painted "Orbit" on it so that the little guy won't get cold at QYRC since it's so drafty here.

Date: October 8, 2002
Security: Friends
Subject: Home

When I got to QYRC tonight there was a new girl, this little baby dyke. She said her name was Chelsea but that she'd rather be called Chris. She kept following me and Billy around, talking about how excited she was to be here. She'd taken three buses including one of the national long-distance busses to get to QYRC from some tiny town just south of Corvallis. She said her mom didn't know where she was and then quickly added that she probably wouldn't care. I think she thought we might rat her out as a runaway or some shit. She said it was her first time being around gay people. I felt really bad for her, so I let her play with Orbit and follow us around. She kept talking about how later in the week she was going to get a rainbow tramp stamp tattoo from some guy in her town. It's weird to think there was a time that this didn't feel like home to me.

Date: October 9, 2002

I woke up really upset today. Piglet woke me up about 2am knocking on my window because it was raining. I didn't hear him until Orbit started barking. I let him in, but after that I kept having this nightmare about James. It was weird, in my dream hy came crawling through the window and tied me up like hy was gonna play with me, but then just left. I woke up all tangled in my sleeping bag and covered in sweat. I could smell that Orbit had pooped somewhere and I wanted to take a shower, but Piglet was in the bathroom. When he stumbled out he thanked me for letting him in and said that the rain had stopped so he needed to go. I went into the bathroom and saw that Piglet forgot to take his damn sharps with him!!!!! He just left the damn needle sitting on the edge of my bathtub. I was mostly mad because if I hadn't woken up Orbit could have gotten it. I turned the water on and threw the syringe out the little window into the airshaft.

I couldn't stop thinking about the dream so I called Buck who doesn't work until late tonight and he offered to come over. Before he got here I decided that the one thing that would really make me feel better today would be to get the anchor tattoo I've been planning. I've never been much of a cutter, but a couple months ago James tried to shove me out of hys car when we were driving over an interstate bridge, and hy told me that no Daddy would ever want me. Hy dumped me back at his mamma's house and went to hang with hys ex-wife.

I had used James' mom's phone and tried to call Buck but he was at work. I was really on my own. James had left hys pocketknife behind so I took it and carved a big "F" for "Fear" into my right thigh. It didn't really make me feel all that much better. When James got back hy was pissed that I used hys knife. Right when I got back to Portland I knew I was going to put an anchor over that scar to help me remember to stay anchored to what really matters. Like my brother, and now little Orbit. I tried to get the tattoo a month ago but the wound was still too fresh and the shop said I needed to let the skin harden better before they could ink over it.

Buck took me to his tattoo shop and they said I could get inked in like an hour. He and I went into a bookstore and looked at little kid picture books for a while. I put Orbit into my messenger bag so the stupid store people wouldn't get all pissy and kick us out. I hadn't eaten anything all day, but Buck had some dried fruit in his bag so I chewed on that while the dude got the stencil situated. Buck held Orbit for me and walked to the back to talk with Hank, this hella hot guy who's the piercer at the shop. I guess he's apprenticing to be a tattoo artist too. He passes really well, but I could tell he was one of us. The shop itself isn't very queer friendly. It's mostly old biker dudes and some young rockabilly types, well, except for Hank. Funny thing is because Hank's such a popular artist already the shop pretty much always has queers swarming all over. Somehow even with all of us, Hank has managed to stay stealth. The only one at the shop who knows is Dave, the old biker who runs the place and that's just because he signs Hank's paycheck. I felt strange laying there on the table in my boxers, but it was all worth it when the tattoo started. It hurt so good.

Date: October 13, 2002
Security:
Subject: Mom

Fucking hell. I saw my mom's car again today. I had been fucking around downtown at the waterfront With Billy and Grace and when I got off the bus back at my place I saw her car just parked there, waiting. She was sitting in the driver's seat. I'm not sure if she saw me or not. I was so freaked out I picked up Orbit, ran into the apartment and locked the door. I can't believe she's already showing up over here. I just told grandma that I moved. I'm sure she told my mom right away, even though I asked her not to. I knew she would. I hate living like this. Worst part, my mom's not even doing anything illegal enough to get the fucking restraining order back.

Date: October 14, 2002
Security: Friends
Subject: I <3 my brother

Buck and I went to the mall together today. God that sounded like we're teen girls spending the day shopping and looking for hot boys or something stupid! Whatever, anyway, we went to the mall because he needed new pants for his job. I didn't really have any plans for the day so I went too. He didn't actually have to try on anything so we avoided all the dressing room mess that always happens when they can't figure out what the hell we are and which little room we should use. We finished fast so we went into the Goth Shop.

As usual it was full of stupid spoiled pre-teens trying to look tough. Buck wanted to stretch his nostril piercing and they have cheap jewelry. He bought a 4 gauge plug, and we walked over to the food court. We got neon colored ice drinks and he started trying to work the new plug into his nostril. It had been at an 8 gauge. I didn't think he could jump two sizes like that, but he said it would work. He handed me his drink to hold as we left the mall, and by the time we got through the parking lot and to the bus stop his nose was bright red, but the new steel plug was in! Last time I stretched anything other than my ears was when I was in the South and jumped my tongue from 14 gauge to 10 gauge. That hurt real bad.

Date: October 17, 2002

I think that Chris kid is totally going to run away sometime soon. She kept saying she was going to stay at QYRC until they closed but I knew the busses back to her house would have stopped running so at eight I told her she really needed to get out of here. She was giving me all kinds of attitude and acting like she wasn't going to leave. Finally I offered to walk her to the bus stop and that seemed to make the difference.

After she got on the bus I headed back to QYRC for a little while and then I headed back to the apartment. I made some pasta and have just been sitting here with Orbit, thinking about what it was like that very first time I came to QYRC. I had to go to the Swift Cut out in the mall and get all my hair chopped off. I wanted to shave my head, but the suburban stylist wasn't willing to go quite that far. Gus gives free haircuts all night long to anyone who wants one, but I didn't know that then. Besides, I'd already decided that I needed to show up looking as queer as possible

Sometimes, I think about that first night. It was late last spring. I'd been couch surfing for a while out in the sticks where I grew up and was trying to not get gaybashed long enough to finish high school. I'd never been anywhere like QYRC before. I brought my homework and sat on the brown couch next to the stage. The cushions had busted open at one point and been stitched back together with thread that didn't match. I don't know why I brought my homework. It's not like we have study hall time or anything. Hell, it's not like anyone else was even still in school. Mostly I was just terrified of walking in alone, and sitting alone, and not knowing anyone and I figured homework would at least make me look busy.

My little corner by the stage was a pretty out of the way and had a good view of everything going on. That first night I pretended to be reading my AP Government textbook but mostly I was reading the graffiti on a rainbow mural splattered with inside jokes I couldn't understand. From my corner I tried to take in the space, which from the outside looked like nothing more than an office complex. Other than the bunch of kids smoking you had to walk through to get to the door.

Inside QYRC is all concrete and spray-paint. To my left was floor-to-ceiling fencing that separated the hangout spot from the basketball area-though no one plays ball there since all the silk-screening supplies are spread across the tiny court. Across the room and to my right was the TV alcove, and towards the middle the pool table; both full of butches like Saucer, Grace, Johnny, Buck and Billy. There were queens doing these crazy dips and spins on the pallet board stage right next to my couch, and a makeshift wall separated the kitchen from the rest of the space. On the kitchen side it was just exposed studs, and facing my couch it was plasterboard turned into a memorial wall for kids who had died.

There was a girl was sitting on another couch, I knew she was trans. I'd never met anyone who wasn't a boy or a girl before. She was even quieter than I was, and I didn't try to talk to her. I was pretty pathetic back then, I just wanted friends but also didn't want anyone to notice me. I got to QYRC right when they opened at four and I must have sat on that damn couch for a good two hours before my bursting bladder finally forced me up and over to the big single stall bathroom. Inside the walls were collaged with hundreds of snapshots, photos of the kids I saw by the pool table and dozens of kids I'd never seen before. Most of the pictures seemed to be from Pride parades and protests. I kept looking at all the faces surrounding me and wondered if these really were my people and if I'd ever belong here.

I opened the bathroom door and walked back into the main drop-in center. I was planning on heading back to the couch, but then I was stopped. Billy introduced himself to me and asked if I wanted to go outside to smoke. Back then I didn't call myself XXX, but I didn't smoke. Still, I wanted to look cool. He was not only the only person who'd talked to me, but he'd

```
also come over from the pool table area,
which meant he had to be pretty cool.
I told him sure, grabbed my backpack and
followed him outside.
```

Date: October 29, 2002
Security: Friends
Subject: Protest!

Last night at QYRC, Gus told us how this fucked up preacher dude from somewhere in the Midwest was going to come with his "Jesus hates fags" signs and picket downtown today! Everyone started making posters for the counter-protest, I found a rainbow knee sock in the free box and made it into a little sweater for Orbit to wear. We all planned to meet up and at ten this morning. When I got back to the apartment I realized that I was supposed to be at work at nine. I woke up early and left a message that I was sick on the answering machine at the dog wash.

The protest itself was awesome. The preacher dude gave up after a little while because there were so many of us queers shouting back at him, dancing and throwing glitter. I'm so glad I didn't miss this to go fold towels. I think I'm going to quit anyway and find something better. Being out at the protest today reminded me how important it is not to tolerate oppression, and my boss is really homophobic.

Date: October 29, 2002

I lost my job today. I called in this morning so that I could be at the protest. It's the first time I've ever called out sick and I didn't think it was going to be that big of a deal. When I got back to the apartment there was a message on the answering machine from my boss. I guess she saw me on the news standing with the other QYRC folks screaming at that homophobic prick and it really upset her. She said I was fired and that she'd send my last check. On the message she said I was being fired because I'd lied about being sick, but I know it's because she saw me at something gay. I was glad Kristin didn't come back from the protest with me. That would have been awkward. I started crying when the message started. I was sitting on my mattress and Orit started crying from the floor. It's just a little mattress on the floor but he's so small he can't crawl up here on his own yet. I held him while my boss, well I guess she's my ex-boss now, said that the rumors she'd heard since my coach kicked me out were true, and that she shouldn't have taken a chance with me. She said I was going to die in the gutter like all of my fucked up dyke friends. Then she hung up.

Date: November 3, 2002

When Billy came into QYRC last night I could just tell things weren't good, and agreed to go to North Portland at ass-o'clock this morning to help him pack. Billy found out that Grace has been fucking Johnny. Grace has this sweet overnight job at the gas station. The cool part is that she has all day to do whatever she wants, she gets to dress like a big dyke at work, and pretty much no one ever comes in, except for Johnny. She's crashing at an apartment only a few blocks from the gas station and it started out that she would just go in to get cigarettes, which she's not even old enough to buy, but then she'd hang out, keeping Grace company. Pretty soon Grace was fucking her every night in the big walk-in convenience store refrigerator, boxers down around both their knees, and Johnny's ass pressed against the past-due milk they always tried to pass off as fresh. It sounds pretty hot, but also totally fucked up. Billy was crushed/destroyed/etc when he found out. He's always been poly himself, but agreed to be monogamous in his relationship with

Grace because she said it was part of being in service to her. I've decided I hate Grace.

Today I had to get up at five to catch the first 6 bus down MLK. I left Orbit at the apartment so I could focus on helping Billy. He and his ferrets have been living in at this big house with Grace, Aurora and Big Billy, but now that he and Grace are broken up he has to leave. The house was mostly dark when I got there; mornings are hard for all of us. Aurora and Big Billy are old, like thirty or something, but I know them from QYRC because they come and teach the leather 101 workshops. I think the funders think that we're just getting basic safer sex shit like how to put a condom on right and stuff. I'm sure if they really knew what was going on, like how they are showing us how to flog and fist and tie folks up they would freak out. I mean, I've seen these folks when they come for site visits to look at all of us. I think they can barely get their heads around the idea that we're having sex at all, which is funny cuz we're practically fucking on the pool table most nights, we just know to try to behave when they come so they don't can Gus and shut us down.

The good thing is that the youth steering committee really has most of the control about what happens in the space and we're all big perverts so of course we have flogging workshops and stuff. I think it's cool that Aurora and Big Billy come. I mean, we're already playing. They just help us to do it without killing each other. Just last week a whole bunch of folks had this crazy scene in the middle of the night down on the waterfront where folks got tied up to the guardrail over the river. I wasn't there, but heard about it the next night at QYRC. I guess a couple folks had been down there as lookouts to make sure the cops weren't nearby.

I wasn't sure if Aurora and Big Billy were going to be home, or awake, but I was really nervous about going to their house. I went early because Billy said Grace wouldn't be there yet. Most mornings she's been leaving work and going to curl up on the couch with Johnny and only coming home in the late afternoon to take a shower before going back to the gas station. I've had a crush on Billy forever and I sorta hoped that in his heartbroken state maybe we could make out.

When I got to the house he was sitting in the middle of his and Grace's room with a shoebox in front of him. At first I thought he was actually packing, but then I realized he was looking through letters and photographs. We only had a couple of hours before he had to be out of the house so I was pissed that he was wasting time. The last thing I wanted was that kind of confrontation with Aurora and Big Billy. Turns what Billy was pulling out of the shoebox was all this sappy crap from their relationship. Poems he'd written Grace on the backs of receipts, pictures from the drive to Utah, and the first needles she'd sunk into him right after they started playing together.

We've all been looking up to Grace and Billy because they play harder than any of us, and living with Aurora and Big Billy meant they had access to the basement that had rigged up into a dungeon. They knew how to take shit really far. Billy was just sorta sitting there in his old hoodie, jeans and boots in the middle of the floor with the ferrets racing around him. I wasn't sure if he even remembered I was there. Then out of nowhere he said that when those needles went in, she pierced his heart. I realized we were so not gonna make out.

I left him to his fucking memories. I don't really get why he was so broken hearted. I mean, the butch is fucking him over big-time with this Johnny shit, and despite that he's the one that has to move out. Aurora and Big Billy said that Grace got to stay because she had been his Master and that gave her priority on the room. I don't really think that makes a lot of sense. Mostly I think that's just an excuse and they're letting her stay cuz she's the one with a job. Billy always makes rent, but it's a scramble. At the end of the month he usually misses all the good shit at QYRC cuz he has to take odd under the table jobs to come up with the last bit of cash. Still though, he was family to them.

I thought Billy and the ferrets were going to be crashing at Saucer's squat but when I got there to start helping him pack he said that fell through and that he'd convinced his mom to let him come stay there for a little while. That seemed like a pretty bad idea to me, since he hasn't lived with her since he was thirteen and

she's never taken the queer shit very
well. I remember him telling me about how
when she walked in on him with his first
girlfriend she threw him down some stairs
and smashed his skull open.

Billy and I get along so well because
our moms are fucked up crazy homophobic
bitches. Anyway, I didn't think he should
go there. I said he could come crash with
me if he wanted to. I was sure that he was
going to say yes, and I was starting to
think about how we could put my bookcase
in the middle of the room to give him a
little bit of privacy since my studio is
so small. He said he thought things were
going a lot better with his mom and that
this time it was going to be ok. He said
if it got bad he would call me.

It took three hours to pack up his shit,
sorting whose boxers were whose, and the
whole time I was terrified that Grace
would walk through the door. It's fucked
up because I hate her, but she's also
really hot and I don't want her pissed
at me. There's the youth play party in
a few weeks, and I kinda want her to
beat me up. I know that's fucked up and
I won't do it if Billy says it's not
ok, but I think it would be hot. Anyway,

thankfully she didn't show up the whole time I was there. I offered to help Billy haul his stuff to the light-rail train, but he said he could do it. He left his key on the counter along with the little bundle of needles from inside the shoebox.

Date: November 4, 2002

Bio dad called and said he needed to meet with me and asked if we could have dinner together tonight. It was weird, but I didn't really feel like I could say no. He asked how work was going, and I was gonna lie and say fine but there didn't seem much point in that. I told him I wasn't working there anymore, but quickly followed that with that I was trying to find another job. He said that he had something serious to talk with me about. He said that since I left birth mom's house he'd continued to send her my child support checks, assuming that she was passing the money on to me.

I was trying to be all polite and shit, but I think I actually laughed at him. My goal is to stay as far away from her as possible so we're certainly not meeting up for her to give me money.

He said that she's been cashing the checks and he thinks that she's using the money for herself. No shit. I guess the checks are going to start coming to me directly now. Good timing. I had no idea how I was gonna make the rent. I suppose this means that for the first time my absentee father is useful for something. I really don't even know the dude. While I was growing up, the courts said I had to see him for lunch four times a year. My mother never wanted me to know him so she always came along. She never even told me who he was. Driving up to meet him for lunch she'd always tell me I couldn't talk to him, I'd just eat my grilled cheese and hope we could leave soon. She said he was a bad man and that if I talked he would take me away. I guess I was in fourth or fifth grade before I figured out he was my bio dad. I never let on to her that I'd figured it out.

Must have come as a big surprise when the courts told him I was on my own. It had been a few months since our last four times per year visit that fell right before my birthday. As usual I had sat there silent and he gave me a birthday card that, as always, my mother had instructed me not to open. He also gave me some clothes she returned and exchanged for herself. When the courts called to say I'd been removed from my mom's house he told the courts he had no idea I was being abused. I guess it would have been pretty impossible for him to know anything. It's not like we'd exchanged more than three sentences since I was born. When the courts first notified him, I was a minor and really scared he was gonna try to pull some sort of bullshit parental control over me and make me come live with him. I don't trust adults, especially parents. I shouldn't have been so worried. Some woman from the courts violated my confidentiality and told him what I was afraid of. He told her that he'd never wanted a kid. He never invited me to come live with him, even when he knew I was couch surfing. I guess on some level I'm still mad. I mean, this was before I went to QYRC and had my pack. I was really lonely. I would have said no, but the offer would have been nice. Whatever, I can't really blame him for not wanting to take me in. Our blood might show differently, but really we're total strangers.

Date: November 8, 2002

The first check came with the return address of his office downtown. I still don't even know where he lives, other than somewhere up in the West Hills where there are a bunch of fancy mansions. There's enough money to cover rent, some food and basic stuff if I'm smart about how I spend it. When the check comes, there's part of me that always wants to say no thanks and send it back. You never wanted a kid? Well guess what? I never wanted a dad, either.

But, jobs are hard to come by when you look like me, and I'm scared to go back to not having a key in my pocket. Besides, now I've got Orbit to think about, and the folks who know they can depend on me for a place to crash if they need it. It's complicated and I don't like to talk about it much, especially when I'm at QYRC. Not even to Buck. But I guess I'll take bio-dad's guilt money and keep my mouth shut about how I pay my bills. I don't know how long it will last, but at least for now it keeps me stable and off someone's couch.

Date: November 10, 2002

Billy and I were chilling out in the smoking area tonight at QYRC. We were sitting at the picnic table and he kept nodding off over his cigarette, his head dropping down onto his folded arms. After a little while I asked if he was ok. He said he was just tired, crashing with his mom didn't work out so good and he and the ferrets had spent the past couple of nights back on the streets and hadn't been sleeping much. Even when things have been really bad I've been able to couch surf. I'm really scared that someday my luck will run out and I'll end up on the streets.

I told Billy that it wasn't that great of a place, but that the offer still stood for him and the ferrets to come and stay with me and Orbit. Billy said he had his food stamps turned back on so he could pay me in groceries, which sounds pretty good. I don't know why he hadn't just asked me himself if he could stay. Maybe he was embarrassed that he turned my place down right when Grace dumped him. Billy got all excited about moving in and went inside to the craft table and started drawing this graffiti tag of our names-he said we could hang it on the wall. We stayed until QYRC closed and then headed back here. Billy seemed to like the place a lot.

He lost the cage for the ferrets when his mom kicked him out. He's got a little carrier that's too small for them to be in all the time, but he can put them into it at night. At least he pretty much carries them around everywhere in his backpack. I said while he's here they can run around with Orbit we just have to make sure they don't play too rough with him. Billy is in the shower now since he hasn't been able to get clean since his mom threw him out.

Piglet said he thought we could dumpster some big pieces of foam from outside the furniture factory down past MLK across the tracks in that industrial area. That's where I scored some good pallets that I turned into bookshelves when I left Buck's place, so I think we're gonna check that out tomorrow. For tonight we'll have to share the futon. Ever since the shit went down with Grace he's been in total Daddy mode, which just makes me want him even more.

Date: November 12, 2002
Security: Friends
Subject: Fisting

Kristin and I hung out at QYRC last night just making out and shit, and then she asked me if I wanted to go to work with her today. I didn't have anything better to do so I said ok. She works as a landscaper and technically she can't have anyone else in the truck with her, but she said her boss would never know as long as we're smart about it. She said I should take the bus up to 82nd (which sucked because I had to wake up hella early) and then wait for her on the corner. She had to go into work first to pick up the work truck. Then she acted like she's on her way out to the first job but stopped to pick up me and Orbit. It was sorta hot to ride around with her in the truck, but it was also boring. I wrote for a little while but then I fell asleep. On our way back to my place to fuck (if Billy could be convinced to go out) we had to stop downtown so Kristin could see Saucer.

Ever since Saucer got locked up this has to happen when Kristin and I hang out in the evening. There are really limited visiting hours at the jail, so Kristin and Saucer came up with this system that sounds crazy but it totally works. The windows on Saucer's holding cell are tinted and we couldn't see what she was signing very well so we figured she could see about as well, but it faces a big parking garage and if Kristin can get past the parking attendant and go up onto the top floor and then use this sketchy metal ladder, she can get onto an electrical box and use all the American Sign Language we've been learning at QYRC because a bunch of really hot queer kids from the state deaf school have started coming.

Sometimes we stay up there a couple of hours. Tonight it was only about one. It was kind of cold so I had Orbit wrapped up in my messenger bag while Kristin filled Saucer in on all the news from the outside. Mostly, what went down last night at QYRC, messages from all her friends, who's broken up with who, and if someone's name or pronouns changed. That kind of shit. Whenever Kristin forgets a sign I have to remind her, but I don't usually get up on the electrical box because I'm pretty sure one of these days the parking lot attendant is going to figure out what we're doing and come up. This way I can get away faster. While Kristin and Saucer talk I mostly just squat in the shadows against the wall and try to work on my zine.

When we got back to the apartment Billy was out. I made macaroni and cheese for me and Kristin and then we started kissing. I thought she was going to fuck me, but then she pulled my hand down into her boxers. We always talk at QYRC about how it's important to ask for what you want, but it's not always that easy. I mean, with James it was expected that I would bottom and take whatever hy knew I needed in the moment, but with Kristin it's different. She kinda makes fun of me, and calls me a "little girl" when I start humping on her and trying to get her to touch me. I don't know why she's like that, but it makes me want to punch her in the face.

She was so wet that when I started fucking her with a couple of fingers it just wasn't enough. She started begging me for more. I kept adding fingers. Pretty soon my whole hand slipped into her and she was rocking so hard on my fist. Inside was hot and smooth and tight. I started pumping into her harder and harder and grabbing at her big nipples. Right when I thought my hand was maybe going to fall off she started screaming really loud and I could feel her cum. It was sorta hot.

Date: November 13, 2002

Gus just called looking for Billy. They said it was really important, that something happened to Scummy. I didn't really know Scummy. He took off for SF right around when I started coming to QYRC. I think I might have met him once, but I can't be sure that's not just me remembering lots of stories about him. Billy had just walked in so I handed him the phone and he started to cry. I've never seen Billy cry like that. Orbit looked worried and ran right over and Billy picked him up. When he hung up he told me that Scummy had died in SF. They couldn't tell if it was a suicide or an accidental overdose. Billy said he had to go downtown and find his sister, Hope. Portland's way different than when I was down south with James, it's so white here. Hope's the only kid of color at QYRC. She gets into a lot of fights with skinheads on the streets who come into Portland from the sticks out where I grew up to start shit with the queers and anyone else they find. It's weird, if I didn't think she'd beat the shit out of me I'd almost say she's a femme. I mean, Hope only wears jeans and would never be caught dead in a dress or anything, but she wears real bras and tight little t-shirts.

Date: November 14, 2002
Security: Friends
Subject: funeral

Today was Scummy's funeral. Everyone met down at the skateboard park under the bridge. I didn't go. I wanted to be there to support Billy and everyone else but I didn't really know Scummy. When I got to QYRC tonight everyone was talking about the memorial. The skate punks did some of his signature tricks while Gus and his street family talked.

After the memorial it took me a while to find Gus, they were curled up on a couch writing in their journal and crying while some adult volunteers handled folks signing in and starting to cook dinner. Orbit jumped up into Gus's lap and started licking tears off their face. I've never seen Gus cry. They're like the perfect adult because they're one of us, and also just so strong. Billy, Hope, Piglet and some other folks got back to QYRC with a bag full of spray paint from the hardware store. They added

Scummy's name to the memorial wall and then just went a little crazy with skulls and stuff. Gus went and ripped a collage that Scummy had made off the wall in the kitchen and brought it out so they could hammer it up on the memorial wall, and Hope had some photos of him from when this photographer came and did some workshop at QYRC.

They finished with the memorial wall a little bit ago, and now it's almost time for QYRC to close up. Billy just came and told me he didn't want to come back to the apartment tonight. He's going to take the ferrets back down to sleep at the skatepark with Hope, Piglet, and Saucer.

Date: November 17, 2002
Security: Friends
Subject: crush

I met a cute boi at QYRC tonight. I was sitting in on the blue couch watching gutterpunks whip some GSA ass on the pool table. His name is Dani, I've seen him around forever but we've never really talked. He's older and not punk. He's doing some kind of internship for school or something, I don't even remember where he goes. He spends most of his time volunteering in the office. He's not really my type. He's no Daddy, but he's kinda cute. I got all shy when he said he's been watching me. The weird thing is, after he told me he thought I was cute I said the place I'm crashing isn't very far away and asked if he wanted to go for a walk with me and Orbit, and he said no! Well, actually he said he still had work to do.

Date: November 19, 2002

Got the foam so Billy and I don't have to sleep together on my mattress. It was a pain in the ass to carry on the bus. I seriously thought the driver was going to freak the hell out and not let us on the bus with this big flapping orange foam, but he did and we made it back to the studio. Billy and I were just chilling out with some pasta, talking about this zine I'm going to write that Billy might illustrate, when the phone rang. It was a number I didn't know so I tossed it to Billy. It was this new girl, Scallion, he's been hanging out with.

I don't like her much. No, that's not true. I like her, I just wish she wasn't dating Billy because he's hella hot and I want to hook up with him. Also Scallion is vanilla, and even though she looks butch, this is her first queer relationship. Mostly, I just think that Billy could do way better. Scallion still lives with her mom up in Washington and her mom's a meth head. Billy and I went up there last week to see her. I don't think her mom liked us much, but it was hard to tell, because after we had been there for just a few minutes she locked herself in the bathroom for a long time. I guess this morning her mom was going through her room and found a drawing Billy did. It's hella good, but she's naked. I guess her mom didn't like that much.

Mom freaked out and called her a dyke and said that she needed to get the hell out. Scallion tried to tell her mom that Billy was a guy, but none of that shit mattered so she shoved a bunch of crap in her backpack and walked to the twenty-four hour diner near the freeway and called me.

Billy told her to meet us at QYRC and they'd figure shit out. I think his plan was to go back to the streets with her, so when they hung up I said that they could both start staying here with us so long as she didn't mind how cold it is. Fucking heat in this place doesn't work. We have to leave the shower running (we don't pay water) to try to make the apartment warm.

Date: November 20, 2002

Kristin finally got on the visitors list to see Saucer. Saucer's been really upset about Scummy dying, he was one of her brothers, but the jail wouldn't let her out to go to the funeral. Kristin said she was pretty messed up. By the time she got in there Saucer's knuckles were bruised and bloody from trying to beat her way out of jail to the memorial.

She wasn't in a good mood and it turns out, Saucer could see us a whole lot better than Kristin thought and wanted to know who the hell was on the parking garage with her every night. At first Kristin tried to lie and say she'd been up there alone which was stupid because Saucer's street sister, Hope, had filled her in on everything like me visiting Kristin at work, and how we've made out at QYRC. Besides, I'm the only one with a little dog and I'd been letting Orbit run around the roof and Saucer had seen him too.

I wasn't thinking about how Saucer was going to get out when I started fucking around with Kristin. I was just thinking about how I'd finally met a girl who was more into me than I was into her and I kinda liked the feeling of being chased. Now it's a fucking mess.

Date: November 21, 2002

I think Billy and I about gave my grandma a heart attack today. I hadn't known she was gonna come over, but this morning she called and said she was at the pay phone up the street and wanted to take me to lunch at the burger place. I wanted to tell her no, but since she was only blocks away and I had picked up the phone I couldn't exactly tell her I was out. I met her on the corner and we drove down the street. I threw a stocking cap over my frizzy blue hair (that last bleaching really fried it pretty good) and had on my work pants and a grungy sweatshirt that Billy had worn last night but that really belonged to Johnny.

Grandma bought me a burger, fries and a shake and we sat at a little plastic table while the lunch rush came in and out. I answered all her questions in as few details as possible. She asked why I dressed like a boy. I said it was comfortable, that kinda shit. She looked like she was going to cry. I've been butch since I left my coach's house but sometimes it hits my grandma harder than others. I haven't seen her since before I went down to be with James so I think

she forgot what I looked like and replaced
me with a memory of the stupid girl my
mom dressed me as. Mostly I just told her
about Orbit.

We finished eating and drove back up the
street. I thought I was about to get away,
but then my grandma said she needed to use
the bathroom. I was pretty sure it was an
excuse to spy on how I'm living, but it's
not like I could tell her she couldn't
come in, especially after she bought me
lunch. I wasn't sure if Billy was home
or not. Thankfully not only was he not
fucking anyone, but he was dressed, too,
and laying on the floor drawing. Orbit
was sleeping on my mattress and I didn't
see the ferrets anywhere, so they were
probably in Billy's hoodie. I introduced
my grandma to Billy and Orbit. I hadn't
told her anyone else was living here.
I think she thinks we're fucking. I wish.

She walked past Billy into the kitchen,
probably to see how gross it was. We'd
just done a bunch of dishes this morning
so it was actually pretty clean. The
problem came when she was walking back
into the living/bed-room. She saw the
main wall that Billy hung his floggers
and ball gag on. Those were the first

thing he hung up when he started staying
here. The large flogger was handed down
to him from Big Billy when Billy took on
his first boy years ago. I was a little
surprised that he kept them after the way
Big Billy fucked him over with the house.
Billy said that leather ran deeper than
that. That even if they couldn't ever be
pack again, they had been, and that still
counted for something.

All the other leather he'd saved up for,
and just ate off his food stamps. Having
his toys on the wall is really sexy.
I don't know what my grandma thought,
like if she knew what that stuff was, but
she looked really uncomfortable. She said
she had to go. When she was going out the
door she asked if I would come over for
Thanksgiving with my birth mom. I told
her no and shut the door.

Date: November 22, 2002
Security: Friends
Subject: shit

Saucer got out of jail. Her parole officer got her out really
fast. She told the judge Saucer knew she'd made a mistake
by shooting up again, and she was "actively volunteering at
QYRC." The judge took pity on her. For some reason I didn't
think through how she was gonna get back out. I don't know

why this didn't occur to me, it's not like she killed someone. Word on the street is that she and Hope want to beat the shit out of me. Billy says I'll be ok.

Date: November 24, 2002

I figured outside of QYRC I wouldn't hear from Kristin since she had Saucer back again which was sorta fine. I like rough butches who can slap me, and Kristin just wanted me to fuck her. But, then she called me, and I wasn't doing anything and was horny so I agreed to go driving around with her. Kristin loves her car and is always talking about wanting to trick it out with better speakers and shit. Her parents bought it for her when she graduated high school. The special ed teachers said Kristin would never be able to graduate, so when she was like fifteen and barely had freshman credits her mom made some stupid promise to her that if she could get her diploma they would get her a car. That's the story she always tells, anyway.

Kristin never binds but she still looked really hot when she picked me up, faded ripped up jeans and a plaid flannel shirt. She doesn't have tattoos or piercings but she just got her head buzzed down and I kept reaching over as she drove and running my fingers over the short hairs at the base of her neck. She had us listening to some stupid rap CD all about 'busting hos' and 'beating fags.' I was really offended, but she was loving it and I didn't want to start something, cuz I hoped we were gonna hook up again. I'd even shoved some gloves in my back pocket before I left the apartment. After it played twice through and we'd driven from downtown over the river into Washington and back she came out with the truth about why she'd called me.

Saucer had headed out to the park and met some of her old friends and shot up without remembering that she still had to pee in a cup for the probation officer. Now she was holed up in the crack hotel on Sandy trying to get herself sobered up. Kristin thought that if she went over there it would be better, but she was afraid to go by herself. She'd paid for the room and didn't want to leave Saucer alone. Except of course Saucer wasn't alone. Hope was there with her and Hope hated me and thought it was my fault that Saucer relapsed again because she couldn't take the stress of whatever it is that Kristin and I are doing.

For whatever reason, well mostly because Billy was going to be there, I said I'd go. Billy always keeps me safe, and has kept Hope from actually jumping me since I started hooking up with Kristin. Billy and Hope are stepsisters and ex-girlfriends, and Hope and Saucer are street sisters, which makes Billy responsible for Saucer too since they are all connected. Also, Billy's known Saucer since they were both little baby butches running around downtown. Billy mostly got himself clean but Hope and Saucer have struggled to make that happen.

See, Billy's mom and Hope's dad had gotten married when they were like fifteen. The problem was, they'd been sneaking down to QYRC and were dating before their parents even met. They both left home a little less than a year later when Hope's dad walked in on them fucking and beat the shit out of Billy, then told Billy's mom who beat him up too, and threw him out. Billy and Hope haven't been together for a really long time, but Hope respects Billy. He's the only person that can calm her down no matter how strung out she is.

I've ridden the bus past the hotel a million times on my way out to the lesbian-owned sex shop with really expensive dildos and nice leather floggers, but I'd never had a reason to go in. The hotel is shaped like an empty square with the office positioned in the middle, surrounded by a strange and dingy concrete courtyard. The hotel rooms make up the perimeter, with outdoor stairwells and catwalks on the second floor. Kristin told me to keep cool as we walked past the office. A bored employee didn't even look up from the small television set balanced on the edge of the counter. We went up the second floor, knocked twice and slipped inside. Billy was alone in the front of room with the TV was on pretty loud, some sort of nature show about creepy looking deep-sea fish. He was wearing my Tribe 8 t-shirt and his faded black work pants. The room was small and dark. The windows faced the catwalk, and were covered by dirty curtains that I think at one point were mustard colored. The ferrets were trying to climb them and running in and out from under the two sloping stained mattresses. I sat on the floor and started watching television, inching further away from Kristin and closer to Billy. It was only after sitting down that I realized the

door to the bathroom was closed and quiet
whispers were coming from inside. After
a while Kristin got up from the bed next
to me and went in.

Billy told me that Hope was in there with
Saucer, trying to help her sober up, and
I got all nervous because I don't really
like being around folks who are using and
I was pretty sure that Hope would kill
me if she knew I was there in the front
room. Billy told me not to worry about
it, that Hope was too busy to care, and
besides, he would protect me. The nature
show wasn't very good but I kept watching
it because there wasn't anything else to
do. It made me think of Mrs. Snow, this
kickass science teacher I had in middle
school. I used to spend stupid amounts
of time in her classroom after school,
and sometimes she'd even write me a pass
to get me out of PE to come hang out
with her classroom pet rats. I used to
think she was a lesbian, and back then
I had a huge crush on her, but it turns
out she was married to some dude. I'd
gone back to see her a couple of times
in high school, and learned she'd had
kids. She lives in Portland and had just
commuted out to that stupid county for
work. The television screen went black

as the camera crew zoomed in on a pissed off octopus. I picked up the phone on the nightstand between the two beds and called information asking for a phone number for "Mary Snow." I didn't really think about what I was doing, and agreed that the operator could connect me.

Mrs. Snow picked up the phone and I said hi. I didn't know what else to say. She didn't know I'd left home. Didn't know I'd been homeless. She didn't know shit, but she'd been nice to me back when I was a little kid and she seemed happy to talk to me now. She said that she'd seen my mother in the grocery store out by the middle school and asked about me, but my mom said I was doing really well. Stupid drunk-ass couldn't even admit she hadn't fucking talked to me in a year.

Hope opened the bathroom door. She was in boxers and a ratty hoodie from the needle exchange and she was chewing on her lip ring and separating her dreads. I don't think she'd known I was there until she came into the main room. She started screaming at me about how I was a little slut, how I didn't know shit about what was going on, how fucked up it was for me to be there, and that she was going to kick my ass once and for all. I told Mrs. Snow I had to go but would call her right back and took off out the door. I started running down the catwalk hallway towards the stairs. Billy must have gotten up too because pretty soon I could hear his boots behind me and he was yelling at Hope that she needed to calm down and that he would handle things. I made it down to the parking lot and hid behind an SUV.

I saw Billy catch up to Hope. He slammed her up against the building. It's fucked up but I was so damn hot and wishing I could piss him off enough that he'd do that to me. I watched them both go upstairs again, Billy's hand on the back of Hope's neck.

I stayed hidden and in a few minutes until Billy came down again, this time with the ferrets peeking out through the neck hole in his hoodie. He asked if I was ok. I said yeah, but that I thought I was going to leave. He thought that was a good idea and started walking me towards the apartment in case there was any trouble. He said he thought Hope might call someone else to try to get me jumped. We started walking down 12th and got all the way back to Hawthorne without anything happening. When we got to the apartment he said he was going back to check on Saucer. She'd shot some really nasty stuff and was having a hard time coming down from it. He said he'd be back later and until then to lock the door and keep Orbit close. I called Buck and told him what happened. He said he was glad I was okay, but that he'd told me to stay the hell away from Kristin and all this drama was my fault.

Date: November 25, 2002

When I got to QYRC tonight I didn't see Sammy. All week we've been playing this stupid flirting game but he's never able to follow through. I signed in and dropped on the brown couch behind the stage. I was in a pretty shitty mood because everyone said they were going to come early but I guess they were running late. It was mostly just GSA kids sitting around playing board games. I decided I was going to take a nap until folks got there since there wasn't anything better to do.

I don't think I actually was sleeping for very long, when I felt someone sit on the edge of the couch. I pretended to still be asleep but opened one eye just a little to try to figure out who it was. All I could see was bright orange so I knew it was Sammy. He wears that same hoodie every single day. I closed my eyes again and felt Sammy reach his arm around me and start to softly rub my shoulder right where we're always knotted up from the way the binding undershirts sit.

I was on my side, and the way Sammy sat down, his ass was right up against my junk. As he rubbed my back I started slowly grinding into him. Then he moved and laid down facing me on the couch. He's a big guy and at first I didn't think he would fit, and then it was so good, I was squished right between him and the back of the couch and finally he kissed me. He started T a little while ago and has these really sexy wispy sideburns. They were kinda scratchy against my cheek when he kissed me. I can't tell Buck this because it would sound really transphobic, but as hot as I think they look, feeling them while we made out kinda freaked me out too. I've never kissed anyone with facial hair before.

Date: November 26, 2002

It's such FUCKING BULLSHIT. This seeing Sammy shit has been mostly weird cuz I don't get what his deal is. I've tried to get him to fuck me a bunch of times, but he keeps saying that he isn't "like that" and wants to "take it slow." I don't know what that even means. We've been sorta seeing each other for like a week now, but we only get together at QYRC, which is awkward cuz he's still got the internship, so it's almost like trying to hook up with someone while they are at work! He never wants to hang out away from QYRC. He says he has school and stuff. Other than Kristin, he's also the only person I know who lives with his parents. It's weird. I'm sure that's why he never wants to see me outside of QYRC.

I'm not exactly someone you can introduce your fucking parents to.

Anyway, so tonight he told me I could walk him to his bus stop when he was ready to leave QYRC. I thought maybe this would be my big chance. We waited for the #15 to come. Finally I couldn't help it and just kissed him. He kissed me back. It was a crappy kiss. His lips were big and wet and it was like he was trying to lick my face off. We stopped kissing. The bus still wasn't there. I started telling him about how I talked to Gus tonight and they told me that all the staff thought it was a great idea for me to write and put together the first QYRC newsletter while we're closed for Thanksgiving. I'd been freaking out about not being able to come to the center for three days in a row, and the stupid holiday, which was why I'd started talking to Gus about the newsletter.

I couldn't tell if Sammy was actually listening or not, but I kept talking about how cool the newsletter was gonna be and how I was really glad all the staff were trusting me with it. Then he said, "They're just letting you do it because they're worried you might fuck yourself up over the weekend. They said so at the staff meeting."

I wanted to punch him.

I almost did, too, but then the bus came and he left.

Now I don't even know what's true.
I thought I could trust Gus, but WTF!!!!!
What if Gus really just says I'm good at
this stuff so I don't go back to slicing
and dicing, which I was always sort of
a failure at, or take a bunch of pills
like I did last summer before James left
me (also a total failure cuz I only took
like twelve).

Now I don't know who to trust.

Date: November 28, 2002
Security: Friends
Subject: Thanksgiving

I called Mrs. Snow back after all the crazy shit at the hotel.
I had to apologize because when I hung up the phone I said
I would be calling right back, and then of course I didn't. She
said it was ok and that since she had heard a bunch of yelling
in the background she was just glad to hear I was ok. It was
only a couple days ago that I called her, and when I filled her
in a little bit on where I've been the last year or so, she asked
if I had thanksgiving plans. I said no. She said I had to come to
her house and have thanksgiving with her family. I didn't really
want to go, but I said ok after she told me I should bring Orbit.

I woke up late this morning, it was hard to sleep knowing this
stupid holiday was going to be there in the morning. Billy was
gone. He spent the night with Hope at her squat because they

had agreed to try to see their parents together today. I didn't even want to come over to Mrs. Snow's place but I'd said I would, so I had to. I asked if I should bring anything and she said no so I didn't have to do any cooking, just get myself cleaned up. I took a shower and re-shaved my mohawk. I thought about dying it again but I was out of green dye and of course everything was fucking closed today for the holiday. My work pants were mostly clean and I put on a black button down that I snagged for fifty cents at the thrift store a couple days ago.

Dinner was awkward. Orbit and I got there right as everyone was sitting down to eat. It was Mrs. Snow and her husband, their two little kids, and another grownup couple with their three kids. I sat at a table with all these parents and little kids and I realized that there was pretty much nothing about my life that was safe to talk about. I ate turkey. The kids couldn't sit still for very long and kept running around the room trying to get Orbit to play with them. They asked a lot of questions about my hair, piercings and tattoos but then their parents would shush them. I wonder what Mrs. Snow told her friends about me. After dinner they were all going to wander around looking at Christmas lights.

Mrs. Snow's youngest kid was cold and had to go to bed so I came back to the house with them. On the way back, Mrs. Snow said she'd run into my birth mom again and mentioned that I'd be coming for Thanksgiving. I know Mrs. Snow probably meant well but I was really angry that she'd say anything about me to my birth mom! She said my mom got really weird and told her to be careful because I was a drug addict. I was so mad. Orbit came and sat in my lap, and I tried to explain to Mrs. Snow what XXX means but she said she had to put the baby to bed. I saw a computer in the living room. I asked if I could check my email before I left and she said of course which is how I'm online right now. I'm getting out of here in a few minutes. I don't know why I tried to get back in touch with her in the first place. I really hope that Billy's around when I get back to the apartment.

Date: November 29, 2002

I hung out with Johnny today, which was pretty cool. I really like her and we always talk at QYRC when I'm not with Billy. They used to be close but now that she's Grace's boy it's hard for him to be around her. Today was the first time Johnny and I hung out on our own outside of the center. She wanted to go out to the lesbian sex toy shop. I didn't have anything else to do, and I really didn't want to be alone so I said I would go with her.

Johnny's only sixteen, so I was kinda worried that they weren't going to let us in when we got out there, but they didn't card at all. Johnny went right through the beaded curtain into the back room to look at cocks. I stayed up front with the books. At QYRC, one of the volunteers brought in a bunch of old issues of a magazine full of folks like me talking about real queer sex. The shop has the latest issue in, but I wasn't that impressed because the cover had this naked fat femme rockstar and it cost six dollars. Then, when I started flipping pages, I started to see hot bois and butches. Johnny came out from the back with a red glitter harness and said she was ready to go. I bought the magazine.

Date: December 2, 2002

I wasn't going to tell Gus about the shit Sammy said, but then I kinda had to.

I haven't been sleeping and I was just so pissed. I finished the newsletter like I said I would so when QYRC opened again today I gave it to Gus. Gus asked if I was ok over Thanksgiving and could tell I was upset. I was going to say I was fine, but then I started crying so we had to go to the back office. I told Gus what Sammy had said. Gus looked really pissed.

Gus said it wasn't true.

Well, they said that of course they were worried about me, and all the rest of us orphans, but that hadn't been why I was asked to do the newsletter.

I think I believe them.

Date: December 5, 2002
Security: Friends
Subject: Untitled

That little kid, Chris, came back to QYRC again tonight. I guess she has to take three busses to get up here from the town she lives in. She keeps trying to hang out with me, I think it's because Gus told her about how I first came to QYRC after I went to the gay rural outreach program that had just started right when I was getting kicked out of home. It was damn good timing. The volunteer leader of our little gay rural group kept telling me that I should go to QYRC but I was scared.

I remember when I walked in here that first time. I was surprised by how out of control it looked. The kids looked rough. I'd never met another homeless kid before. Fuck, I'd only ever seen maybe five gay people in my whole life! When I came out, all the kids at my high school were scared of me. A bunch of parents had called the guidance councilor to complain that my GSA was "leading kids down a path to hell." This place changed everything.

Date: December 11, 2002

Piglet is sleeping again, curled up behind some backpacks. His mouth is hanging open. I know Billy keeps watching to make sure he's still breathing. His eyes were all glazed when he stumbled into QYRC a few hours ago. We were all standing outside and he came up and said he needed to sleep for a while. He was stuttering real bad, but he always is. Johnny tells me that before Scummy died things used to be better, it seems like Piglet's always been this way to me.

Technically we're not supposed to sleep here, but Piglet needs to. Once QYRC closes he'll be up all night wandering around under the bridges, along the waterfront, and up towards Paranoia Park. Gus knows what's going on but so long as we don't flaunt it the volunteers won't have to bust him for sleeping while he can. They won't say it, but I know with Scummy gone, Gus expects Piglet to be next.

Someone recently donated the whole first season of some faggot sitcom, so we're all curled up on the beanbags with some burnt microwave popcorn, watching these rich faggots dancing on the screen. It's just dark enough that none of the GSA kids can see Piglet sleeping and rat us out.

I always feel this pressure to make sure everyone knows where my allegiances are. When I first came to QYRC I was a little contentious cuz technically I was a GSA kid, but it was quickly decided that I was different. I was in school but just barely and I didn't have any parents. I went to the GSA but it was different, since I started the first one my high school ever had. That was after my coach kicked me out and I was couch surfing with my best fag friend. I'd take the bus a couple hours to get to Portland and come to QYRC. All the street kids thought that made me pretty tough because my high school was way out in Clackamas which is one scary-ass county.

After a couple of weeks of just coming to QYRC every night and keeping to myself folks figured out I wasn't like the other kids still going to high school. It helped that I made friends with Billy quickly. He vouched for me when Hope and Saucer would start giving me a hard time.

For once it feels good to belong somewhere, and to know that someone has my back. We don't tell the GSA kids what we think of them, that kinda fighting would get all kicked out of the space for the night, even though I'm pretty sure staff like us best. Instead we're commanding control of the VCR and spreading out to let people sleep and fuck in the shadows and daring the GSA kids to cross us.

Date: December 13, 2002

All we really have is each other. Scummy dying messed with everyone's heads real bad. Last night Billy said that he just couldn't handle this bullshit anymore. I think the drama with Hope and Saucer is finally over. Billy and I were talking late last night, curled up in my bed because it was so cold, and he told me he'd fixed everything with Hope. I'm always looking over my shoulder in case birth mom pulls some stupid shit, but I've also spent the last little bit watching out for Hope and her gang. Every time we've run into each other at QYRC she'll hip check me and threaten to get me jumped. I thought about telling Gus, but being labeled a snitch would not help my reputation at all. I guess Billy was tired of being in

the middle and he told her that he and
I were family that he had my back and
she needed to really call her pack off
or they would be answering to him. Being
stepsiblings, he's probably the only
person that could get by with talking to
her that way.

Tonight she came up to me at QYRC and
gave me a hug like I was anyone else in
the space. I was a little worried she was
going to stab me or something but Billy was
next to her and he nodded that everything
was ok so I went ahead and hugged her.
Later, Saucer asked if I wanted to play
pool with her. She and Kristin are still
seeing each other, and while I'm sure
she doesn't love that I fucked her girl,
I think she's also realized it wasn't
anything serious.

Date: December 14, 2002

I ran into Dean at QYRC. I hadn't seen him
for a while, so it was good to know he was
ok. He's off the streets, but staying with
his grandmother again. From his stories,
things have always been pretty bad there,
but it's been raining for weeks, and he's
got a cough that won't go away. We talked
for a long time outside while he smoked

cigarette after cigarette. Orbit came and curled up in his lap. Right before we went in to watch the practice for next week's drag show, Dean asked if I'd go to church with him the next morning. I was kinda surprised because we're not even that close of friends.

Dean said it was a big thing to his grandmother. Live under her roof, pray to her god. That meant church every Sunday. Dean said he was seeing how long he could take it, but he was starting to feel better which meant he was thinking of running again.

I haven't been to church in years, since I was in the seventh grade. It was this wannabe mega church that all the kids from my school were going to. My parents went to a smaller one with mostly senior citizens. I was taking a stab at being one of the Jesus freaks. They were always looking for folks to save, and took me along to one of the youth groups, and rock services. I tried hard, but couldn't even do that right. I was such a clueless baby back then, but other people were on to me. The whole school knew that I was a dyke, and pretty soon god did too. I haven't been in a church since.

Even though Dean's grandmother's church was really early in the morning, like ten or some shit, I told Dean that I would go with him. I am never even awake that early, let alone clean and coherent enough to interact with straight people. I think the last time I agreed to do something so early was when Billy got his food stamps turned off for not meeting with his case manager, and had to go into the welfare office to get them turned back on, and needed someone to go with him. Dean said he had some clothes that I could borrow, which meant I had to get up even earlier to get to his grandma's place in time to change. I didn't really have a choice. My nice clothes are an old pair of work pants and a bleach stained button up flannel shirt.

When I left the apartment Billy was still sleeping so I tucked Orbit into bed on the futon with him and the ferrets and headed for the bus stop. When Dean moved in, his grandmother bought him a bunch of dresses for different church functions. Dean may have been sick, but he wasn't desperate enough to go for that shit. Right away, he snuck downtown and with a little cardboard sign and a sob story about being stranded and trying to get home, spanged enough cash to buy a button down. He stuffed a tie into his pocket when the clerk at the thrift store wasn't looking. Then he found a second button down in one of the bags of donated clothes at QYRC.

We offered to meet her at church, but his grandmother didn't think it was appropriate for two young ladies to take the bus, so we had to ride in the back of her car. I kept tugging at my tie and adjusting my binder when I thought her eyes were away from the review mirror. Dean sat quietly next to me. When we got to church, Dean's grandmother disappeared into a crowd of women, leaving us alone in the church hall. I nudged the red velvet-covered kneeler in front of me with my boot. I started thinking about how hot it would be to suck Dean off, right here in the pew. Before services started, Dean's grandma joined us with a stern look. On the drive over she had lectured the two of us on proper behavior when in the house of God. I think that was mostly for my benefit. Dean had the fear God in him and knew how to behave. She seemed stuck between her dislike of me as I was not a proper friend for her "granddaughter" and her Christian duty to fear for, and care for my soul.

The service was mostly pretty uneventful. The preacher talked about duty, honor, and family values. All these folks seemed like unlikely experts on this stuff to me. I kept wanting to pop up and say something, but Dean could tell I was getting upset and would stick his elbow into my ribs. He didn't want to go back to the streets. Dean looked scared. I guess he could live with the cost of the bed at his grandma's, and he couldn't afford for me to mess it up. His grandma's eyes never left her ratty over-highlighted Bible. I kept my mouth shut.

After the services Dean and I slipped away to the fellowship room scarfing down donut holes and burnt coffee while his grandmother chatted with her friends. I wanted to go downtown, but couldn't just abandon Dean. Finally, his grandma had enough gossip to last her until Wednesday bible study, and she motioned that it was time to go. I thought the whole thing was over, but then I saw the pastor standing between us and the parking lot, shaking hands with the congregation as they left.

I tried to duck around him, but he was already gripping Dean's hand, shaking it firmly up and down. Then he grabbed mine.

"You have lovely grandsons, strong, respectable looking boys," the pastor commented to Dean's grandmother. She blushed, hard, then tried to stammer out a correction, but ended in a thank you and quickly led us to the car. She dumped me at a nearby bus stop and sped away. I tried to wave to Dean but he never turned his head away from the windshield.

This morning I saw Dean sitting with his backpack by the fountain under the bridge. The stupid-ass church clothes gone. He looked hot sitting there with a notebook, in his old hoodie and mud on his boots and on the bottom cuff of his ratty work pants. He looked tired, and was coughing again.

Date: December 17, 2002
Security: Friends

Hope got proposed to last night at the QYRC open mic. If I hadn't been there, and I almost wasn't because I almost went gay line dancing with some folks, I wouldn't have believed that it happened. She's been dating Tristan, this cute little blond butch, for a while now. Tristan moved here from Texas a few months ago and hooked up with Hope right away. She's always wearing cowboy boots and Wranglers and goddamn, if she weren't dating Hope I'd so hit on her because she reminds me of all the good things about growing up in the country.

I don't know Tristan very well. Johnny's best friends with her and said she hadn't told anyone she was going to do it. I guess Tristan wanted it to be a real surprise, which it was, but still that's the kind of thing you tell your best friend about. She was reading this sappy poem she'd written about how Hope was the best thing that ever happened to her, and how she couldn't imagine the point of life if Hope wasn't in it, that sort of thing. She made Hope get up on the stage with her before dropping to one knee and pulling a diamond ring out of her jeans. It's a good thing she waited until the end of the open mic, because no one was paying attention to anything else after that.

Later, out in the smoking area, Tristan made a big deal about the ring being real. She was really proud of how it wasn't thirteen dollar glass from the super store. She said she'd been saving all the money from her second fast food job for a long time to buy that ring. I'm sure Hope had just assumed she'd started using again, with the rate the money was disappearing. Hope looked both excited and embarrassed standing there with all her ex's out in the smoking area.

When QYRC closed last night, we went with them to the all night convenience store to get the sixty dollar money order. The girl behind the counter looked pissed about having to count up all the crumpled ones and fives. First thing this morning they went to the county registration building and handed over last of the money that had been saved up. Hope and Tristan walked out of the county building with a certificate of domestic partnership and brought it to QYRC right when it opened today. None of us could stop looking at it and how official it was. Printed on the paper right next to each other right above a fancy seal were their names! Well, not their real names, it was just their government issued names. But still.

Tonight to celebrate, Johnny and I cooked pasta for everyone, and when we were mostly alone in the kitchen, she told how she'd heard Hope and Tristan had to lie a little bit in order to get it. The city mandates folks entering into domestic partnerships live together for six months. I guess they wrote down QYRC as their primary shared residence. That wasn't really a lie. They were living together but just didn't have a steady address or anything. Everyone was obsessed and kept asking to see the certificate. Now that it seems like Saucer and Kristin are doing well, Hope is done fighting with me. It helps that Billy told her she'd have to go through him first to get at me. Still, I tried to play it a little cool and not be all gushing and shit, but that was kinda hard.

Date: December 25, 2002

It's so weird not to be able to go to QYRC. I get why they have to be closed and shit, but for those of us without fucking family it really would be nice to have somewhere to go. Last night a new dyke moved in down the hall. I was surprised to see anyone moving in the day before Christmas! She was hella cute in her overalls and thermal shirt and bright red hair. We stood and talked in the hallway for a while until she said she needed to go check on her son but that I could come in with her.

I must have made a face because she looked really hurt. She let me follow her into her apartment anyway. It's a little studio smaller than mine even. There were boxes everywhere and a little kid, maybe about three, coloring on one of them. I got down on the floor and tried to play with him but he seemed scared of Orbit. I asked what he was drawing and he said Santa, but then got scared and ran behind his mom. She said he learned bout Santa from daycare. She hadn't planned to tell him, since with this unexpected move she couldn't afford to get him anything.

I asked how they were going to fit in this little room. She said she hoped to get a bigger place someday, but for now she'd figured out that when he was asleep she could go read in the bathroom so the

light wouldn't bother him. I said I had
to go and went outside instead of back
into my apartment. It was weird to see
a little kid the day before Christmas
and know he wasn't going to get shit.
I started walking and ended up by the
super store that was still open. I went
in and wandered the toy aisle for a while.
I don't know what the fuck little kids
like. I hadn't remembered how gendered
toys were, what does a little boy wearing
pink pajamas with a dyke mama want to play
with anyway? I settled on a rainbow set
of putty and then on my way to the cash
register found a little tiny Christmas
tree, seriously it's like the size of my
hand, in a little red pot, and grabbed
that too.

I have no fucking idea what I'm doing.
Billy thought I'd lost my mind when he
saw Orbit and me walking back in with
this little tree. He knows how much
I hate Christmas. I told him the whole
story though and then he thought it was
sweet and got all into it. Right now he's
drawing Santa and his reindeer all over
the pot. We figure at midnight we will go
sneak down the hall put them in front of
the kid's door, knock, and then run back
to our place before his mother gets to

the door. That way when she and the kid
pop their heads out they will just see
what Santa left.

After that I'm going to bed and not waking
up until this bullshit holiday is over.

Date: December 28, 2002
Security: Friends
Subject: approved

The Steering Committee at QYRC is mostly just everyone who founded the space: Billy, Hope, Saucer, Sean, Scummy before he died, and a couple other old folks like Johnny. Essentially it's written in the mission statement that they get to make all the major decisions about the space, like what programs happen and what staff gets hired. I knew that they were looking for another person to join steering committee but after I fucked everything up by going to be with James in the south I never thought I'd have another chance. Tonight Orbit and I walked in, and Billy told me the group had voted for me to join! I guess they saw that my loyalties really are here now.

We went right into my first meeting, and they said that I got in because I'm one of them, old school. I know what it means to be on my own and can be trusted. We had a long meeting to interview about this new group of adults who applied to be volunteers for during drop-in.

Most of them were ok, a couple of lesbians, and one gay guy who wanted to do art programming. I wasn't in love with them, but they seemed harmless.

Then there was this little group of graduate students who wanted to volunteer together. They're working on some bullshit study about homeless queer kids and thought it would be great to volunteer at QYRC in order to learn more about our world. I think they were really uncomfortable with having to interview with youth. They so don't belong here. It was a unanimous vote to not let them back in the space, ever, and that the other folks could move onto the orientation phase where the community educators and I will teach them the basics for how to understand folks around here and be "culturally competent."

We called the students on speaker phone to let them know that they would not be moving to the next stage of the interview process. They seemed pissed and wanted to know why. We told them that they weren't an appropriate fit for the space. That's the nice way of saying "suck my rubber cock."

Graindaughter ~~Natalie Styles~~ Zander ~~Nate~~ Click

Burthday May 16, 1984

~~3258 St Jude St Clackamas Oregon~~
~~c/o Linda 123523 rural road 5 Oregon City, Oregon~~
~~c/o Frank 1345 highway 8 Molalla, Oregon~~
~~2344 9th ave, basement SE Portland, Oregon~~
~~c/o James 2345 Heart St Jacksonville, Florida~~
~~974 apt 66 35th ave Jacksonville, Florida~~
~~c/o Mrs Jahn 2345 Beach Drive Jacksonville Fla~~
~~c/o Buck 1469 apt 5 NW Portland, Oregon~~
~~133 Hawthorne Blvd Apt 3 Portland, Oregon~~
67 East 75th St Portland, Oregon

Date: January 4, 2003

Sunny has been dating Cody for six months now. That's practically like being married around here. Sunny's a funny one, hella genderqueer, like one day she'll come in with a baby doll t-shirt and bondage pants, and the next day she'll be binding and wearing a hoodie. Cody's all boy but not punk. He dresses all preppy but has piercings and stuff. He's so ready to turn eighteen so he can start on T, it's pretty much all he talks about. They met when he was on vacation from the state deaf school where he has to live most of the year. It was a big deal, cuz Sunny didn't even know how to sign at the time, but she learned fucking fast. I mean, we've all gotten pretty good since folks from the school started coming up here regularly. Sunny had been sleeping in her car for a few months ever since her mom kicked her out, so she and Cody spent a lot of time just driving around together, him giving her gas money and shit. After about a month of that his mom got tired of not knowing where he was and said that Sunny could come and live with them. His mom didn't even make her pay rent or anything from her job at the call center,

so she quit it, to have more time to spend
with Cody who has pretty much dropped out
of school.

See, Sunny came from a little farming
community about an hour and a half south,
which is why she and I became friends.
I grew up in the sticks too, and was
all into that country shit until being
queer got in the way, and I woke up and
realized how fucked up all that shit is.

Sunny and I were talking out in the smoking
area at QYRC last night while Cody was in
the trans youth group. At first we were
just talking about what events we were
going to go to this week. She was trying
to convince Cody to go to the bondage
101 workshop because she thought it would
be really hot to tie him up. So far at
least, he wasn't going for it. He didn't
like the idea of not being able to talk.
She countered that she'd let him stuff a
ball gag in her mouth, but he said it was
different because without his hands free
he couldn't communicate at all. Then we
started talking about how I hadn't hooked
up with anyone for a little bit and she
asked if I would be willing to let her
set me up with one of her friends.

Now, by friend she meant ex-girlfriend, well, boy now, but girl back then. Anyway, the whole thing sounded possibly a little dramatic, lesbionic, not to mention pathetic. Do I really need someone to fucking set me up? Sunny promised me it was none of that. She said his name was Hunter, and explained that he lives down in a tiny town on the way out to the coast, and she wanted to make sure he hooked up with good folks. She also said he was way hot. I said she could give him my number. I wonder if he'll call.

Date: January 5, 2003

Hunter called me this afternoon. Billy wasn't around and I was just about to jump into the shower when I heard the phone ring. I ignored the big windows that were open and facing the walkway to the building and ran across the apartment, tripping over Orbit which made him start barking. Hunter said that he was thinking of coming into Portland tonight and wanted to know if I'd be at QYRC. I almost laughed at him. Come on, where the hell else would I be? I decided laughing at him might not be very nice, especially if he was talking about having to take all kinds of county transfer busses for hours, pretty much just to meet me. It was awkward being on the phone, but he sounded hot and kinda bossy. He said he thought he'd be to QYRC by eight. When we got off the phone I realized I needed to find something really good to wear. I ended up settling on my "heretic in good company" t-shirt that lists all the names of these kick ass folks through history, lots of them dykes that really fucked shit up, and my work pants and boots, of course.

I went to QYRC early and was super glad that Sunny was already there. I was going to tell her that Hunter called, but she already knew. She said that he called her right when he hung up with me, and that he said I sounded hot and couldn't wait to meet me. Things at QYRC got busy and I lost track of time. Every so often the youth phone would ring and someone, usually Sean who's this hella queeny fag who was always sitting by it hoping his boyfriend of the week would call, would yell for Sunny.

Turns out that the county transfer busses were running enough to pick Hunter up, but when they got to the next biggest town they stopped running cuz it was too late.

Hunter kept calling her from pay phones trying to figure out what to do. I think he wanted her to come pick him up, but she didn't have enough gas and Cody would be pissed if she went off to get her ex. After the third call I was pretty sure he was not showing up tonight, and I was not going to get laid. Sunny didn't seem worried. I guess Hunter decided to blow the last of his cash on a the private bus ticket and rode the last leg of the trip into Portland in style.

It was almost ten by the time Hunter showed up at QYRC. His hair was dyed red and cut into a bowl cut and he had on all these studded leather bands around his wrists and baggy jeans with a plain black t-shirt. He has dates of concerts tattooed all over his left arm and his eyebrow and lip are pierced. I love kissing people with facial piercings because of how hot it is when they hit up against mine. He's about my height so kinda short and a little round in the best ways. He was binding flat and winked at me when he walked in the door. Sunny must have told him what I looked like.

They talked for a little while, but then Cody started getting really pissed off. I could only understand about half of what he was signing because it was so fast. Sunny said they had to go.

Hunter and I went out to the smoking area and talked for a while. He thought it was cool that I don't smoke, and weird that I am XXX. I guess he's working on being clean. He said he'd done a bunch of stuff, but mostly meth for a long time. He started telling me about driving in the middle of the night from his mom's house to Sunny's mom's farm, steering with his knees while shooting up. I guess I looked a little nervous about that, because then he said all that was far behind him now. He leaned in and kissed me. Even before we went back to my place, I let him leave hickies all over my neck. When I went in to say goodbye to everyone folks kept giving me these goofy grins. I asked Billy when he thought he'd be home. He said he would stay at QYRC until midnight, and then walk home slowly. Our place is only about ten blocks from QYRC. Hunter and me had to hurry.

When Billy got back to the apartment we were done fucking, barely. I'd gotten all shy for a second when we first got back to my place but then Hunter took charge. He slapped me around when we were making out and then ordered me to take my pants off. He fisted me hard, hand sticking through the fly of my boxer shorts and his other hand right in the middle of my chest pushing down so I could barely breathe. When I heard Billy's key in the door Hunter had all his clothes on but I had to scramble to pull on my shirt. We all ate some hotdogs and then Hunter and I decided we were going to take a walk. Before we left, Hunter asked if he could borrow a little bit of money. At first I thought he was going to fuck and run and was planning on buying a bus ticket, but then he explained that he wasn't going anywhere and that he wanted to buy me a present. He said he needed ten dollars.

I told him he didn't have to get me a present, after all he'd already bought a bus ticket tonight but he said he wanted to, so I gave him the money. I left Orbit with Billy, and Hunter and I walked over the bridge into downtown. Orbit was really upset when we left, I could hear him crying when we walked down the hallway. I never leave him alone at night, so I think that's why he's upset. Hunter also doesn't like dogs very much so he hadn't really given him any attention all evening. All that was open was the shit that never closes: the 24 hour diner and the leather shop. When we were walking past Paranoia Park I saw Johnny who hadn't been at QYRC earlier. She and I started talking and Hunter said he'd be right back.

It took Hunter about twenty minutes to get back to the park. I had started to wonder if he found someone hotter. It was late, so we started walking back towards the apartment place. We were talking mostly about our fucked up families, what we liked to eat, and I was babbling on and on about Orbit, that kind of shit. I was telling him about this zine I was starting to working on and then he got all quiet. We were right in the middle of the bridge. He said he wanted to give me my present. I'd forgotten all about it. He told me I had to get on my knees and close my eyes. I was kinda freaked out because the bridge isn't super safe and anyone driving by could see what was happening, but I did as I was told.

Hunter grabbed my right hand hard and I wasn't sure what he was going to do but then I felt something warm and stiff slip around my wrist and heard metal snap together. He told me I could open my eyes. There was a leather band around my wrist and as a car drove by the headlights caught the metal studs pressed into it that spelled out "Daddy's Boy." Hunter pushed up his ratty sweatshirt to reveal the matching "Daddy" cuff on his left.

"Thank you Sir," was all I could say, and he started walking. I picked myself off the concrete and scrambled to catch up. I couldn't wait to get home and show Billy.

When we got back, Billy was laying on the futon with Orbit reading a zine some girl gave me at the bookstore. I showed him my present and he got all excited about it just like I knew he would. He's been collared several times, and knew what a big deal it was for me, especially after James. He asked if we wanted him to go out for a while but it was really late so I said no. I don't think Hunter really liked that, and said he wanted to see me in the kitchen. I handed Billy my Walkman so he could at least have some headphones, not that it really makes much difference in this little space.

Hunter pushed me hard, face first against the counters and kicked my boots apart. He pulled my shirt off but let me keep my sports bra. I could hear him take a couple of steps away and then my back lit up. The leather falls bit into my shoulders again and again. For a second I got distracted, wondering where the flogger came from. He hadn't brought a backpack with him to QYRC and I know that ten dollars barely covered the cuffs. It doesn't really matter, but something tells me he can't go back to the leather shop anymore.

Date: January 8, 2003

Hunter had to leave me today to go back down to his old place to get the rest his clothes and cats and stuff. I told him that he could start living here with us, I mean he's my Daddy and he needs a place to live so obviously I wasn't going to tell him no. Billy seemed cool with it when I told him this morning. He understands that there are things you have to do when you have a Daddy. When

I said Hunter could move in I didn't know he had cats, but it's not that big of a deal really so long as the landlord doesn't know. I mean the landlord just thinks it's me living here, they don't know anything about Orbit or Billy's ferrets or Billy for that matter.

When Hunter left this morning I made beds on top of the kitchen cabinets out of some old t-shirts so when the cats got here they could have their own private little space and Billy and I went and dumpstered an old pallet. He and I used it to make a little ramp from the top of the refrigerator to the cabinet to give them even more space. It was good to have the cat ramp project to focus on, because I was really freaking out when Hunter left this morning. I was worried that he wasn't going to come back. I guess I'm still kinda fucked up about the James thing, but I have to keep reminding myself that it's different this time, I have a real Daddy who's never going to leave me. He left on the bus to go down there early this morning and one of his buddies had agreed to drive him back tonight. It's who he used to get high with so I was nervous about it, but he promised me he's done with meth and the only thing they might do was smoke.

I don't think Hunter really understands how XXX I am.

The cats are settling in pretty good I think. Orbit sniffed the backpacks Hunter had driven them up in but then jumped back onto my bed, and the ferrets haven't even noticed them yet I don't think.

Date: January 9, 2003

I ran into Buck by the fountain down by the light-rail tracks under the bridge. I was wasting time before QYRC opened. Hunter went downtown with me, but said he had to meet up with someone up by the pizza place and that he would be right back. I had my notebook with me and started working on this story about that preacher protest where I lost my job. I think I'm going to be talking about it in my next zine. I was sitting there writing when Orbit started barking and startled me. I looked up and Buck was walking towards us. I guess he was on his lunch break cuz he was wearing the

dopy polo shirt uniform. He asked me if
I was hooking up with anyone. It was a
weird question. I knew someone at QYRC
had probably ratted me out about Hunter.
I was pissed. I needed to tell my brother
about it myself.

I hadn't even replied yet when Buck said,
"I don't like him."

"Who?" I asked, trying to play innocent.

He grabbed my faded saggy mohawk and
pulled me into him and whispered into my
ear, "Don't fuck with me, little brother."

I was shaking. He sat me down back to the
concrete base of the fountain and I told
him all about how Sunny set me up with
Hunter and that things are going really
good. I even pulled up the sleeve of my
sweatshirt to show Buck the leather cuff.
He asked me if Hunter is still using.
I told him no.

Pretty soon he had to go back to work.
I stood up too and he grabbed my face in
his left hand so I had to look him in the
eyes. "I didn't get you back from Florida
to lose you to some wannabe Daddy."

Buck kissed me on top of the head and started walking back towards work. I saw Johnny and Grace and asked if they'd seen Hunter anywhere. I was getting worried. Johnny said she'd seen him up in Paranoia Park with some dudes she didn't know. I grabbed my messenger bag and started jogging up Burnside. When I got to the park there was just a bunch of folks tweaking but I didn't see Hunter anywhere. Paranoia is only a half block big so it's not like there are many places to hide.

Orbit took off running towards the bathrooms, so I followed him. They are these little concrete cubes that are always open and the only places this side of downtown where you can pee without having to buy something. The city doesn't really clean them so they're nasty most of the time and the next stall over almost always has someone shooting up in it. Hunter is a neat freak, he refuses to piss in dirty bathrooms, which was why I was so freaked when I saw him stumbling out of the women's bathroom.

His hair was all messed up and my flannel shirt he was wearing was all lumpy from where the buttons and holes had been unevenly put together. The thing that

```
scared me most was that he wasn't binding
like he was when he left me at the fountain.
I ran over to him worried that something
had happened and worried even more that
he'd be mad I came up there looking for
him. He looked more confused than angry
and said his stomach was upset and he'd
had to puke. His eyes were super big
and he was talking really fast. I started
walking us out of the park, him leaning
against me and stumbling as I took him to
the bus.
```

Date: January 13, 2003
Security: Public
Subject: moving

Ugh!! I knew could happen, but I never really thought it would. Some dumbass neighbor must have figured out what was going on and called the management company because I got a fucking notice in the mail today that we had ten days to get out of the apartment. Well, they said I had ten days to get out everyone else out.

I really don't get what their fucking problem is. I know it's a little studio, and Billy and Hunter are living here and then on and off other folks sometimes crash and that's a little crazy, but folks need somewhere to go!!!! Besides, it's not like we're not paying rent.

I'm sure it doesn't help that we're on the first floor and the windows open right onto the front walk so folks can easily look in and see all of us.

I've been freaking about it and carrying the letter around in my back pocket. I guess that means I'm flagging "soon to be homeless again." Billy came up to me and said he could go back to the squats or find somewhere else to crash. Hunter just left when I told him, and came back a few hours later drunk. I know he's angry with me because I can't stop it from happening. If I were a good boy I'd solve it. I told Billy he wasn't going anywhere. I'm responsible for what happened and I take that seriously. I'm going to figure everything out.

Date: January 17, 2003

Hunter and I had a big fight tonight. Orbit and I went to QYRC for a steering committee meeting. We were trying to come to a consensus about rules for how much food folks could eat, and if it was ok for the GSA kids to mooch off the donated food when they don't need it, so the meeting ran a little late. I thought that Daddy and I had plans to go with Billy to the solidarity gathering at the feminist bookstore to respond to some stupid anti-sex feminists who ripped the covers off every fucking SM erotica book in the store (and it's not like there were all that many to begin with). Billy, Orbit and I got back to the apartment after steering committee and the only ones home were the cats and ferrets! I was pretty upset, but mostly worried that something had happened to Daddy.

Billy convinced me to go to the bookstore with him by saying that maybe Hunter had gotten tired of waiting for us and was already there. I popped Orbit into my bag and we took the bus up to the shop, but Daddy wasn't there. The event was boring, mostly just people talking about how to better communicate to other people in the community about the dangers of censorship and book banning, but nothing about why it's not ok to be hating on us as Leather folks. That part really pissed me off.

Daddy wasn't at the apartment when we got back, either. I was really glad that Billy and Orbit were with me because I was worried and stressed out. He came stumbling in about two. Billy and I were still up, we'd been talking about the bookstore event, and then he just came in like nothing had happened! I asked where he'd been and he said he went for walk and lost track of time and all he wanted to do now was get some sleep.

Date: January 18, 2003
Security: Friends
Subject !!!!!!!!!!!!

We're moving!!!! Finding the place was kinda weird. I'm not supposed to talk about it cuz it technically broke some QYRC rules.

I was talking about getting evicted at QYRC, and one of the adult volunteers said that she had a brother who had a house for rent. Really it's an old shed that someone made into a sorta house at some point. Anyway, he owns the place and it was vacant and she said he'd rent it to me for two hundred dollars a month. It sounded way too good to be true and I was ready to take the fucking place sight unseen, but she said I had to go see it first.

It's in mostly an ok area, you just have to keep your wits about you. The only way to get here is on the 59 bus. There's folks down the street cooking up meth, but they seem like they will mostly keep to themselves as long as you aren't snooping around. It's the other neighbors that have me the most uncomfortable. It's like living next to my fucking brothers and cousins, goddamn rednecks threw glass bottles at me from their trucks when I walked up from the bus stop.

That shit I can take, though. I mean I grew up around it. I know how to protect myself. It was pretty much just like she'd said. Weird little shack like house, but just about everything I could want. The landlord said it's a little two-fifty square foot box that someone split into four equally sized rooms: bedroom, living room, kitchen, bathroom. It makes for a huge bathroom compared to everything else, but at least it's an extra spot that someone could sleep in if it gets really cold out and we have more folks over. I don't like how thin all the walls are. The ones inside are pretty much cardboard and if you close a door too hard the whole thing shakes. The outside walls are a little better at least.

I told the dude who owns it that I loved it, and he gave me the keys right there! Gotta find folks to help us move.

Date: January 20, 2003

Since we're moving into the house real soon I thought we should get another dog to keep Orbit company, and Hunter is always talking about how growing up he wanted a big dog but his mom was so unstable they couldn't really have pets. Hunter said he didn't know if it was a good idea, but I know that he'll fall in love with the dog, and it will bring us even closer as a family.

I called Sunny, we haven't really hung out since the night she hooked me and Hunter up. I asked if she wanted to go to the Humane Society with me to look at dogs.

She grew up on a farm, so she's usually up for anything with animals involved. I told Hunter that he should go with us, but he said it was weird to hang out with Sunny since they are ex's. When Sunny and I got to the shelter we walked through the whole dog area. There were lots of cute dogs, but I didn't really feel a strong pull towards any of them, which I was kinda disappointed about. I know you can't rush these things, but I'd gotten my hopes up that I'd be getting another dog today. We walked back through again, and this time I saw a border collie that seemed a little neurotic but mostly cool. He had a tennis ball in his pen and he kept dropping it and chasing it over and over. The info sheet on the front of the pen said that the dog's name was Tyler, and that he was a neutered male, border collie mix. I asked the shelter staff if we could take him out for a meet and greet.

They put us in a little room with concrete benches and a bunch of toys. They brought Tyler in and said that he was about three years old. I avoided being snotty and telling her I knew that much from the info sheet on his pen. The woman said he was really high needs, and asked if

I had any experience with border collies.
I pulled at my lip rings hard to keep
from crying, threw the ball across the
room again and told her about my past in
dog sports. I told her about the number
of titles I'd earned, the years I'd spent
training, and about apprenticing with my
dog trainer. It was clear really fast
that I actually knew more about dogs than
the adoption volunteer who'd been put in
the room with us, because she stopped
asking me questions.

I didn't tell them about losing my dogs
because I was too worried that they would
think I was unstable and not a fit home.
I asked her what they knew about where he'd
come from. The volunteer flipped through
the chart she was holding and said that
he'd been found on the streets almost a
year ago, and they didn't know anything
else about him. That was when I started
coming to QYRC and I liked that we'd been
homeless at about the same time.

After twenty minutes of throwing a soggy
tennis ball I was completely in love and
said I wanted to adopt him. The adoption
lady asked about other pets in the home
and I mentioned Orbit. She said that even
though Tyler was good with other dogs,

they wanted to make sure everyone got along and that I'd need to bring Orbit in before they could finalize the adoption. Sunny said that she would drive me to the apartment to get Orbit, and back to the shelter. I was really panicked that someone else would adopt Tyler before we got back, but the shelter people promised me they had put a hold sign on his pen for the rest of the day.

Sunny was hungry and we had to stop for drive-through before we could go back to the apartment. I bought her a burger and fries for being such a good friend and helping me out with everything. I bought a meal for Hunter too, figuring he probably hadn't eaten anything since I'd been gone. I hoped the treat would put him in a good mood.

Sunny stayed in the car while I went into the apartment. Billy wasn't around, which was good since I didn't bring him any food. When I came in, the TV was all static and Hunter was fumbling with the antennas, so I figured he probably wasn't in a very good mood after all. I closed the door, dropped to my knees and offered the paper bag above my head towards him. I could hear him curse over the sound of

static. I think he was cursing was at the
antenna, and not me. After a few seconds,
I snuck a peek. The grease from the fries
was starting to bleed through the paper
bag.

Hunter stood facing away from me with one
of his cats balanced on his shoulder.
I dropped my eyes again before he noticed.
Finally the sound of static went away,
and I could hear commercials for some car
and then the theme song for a talk show.
My arms were starting to burn a little
bit from holding up the bag of food.
I heard Hunter sit on the mattress next
to me, and then he snatched the food out
of my hands.

"Where's the new dog?"

I explained that I'd found a really good
dog for us, and that all I needed to do
was bring Orbit back to meet him to make
sure they got along. I asked if Hunter
would go with us, but he said no and that
he was busy and he could meet the dog
later. I was disappointed because Orbit's
my dog and this dog (whose name will so
not be Tyler) is supposed to be for us as
a family. I really wanted Hunter to take

more interest in the whole thing, but
even if I beg it's not like I can make
him do anything he doesn't want to do.

I got Orbit leashed and headed back out
to Sunny's car. I started getting more
nervous. When there's something I really
want I'm always convinced that something
will go wrong. Today it was all about being
worried that the shelter folks hadn't
remembered to put up the hold sign, and
someone would adopt Tyler before we got
back to rescue him. I think I was worried
that they didn't take me seriously, that
they just saw me as an irresponsible kid
who wasn't serious about taking this dog
home and giving him a good life.

When we got to the shelter the receptionist
thought I was there to surrender Orbit and
tried to hand me a packet of forms,which
really pissed me off. I told her we
were actually there for a family visit
to finalize the adoption of Tyler. I had
to fill out a bunch more forms with our
address and stuff, so I just put down the
new house figuring telling the shelter we
were moving would confuse them. We'll be
there soon enough anyway. I was glad they
didn't want to talk to the landlord or
anything. I mean, he said he doesn't care

about pets, but I think it would still be weird for him to get a call about a new dog before we've even moved in. Tyler and Orbit met and got along pretty well. Actually they didn't really care much about each other. Tyler was way more into his tennis ball than anything else and Orbit knew that I'd been stressed about everything and stayed glued to me. I finished filling out the paperwork and handed it back to the adoption folks. They left Sunny and I in the meet and greet room with the dogs for a long time and finally said that the adoption was final and I could take him home!

I asked if Sunny wanted to come into the apartment with us but she said no. Probably good, since Hunter had been being so weird about her earlier. Billy was in the kitchen but he ran to the door because he was so excited to meet the new dog. The ferrets were in his hoodie and they crawled out the sleeves when he bent down to pet Tyler so they became the first critters in the apartment to really meet him. I was a little worried about how he would respond to them but he just sat there like a good dog. The cats were totally not interested and watched us from their spot on top of the cabinets.

Hunter said that he was cute, and petted him a little bit but wasn't anywhere near as excited about him as Billy was. He did agree to come to the park with us. Orbit ran off into the bushes like usual, and Hunter actually got into throwing the ball for our new dog while I pulled out my notebook and started making a list of all kinds of better names for him.

Date: January 21, 2003
Security: Friends
Subject: Cosmo!

Hunter and I adopted a new dog! His name is Cosmo and he's a former street dog who really likes to play. He's so goofy and happy and just a lot of fun to have around. I brought him to QYRC tonight to meet everyone. I let them off leash once we got here and Orbit ran around introducing him to everyone. Once we move into the new house he won't be able to come so often because it's too far to walk, so I'm glad that he was able to meet everyone tonight.

Gus thought there was an old Frisbee somewhere under the stage so Buck and I started going through the boxes to try to find it. We found a bunch of lube leftover from Pride, more zines for the library, and a bunch of chains and other bike parts. Finally under all that we found the Frisbee. Orbit was hanging out with Piglet's new kitten so we left him inside while Buck and Gus and I went outside into the smoking area to see what

Cosmo thought of the Frisbee. I think it's about time to head back to the apartment and see what Hunter's up to, but it's been a really good night.

Date: January 26, 2003

So pissed. Bio dad called today. He knows I'm moving, and he asked if I'd told my grandma about it yet. I was sorta planning on never telling her. When I was a little kid, she and I were hella close, except she knew my mom and stepdad were beating the shit out of me and she never even asked about it. When I left my mom, she told me nothing happened, and ever since I don't really want anything to do with her. I disappeared from grandma for a little while, but then she and bio mom got all scary stalker so I've been telling her where I'm at, seeing her maybe every few months and calling every few weeks so she leaves me along the rest of the time.

That's been working ok, but it also just pisses me the hell off because I know that everything she sees or I tell her goes straight to my fucking birth mom. My grandma is just a fucking spy for her and I don't like that, so I was thinking I might try to disappear again. Bio dad is saying that he's gonna stop sending the child support if I don't tell my grandma where I'm at. He gave me this sob story about how when he and my mom got married he cut off contact with his parents for a couple years, and when his dad died he felt real guilty. I told him it was different. He told me it wasn't.

My rent for the new place is due. Most people don't know where my rent money comes from, and I know if I tried to complain about this shit they would just think I was a spoiled brat. I have to fucking call her.

Date: January 28, 2003

Hunter's mom called yesterday morning and asked if he would come and spend the night at her place. She lives in this little town a couple hours outside of Portland. She's really been struggling with staying off meth and I guess Hunter's newest stepfather had to work overnight again at the gas station, and Hunter's mom was worried bout being alone all night in the house. I wanted to go with him, but Orbit and Cosmo couldn't be alone, his mom hates dogs, and Billy is spending the night with some girl he's trying to turn out.

I had to give Hunter the bus money to get
to his mom's and back. I made macaroni for
myself and fed Hunter's cats, who mostly
just stay on top of the kitchen cabinets
if he isn't around. Orbit, Cosmo, and
I got into bed with the bowl of noodles.
I don't remember falling asleep, but
for once I didn't wake up panicked in
the middle of the night. I woke up this
morning with my finger looped into the
leather cuff on my wrist like Hunter does
when we sleep to remind me of my place.
He stumbled in a little bit ago and said
he was tired, didn't want to talk, and
needed to shower.

Date: February 1, 2003
Security: Friends
Subject: Hunter

I probably shouldn't be writing about this on here, especially
when I'm at QYRC. Today Hunter went down and saw this crazy
ass shrink who's a trans guy. Pretty much all any of us have
to do is show up at his office, say we're men and that we've
always known we're men and he'll give us a letter to get started
on T. It's a good system, cuz then we go see this old trans
woman doctor. Everyone says she's writing a book about trans
folks, some kind of medical study. I don't know if that's true or
not. It doesn't really matter I guess, cuz pretty much she'll give
everyone their hormones, so long as they show up with our
letters from the tranny shrink.

Hunter had his appointment last week. He was all fucking scared about going because when he was a kid his mom locked him up in the psych ward and he was afraid it would be that sort thing again. He had been practicing telling his story to be sure not to include things like the drugs or the drinking, and he was planning to wear a button down that would cover all the cuts and scars on his arms. It ended up being just like everyone said it would be. Just a quick fifteen minute meeting, tell the shrink what he wanted to hear and get the hell out with the letter. Today Hunter went to see the lady doctor, and he got his prescription, which was way cool.

I had to do his shot tonight. The doctor gave him this brochure that told you how to do it. Hunter told me that his shots were my responsibility, so I better study it good. That's just about all I did most of this afternoon. Everyone's really excited that I can do shots now, because most other folks are too triggered by it. I guess being XXX really does have its perks. Hunter was bragging about how useful his boy is, and that made me feel really good. It sounds like I might start doing shots for a bunch of guys. I guess we'll have to see.

Date: February 3, 2003

I'm the worst boy in the entire world. Daddy hasn't wanted to fuck or play with me for a while now, and tonight he actually turned off the TV and said he was interested, but I had to do exactly as he said. He said I wasn't allowed to talk and it was my job to beat him until he called "red" and then to fuck him hard. He threw his flogger at me, and braced himself against the arm of the futon.

I've never beaten anyone before. I tried to quiet my breathing and tried to remember the best beatings I've ever had. I started out ok, I think. I've never really held a flogger before so I know I was hesitating a little between strokes and I could tell he was getting frustrated. Then I really messed up. I misjudged the distance and the flogger landed right across his spine. He was so mad. Daddy flipped around and started yelling that I couldn't do anything right, and that James was right when he said I was such worthless boy. Daddy told me I was dangerous to play with, and I didn't know what I was doing.

I was so flustered that I lied. I fucking lied to my Daddy and said that I thought I landed in the safe zone. I should have taken responsibility for my mistake, but I didn't. He ripped the flogger out of my hand and threw it across the room. Then he pulled his binder and shirt back on, grabbed his wallet, and said he was going out for a while. I'm sure he went to The

Hotel or Safety Net and is hanging out with the guys and telling them about how much I suck. I tried to call Buck but his new Daddy said he couldn't come to the phone right now. I'm glad he's finally found a good Daddy, but it's hard when that also means he can't be around when I need him.

Date: February 5, 2003

Piglet's new kitten, Trash, is so cute! Piglet found him down at the skatepark under the bridge. I guess he was down there to visit Scummy's memorial and then he heard this little mewing noise. He was pretty high, so he told us that when he first heard Trash, he thought it was Scummy trying to communicate with him from the great dumpster in the sky or something. It's a miracle that Trash is alive. He's so small that if Piglet hadn't found him right then he probably would have died.

Piglet struggles to take care of himself sometimes when he's really high, so at first I was worried about Trash, but I've been watching how Piglet's been with him and he's doing such a good job. He's got this supply of cat food he keeps stashed under the stage at QYRC and has

made his backpack into a nice little nest
for Trash. I think it's really good for
Piglet not to be lonely at night when
he's wandering around.

Date: February 10, 2003

Hunter is getting this stupid pumpkin
tattoo. It's cuz he went to a big concert
on Halloween a couple years ago. He's
already got a few of those kinds of
concert tattoos, and he says he wants to
someday have a whole sleeve of tattoos
about concerts. I think it sounds kinda
dumb, but whatever. It's his arm.

I came to the appointment cuz it's an
excuse to hang out with Hank, our tattoo
artist, while he works on Hunter. He's
hella hot but he's so straight it hurts.

While I was waiting, some lady came in
wanting a tattoo, some tribal nonsense.
Hank didn't stop working on Hunter and
just pointed to some framed flash next to
where I was sitting. Mostly hearts with
banners and shit. Hank took a break to go
out and smoke. I left my chair and went
to talk to Hunter who was all bloody and
inky. I told him I thought it would be
cool to get a tattoo that said "Daddy."

He told me that was stupid. I told him
to fuck off. Right then is when Hank came
back in. He told me to respect my Daddy
or he would kick me out of the shop.

Date: February 12, 2003
Security: Friends
Subject : Neighbors

I can't quite get a read on the neighbors out here. Mostly they
wave at me when I come and go, but only if I wave first. I can
tell they're uncomfortable. They never let their kids get too
close to me. This woman and her kids and her mother live next
door. They reminded me of the folks I knew growing up. I think
there is part of me that wants to be friends with them. I mean
not real friends, but like sorta friends. I love my queer world,
but there is part of me that remembers being out in the woods,
and farms and shit back before I got kicked out of the Future
Farmers for not wearing a skirt and starting a GSA in the high
school. I thought maybe I could make friends with them, and
have my own little place here. Stupid shit, obviously.

Date: February 14, 2003

Saucer was at QYRC tonight, I didn't see
Kristin. I am so glad that the drama with
that messy love triangle is over. Saucer
was tired and in a bunch of pain cuz
she's actually started the tattoo removal
program. The homeless health clinic has a
program where they will pay to get the gang

tattoos taken off of her face and hands. She told us all to think a lot about what we put on us. She started getting tattoos when she hit the streets at twelve, but is trying to turn stuff around now. The skin where they zapped her with the laser looked really swollen and nasty. Everyone was hanging out around her wanting to see how it looked after the first treatment. She didn't even seem upset when I walked up to take a look. I know it's stupid because I fucked her girlfriend but Saucer is one of the hottest people I've ever seen. She's huge like maybe six feet and built. She walks around in her a-shirts and sports bras with boxers hanging out of her jeans like she's not scared of anything. I love looking at her, all the tattoos and all the stories behind them. This round of removal mostly will just fade the ones on her face, but her hands are covered in little blue pictures. God. Her hands are huge and so sexy.

I can't even imagine getting my ink taken out. I've gotten a few more pieces recently. Four stars on my forearm, after all, Gus always tells us about how gender is a universe, and we are all stars, and

```
I got a portrait of Orbit on my bicep,
it's of him as a little angel cuz god
knows that little dog is saving me.
```

Date: February 20, 2003
Security: Friends
Subject: Name Change!

Best news ever! I'm gonna get my name changed for real. The homeless medical clinic downtown got this new grant that's gonna pay for any trans kid who wants to get their name legally changed! They have staff who will go with you to the courthouse and fill out all the papers and then go back with you when you have to see the judge! I found out because a bunch of folks already did it, and now Hunter and I are gonna do it, too. Hunter said that he should get to go first because he's been trans for longer, but I think I convinced him it would be ok for us to do it at the same time.

I told bio dad about it today since once it happens he's one of the people who will have to know. I was worried he was going to freak out, but he didn't even care. The only thing that pissed me off was that he said I had to tell my grandmother. I was hoping I could avoid that, create a little distance so that someday I'd be able to move and she and my birth mother wouldn't know what happened to me, but rent is worth more than that dream right now.

Date: February 25, 2003

Two years ago I became homeless. It's when I got kicked out from my coach's house and I lost the dogs. I'm remembering what it was like to sit in my fucking high school and realize I didn't have a family or a home anymore. I planned on just taking it easy today so I wouldn't go crazy. I ended up calling Buck, and I didn't even have to tell him what day it was. He knew and asked what we were going to do. I don't know where I'd be without my brother, I really don't.

He came over and we took the dogs out to the park. After a while we just sat down quietly on the grass together and threw a ball for Cosmo. I know it sounds dumb but I curled up in Buck's lap and he just held me for a long time. I could feel his heart beating all the way through his binder and t-shirt and hoodie. He kissed the top of my head when we were about to go back. I wanted to ask him to stay for dinner but I knew Hunter wouldn't like it. He was pissed enough that Buck and I went out today. He always says I shouldn't dwell on the past. He reminded me of that this morning when he said I was in a sour mood. It's different for him, he loves his mother even if she did get him hooked on drugs and let her boyfriends fuck him up.

Date: March 1, 2003

Billy came in really late last night. Hunter and I had already gone to bed, but I knew that Billy was out on the prowl because things with that vanilla girl are fizzling out. I knew they would. She's so not his type. Hunter had his hand wrapped around the leather cuff on my wrist and his leg flung over me, but I carefully detangled myself and crawled onto the foam bed to wait for Billy to come out of the bathroom.

The damn streetlight means the room never really gets dark so I could see him smile at me when he came out in a t-shirt and pajama pants. He crawled into his bed next to me and we pulled his unzipped sleeping bag over us. He smelled good, like sweat and cigarettes. I asked how his night went and he got all quiet which seemed strange because usually he's excited to tell me everything he gets up to. Finally he blurted out that he'd been with my brother. It was weird to

think about Buck and Billy hooking up!
Billy quickly clarified that they hadn't
actually fucked.

Billy was hanging out down on the waterfront
tonight and Buck must have wandered down
there when he got off work. Billy told me
about how they went off on a walk along
the water together. They were talking
about life and leather and all kinds of
stuff. Buck's girlfriend is vanilla and
sometimes he talks about missing having a
Daddy and the power exchange that happens
in that kind of a relationship. I'm
guessing he was talking like that with
Billy tonight. Billy told me how they
walked all the way down the waterfront
to the south side where these new condos
are being put up but the shipyards used
to be. Billy told me how he couldn't
help but slam Buck up against a fence.
He told me how hot it was to hear Buck's
body hit the chain link. He told me about
pressing into him, and how hot it was
when Buck moaned, but how then he'd said
he couldn't do more because he couldn't
cheat on his girlfriend.

I know I have a Daddy now, but there's
part of me that's still really jealous
that Billy is into Buck like that.

Date: March 3, 2003

This fucking GSA kid almost got his ass kicked at QYRC tonight. This dumb little spoiled faggot was hanging around and listening when Saucer and I were talking about our fucking mothers and all the shit they pulled back in the day when we were little kids and how the best damn thing we've ever done was get the hell out. This little snot nose picked that moment to jump in and start talking about how we needed to really show more respect for our parents and how he was sure they loved us and how it was our job to forgive them. I was about to fucking rip this kid apart but Saucer was already on her feet and had him slammed up against the wall by his throat.

Gus broke it up. I thought we were all gonna get kicked out for the night, but when they found out what had happened it was just the dumbass little GSA kid that had to get out. He was fucking pissed about that, too, and said he was gonna have his mom call to complain. Saucer and I just laughed in his face. Complaints like that go to the youth steering committee and as a steering committee member I can guarantee that complaint ain't going nowhere. We were all standing out in the smoking area when he stormed out to his car. Right before he slammed his door he said we were all gonna die in the gutter. Fucking spoiled little brat better not show his face around here anytime soon.

Date: March 4, 2003

Buck called today. He and his girlfriend broke up. He's going to be staying with this guy Luke who's friends with Big Billy. I don't really know him, but I've heard about him from Billy and I guess Buck randomly met him and they've been hanging out. Buck said he's really excited about being his roommate because Luke is all heavy into leather and he thinks Luke might be someone who could be his Daddy someday. I told Billy about it and he said Luke was good people, so I'm glad that Buck will at least be in good hands.

Date: March 5, 2003
Security: Friends
Subject: Canada

I wonder how difficult it would be to leave the country? Hunter said that if Bush does declare war he's leaving. I think he's serious and I don't want to get left behind. We just bought this really shitty car from his stepdad because Hunter said he could get a job delivering papers like he used to with his mom when he was a little kid, but he needed a car to do it.

It means we don't have money for any extra food beyond what his food stamps will buy, but now at least we have a car. We just have to be careful, cuz he doesn't have insurance yet. The car's mostly trashed cuz his stepdad got into a really bad accident in it, and then sorta got it running again, but I think it would get us and the dogs to Canada if we made a run for the border.

Date: March 7, 2003

Sometimes things are bad, but when he puts his hands on me, Daddy knows how to make everything better. Tonight I fell asleep on the futon. It had been a fucked up day where I saw my birth mom's car drive by the house like three times so I was too afraid to go to QYRC. We made frozen pizza for dinner and Hunter started watching a horror video that he borrowed from someone, but I fell asleep. I'm a really deep sleeper, one of the good things about being fucked with a lot as a little kid. I didn't hear him get up, and he must have moved fast because when I woke up my wrists were tied to the pipe frame of the futon, and his hand was pressed over my nose and mouth.

I couldn't breathe and started to freak
out. I realized my hands were tied was
when I tried to get away from him. Then,
everything got real calm and quiet.
I love sceneing with Daddy especially
when I don't know what's coming. Back when
I was with James it was good, I mean he
was my first Daddy, after all, but I also
just didn't know what I was doing and I'd
get scared over stupid shit. Being with
Hunter I can really just let myself go
and give myself to him the way he likes.
He fucked me so hard I was bleeding by
the time we were through. I remember
thinking right before I came that I was
safe. I don't know the last time I felt
like that.

Date: March 10, 2003

Really bad night. Hunter's been in a bad
mood all week, but tonight was extra bad.
Nothing I could do was right. I even made
him frozen pizza. Before I cooked dinner
I went through all of our pants and found
enough change to take to the convenience
store down the street and buy him a soda
to go with it. Billy was out most of the
day, but when he came back Hunter was even
more pissed. I think he's angry about how
close Billy and I are, and that we never

really have much privacy. That said, it's not like he wants to be without Billy's food stamps, which mean we can afford to buy him frozen pizza all the time.

Right before Billy walked in, Hunter had started laying into me because Cosmo had shit in the bathroom when I'd been out at the store getting him soda. I don't know if Cosmo didn't tell Hunter he needed to go out, or if Hunter just hadn't wanted to get off the couch, but whatever the reason, he pooped on the bathroom floor. I found it first and was trying to get it cleaned up before Hunter saw it because I knew he'd be really pissed. Hunter walked into the bathroom and started yelling about how much he hated my dogs and what a bad trainer I clearly was if I couldn't even keep the dog from shitting in the house.

I was down on my hands and knees trying to get everything cleaned up and he was yelling and worst of all I started crying. I fucking hate myself for that, because I know that when I cry it just pisses him off more. Then he kicked me in the ribs and my face was in the shit and I couldn't stop crying.

I hadn't heard Billy come in over Hunter's yelling, but when I got back to my knees and opened my eyes he was standing there looking like he might seriously deck Hunter. "Leave hir be," Billy growled, and I could tell that Hunter was even more mad than he was before. He stormed back into the living room with his pizza and soda and turned on a movie really loud. I was crying even harder by this point but at least the floor was cleaned up.

I tried to close the bathroom door so Billy couldn't see me crying but he wedged his boot in the door and forced his way in. The dogs followed. They seemed upset and didn't understand what was going on at all. I was curled up leaning against the bathtub and Cosmo dropped his tennis ball at my feet and I threw it into the kitchen. Billy sat next to me and I flinched as he wrapped his arm around me. I couldn't stop crying and he just held me tighter and tighter. He didn't even make fun of me for crying, but I'm sure he must think I'm such a big baby.

I was worried that Hunter was going to need to piss and come in and find us and get mad all over again, but it felt so good to be held. Finally I stopped crying. Orbit was in my lap and one of the ferrets had popped out of the pocket on Billy's hoodie and made me giggle a little bit. Billy squeezed me hard one more time. Before getting up, he reached down and pulled me to my feet too. "You really are a good boy," he whispered, looking me right in the eyes. I wish I could believe him.

He led me out of the bathroom and into the kitchen. Hunter had eaten all the pizza so I poured Billy and me some cold cereal and we went to watch the movie. I sat at Hunter's feet just like he prefers but he just ignored me and went right on watching this stupid violent movie. I kept looking over at Billy. He wasn't watching the movie at all. He was watching me and shaking his head. I'm so embarrassed about everything.

Date: March 12, 2003

I don't know what to do. Today Billy came and said he needed to talk to me. Alone. Hunter was really pissed. Anyway so Billy and I went outside with Orbit and Cosmo and sat in the very back of the yard. I could see Hunter watching us through the little kitchen window, but we were far enough away that I know he couldn't read my lips or hear what we were saying.

Billy told me that he couldn't handle being around Hunter anymore. He said a lot of people at QYRC were pretty sick of the shit that Hunter was pulling, too. Billy said he loved me, but couldn't handle Hunter's temper tantrums, and that he was going to go stay with Saucer for a while. I asked if he meant for just a couple of days, or if he was actually moving out. Billy said he was leaving.

We went back into the house and Hunter was watching small claims court TV in the living room. He was sitting on Billy's bed, but Billy didn't say anything about it. He just started shoving clothes and colored pencils and all the ferret stuff into his messenger bag.

"Billy's going to move in with Saucer," I told Hunter. He didn't say anything, just grunted and turned up the volume on the TV. It didn't take very long for Billy to get his stuff together. I almost offered to walk him and the ferrets to the bus stop, but I thought that might piss Hunter off even more. Instead, I walked

Billy out to the street. He gave me a big hug and I told him I'd see him around at QYRC.

"I'm worried about you," was all he said before walking away.

Date: March 13, 2003
Security: Friends
Subject:

Billy moved out, he's going to go and stay with Saucer. I love Billy, but it's nice that Hunter and I can just be our little family, the two of us and the dogs and cats. Billy and I can still see each other all the time at QYRC.

Date: March 17, 2003
Security: Friends
Subject: Call me Click

Went to court today with the folks from the name change clinic. I was freaked out that the judge would give me a hard time about my name, or say no or something. The staff told me it would be ok, but I didn't believe them until I walked out of the courthouse with the notarized form saying my name is officially changed! Hunter got his name changed too, so after court we went to the diner to get pancakes to celebrate.

Date: March 18, 2003

Today has been a fucking long day. Hunter woke up in kinda a bad mood, but we didn't have a whole lot of time to fight cuz we were already running late to get him to work and I had to get Orbit and Cosmo set up to be alone for the day. I had to feed Hunter's cats too, because he needed to shower.

Hunter has been selling his plasma for a few months. You're only supposed to do it once every thirty days, but if you go to all the clinics you can do it every week or so. Today's appointment was the one way the hell out on 82nd and it takes forever to get there, but it pays well. Every time you give, they will give you fifty bucks. The place is wicked far out though, so it's an all day thing. Hunter gets so triggered every time we go, so he makes me go with him. We sat on the stupid-ass 12 bus for hours while it stopped every few fucking feet and until we got out to the sketchiest suburbs.

It's the same rules about giving blood, no faggots. Problem is, Hunter is a faggot, just not the sort of faggot they are actually caring about. For their purposes he's a woman who has sex with other women. This pisses him the hell off. I've got the bruises to prove it. They always make him fill out this questionnaire swearing that he isn't in any of the high-risk categories. Of course he's in all of them—new healing piercings and tattoos, former IV drug user, faggot. It's obvious the piercings in his face are always fresh and changing and he's healing tattoos right where they take the blood from, but so long as you sign on the form that it's old they don't care. I don't even really know why I have to go with him. It's boring as shit and there is nothing for me to do, but he says I have to come, says it's an order.

Mostly I have to be there because needles freak him out, same reason I have to do his shot. Also, the clinic is in tweakerville and it's so hard for him not to leave and go blow the cash on meth. He says he didn't, but I'm pretty sure he did that the couple of the times I refused to go. He'd call hours and hours later saying they hadn't been able to give him work that day so he didn't have any money. Then he'd say he was going to go visit an old friend and would be home later. If he goes to see old friends he doesn't come home for a couple of days.

It's the deal we have that after plasma he gets to blow some of it on greasy delivery pizza. I don't understand why he fucking likes it so much. It seems like a huge waste of money when we can get ten frozen pizzas for the same price, and now that Billy's moved out and we don't have his food stamps anymore, we need to be saving money, but whatever. It makes him happy, for a night, so I don't complain too much. The rest of the money mostly goes to rent and shit.

Tonight, after the pizza came Hunter and I got into a fight. It was a big one, and I don't even know why the whole damn thing got started. I asked him to help me get the laundry together after he finished eating. It's been about a month since we did laundry. He didn't even think we had to do it today and was upset I was wasting his plasma money on it but I've had to go commando for the last two weeks and I want my fucking boxers back. I still don't know why we thought black sheets were going to hide cum. They're so gross. Even I don't want to sleep on them. The closest laundromat five blocks away, and I could do it by myself, I guess, but not in one trip. And besides, if I have to wash Hunter's crusty ass pants, then the least he can do is help me carry the shit.

The fight started cuz I said he should maybe think about washing his binder and he didn't want to do that. He said I was being insensitive and not respecting his gender. I was so fucking mad. It had nothing to do with his gender, and everything to do with the fact that he stinks. He said the only way he was going to wash his was if I gave him mine to wear. This of course totally defeats the point of doing laundry cuz it ain't like mine has been washed in a month either! I told him he could handle binding with something else for a couple of hours. I even said he could have the ace bandage and I'd wear the sports bras. I was trying to be nice but he thought I was making fun of him and started screaming. I don't even know what he was so pissed about, so I kept gathering up the laundry. He punched a hole in the bathroom wall, one more reason we're never going to see the deposit back on this fucking place.

With my binder and a baggy sweatshirt on, he was finally willing to leave the apartment and help me lug the trash bags down the street towards the laundromat. I thought things were better, that punching the wall had gotten him over whatever shit he was in the midst of but I was totally wrong. He's always quiet after he gets mad like that, so I started babbling to fill space. I was talking about some of the dykes from QYRC and how I thought we were going to meet up and take our zines to the feminist bookstore next week and see if maybe they would sell them.

He normally likes it when I'm selling zines, cuz it brings in a little extra money, but tonight he got all pissed off again. He said I shouldn't be hanging out with girls, and that it made him really uncomfortable that my friends were dykes. I don't get what the big fucking problem is. I'm genderqueer, but I'm a dyke too My friends have always been dykes. I mean, sometimes they stop being dykes and become dudes or whatever, but that's never had any effect on who I'm friends with.

When I said that, Hunter dropped the laundry in the middle of the street. Of course he hadn't let me tie the bag closed before we left, so my shirts and shit started spilling out onto the muddy concrete. He said that I was spending too much time with them and it looked bad for him. I started picking up my clothes and shoving them back into the bag, trying to figure out how the hell I was going to carry this shit myself.

I can't say this, but I think he's full of shit. So what if I'm friends with the dykes? It doesn't mean that anyone sees him as one. He picked up the bag and kept walking towards the laundromat. Thankfully it was empty. After we got the clothes into the washer I thought things cooled down. We were sitting next to each other and fucking everything. I pulled my notebook out of my bag and started working on designs for this new zine. It wasn't very smart, I guess, since we'd just been fighting about zine related shit, but I needed to get the design done. I could tell he was getting pissed again so I put my notebook back, but it was too late. He started telling me how every time he goes down on me it makes him feel like a lesbian, how he thinks I'm just playing around with this trans shit and not serious like he is. He said he didn't know if he could be with someone who still identified as a dyke even just a little bit, let alone someone who flaunted that shit like I did.

I got up and started kicking the fronts of the folding tables. I knew I was about to cry, and if he saw that, everything would be fucking over. The tables made a satisfying clunk when my steel toes connected with them. I love him so fucking much. I mean, I know he's an asshole and no one really understands why I put up with this shit, but fuck. I've never felt about anyone like I feel about him, not even James. He's my Daddy, there is fucking nothing I wouldn't do for him.

I turned around and asked Hunter if starting T would make a difference. If that would fucking prove that I wasn't a dyke.

He sat for a stupid long time watching the clothes tumble through the graffiti front of the dryer. We didn't fold the clothes there, we never fold our clothes

at all. We were shoving them back into
the trash bags when he asked if I was
serious about starting.

I'd never really thought about it before.
I'd never really thought much about T,
for me at least. I shoot T into a bunch
of guys asses, but never really wanted to
do it myself. I mean I've identified as
genderqueer for a bunch of months, and
for me genderqueer is a type of being
trans, so I mostly just kinda let people
assume what they want about me. I mean,
fuck, it ain't like I look like a girl or
anything.

I told him I've been thinking of starting
for a while, and I was ready to leave
behind this dyke shit once and for all.
I could tell even though we were carrying
all these fucking clothes that he was
relaxing. When we got home, he microwaved
some hotdogs and then went into the
bathroom. He came out with his shit. He
said if I was serious I should start now,
that we'd go down to the clinic tomorrow
and get my prescription and I could pay
him back the shot. He started kissing me
and laid me down on the futon. My pants
were around my ankles and I thought he
was going to fuck me but then I jumped

as steel punctured my ass. I guess doing
shots for other people doesn't trigger
him. It was over in about ten seconds and
then Hunter started fucking me. I guess
when he went into the bathroom to get his
shit he got his cock on too. I hadn't
even realized he was hard packing when he
came out.

I guess I'm on T now.

Date: March 19, 2003
Security: Public
Subject: T

Ok, so I said I wouldn't do this, but really it's cuz I was afraid
and thanks to the pack I've worked through my shit. I decided
to start T !!!!

Had my first shot this week and I'm feeling really good.

Date: March 19, 2003

My brother called. He hadn't seen me in
the park blocks for a while and I guess
he started freaking out about it. I don't
like to leave Hunter alone, because I'm
always worried that he'll go out and get
trashed or something.

Buck must've already read my online journal, because the first thing he wanted to talk about was how and why I was on T. I don't get what his problem is, he says that he's all dude identified and he's always given me a bad time for being so gender fluid. I thought he would be into it, especially because I made it sound like I'd really thought through everything and decided that this was the path for me.

We talked for a long ass time and he asked a bunch of stupid therapist questions. He wanted to know what had changed for me since I said I wasn't going to go on. I told him that we all grow up and realize that things need to make sense in the world and that sometimes the way that we live just isn't translatable. He seemed to get that at least.

Date: March 20, 2003
Security: Friends
Subject: War

So fucking crazy! I've been looking at the front page of newspapers in the bus stop news-boxes downtown for the last few days so I sorta knew this was coming. Still, how crazy is it that we're at war?! The TV reports look all scary and shit and it's just looping this video of bombs falling and some dumb reporter dude on a rooftop in Baghdad. I don't know what to think. I remember as a kid I was convinced a bomb was going to come through my bathroom window. Only, I didn't really know what a bomb was. I thought it looked like a wrecking ball. This was in the Gulf War. My mom was always drunk and would pass out in front of the TV with the news on and I was really little so I guess that's where I got the idea.

Anyway, everyone freaked out when Bush got on TV. Hunter and I were over at the Clit Shack which is this big pink punk house in north Portland that's been around forever, like since the start of Riot Grrrrrl. Hunter's crushing out real hard on this girl Sarah who lives there, so we've been hanging out a bunch. I'm actually doing pretty good with the whole poly thing. James fucked me up bad by cheating on me with hys ex-wife but it feels different with Hunter. I know that I can trust him.

The Clit Shack has an old TV and we turned it on because someone called and we could hear them leaving a message on the answering machine that if anyone was home (everyone knows they never pick up cuz it's usually bill collectors) they should turn on the TV because something big was gonna go down. Right when Bush started talking and said we were at war, Sarah started calling folks. We knew there was gonna be a big protest downtown with people trying to take the Burnside Bridge so the yuppies couldn't get back to the suburbs. I just sat there holding Orbit and trying not to freak out. I tried to call Buck to see if he was going, but he didn't pick up. He has a gas mask that he used to carry around to protests when he was fourteen and living on the streets in New York. I'm sure he's already downtown. I just hope he's ok.

Date: March 22, 2003

Getting a prescription wasn't as easy as I thought it would be. I should have just started at trans guy shrink but I thought it would be easier just to go with the case manager man at QYRC. He helped me out a lot, back when I was in high school and dealing with the courts and the restraining order, but we haven't met in a long time. I called and asked if we could have an appointment and he suggested we meet at a coffee shop. I told him that I was ready to start T and just needed a letter. He's written letters for bunches of guys the minute they turned eighteen, so I didn't think he was going to give me a bad time about it, but he did.

He said that he didn't feel comfortable writing the letter for me. I told him that me starting T wasn't about him and what he thinks. That's the problem with fucking adults, they always think they know what's right for other people. He told me that he couldn't clinically support my decision to medically transition because

my gender had been too fluid. That's when
I stood up and right in the middle of
the coffee shop told him to go to hell,
that I'm already on T, and that it was
clear that QYRC couldn't really help me
anymore. Then I just walked out of the
coffee shop.

Date: March 24, 2003

I was at steering committee tonight for
a meeting about trying to come up with a
good fundraiser for the space. I haven't
seen Billy since he moved out so it was
really good to see him. Jacob was at
steering committee with Trash, Piglet's
cat. At first I thought maybe she was just
watching him for Piglet, but then she
started talking about needing to go to
the grocery store after the meeting to
get some cat food. She'd been downtown
before the meeting and run into Piglet,
who told her that he needed to get out
of town.

He's been struggling a lot more recently,
and just really strung out every time
I see him. He decided to train hop out
to Detroit because he knows someone out
there, but he didn't think it would be
safe for Trash. He gave him to Jacob and

then took off for the train yard. Jacob
seemed excited about having Trash around,
and she's got a room in a house out in SE
so at least she's got somewhere to take
the kitten.

Date: March 25, 2003
Security: Friends
Subject: coming out (again)

Sent a letter to Grandma today telling her about starting T. I'd actually never come out to her as trans before, and this seemed like a pretty good time to do it. I said, "So you know how I dress like a boy? Well, I decided that I'm going to become one. I talked to my doctor and started hormones. My voice is going to drop and I'm probably going to grow a beard. I already started taking the hormones so there isn't anything you can do to stop me, I'm just telling you so you don't worry when I start looking and sounding different." Wonder how she's going to take it.....

Date: March 29, 2003
Security: Friends
Subject: "M" is for MALE!

Went to the DMV today and now I'm legally a guy! So grateful for the homeless health clinic program helping me to get my name and gender changed! The social worker met me downtown outside the DMV and helped me fill out all the papers, walked to the counter with me, and explained everything about the process to the clueless guy working there. It took about an hour and we walked out with my new ID!

A bunch of folks were hanging out at the Clit Shack, so I went and picked Orbit up (I knew DMV would kick him out for sure) and headed over to show off my new ID. They all did theirs last month, and were telling me about how they just found out there is this lady at the social security office who's changing the gender markers for people with just our DMV gender identity letters, without the proof of surgery like you're technically supposed to have. The lady said to spread the word that she works at the desk in the mornings. Hunter and I decided that we're gonna try to go and see if we can get that changed too.

Date: April 1, 2003
Security: Friends
Subject: Passing

Holy shit. I don't talk to my bio dad like at all. I didn't know him growing up, and I really don't want to know him now. Sometimes he acts like he wants to try to be in my life, but most of the time we just exchange occasional awkward phone calls so he knows that I'm alive. He called me yesterday, though, and asked if we could go to dinner, his treat. I didn't really want to, but I also wasn't going to turn down the free food.

I left the dogs at home and we met downtown and ate Italian food. I think Hunter was pissed that he wasn't invited and had to stay out at the shack with the dogs. I told him I wouldn't eat all my dinner and would bring most of it back for him. The food was ok, but the conversation was awkward. I was worried bio dad would start talking about the war, but he didn't. I'd told him that I was legally changing my name and he hadn't really said anything at the time other than that I had to make sure my Grandma knew. I guess that's why we had to have dinner tonight. He said he didn't understand why I would give up such a beautiful name but that he would make me a deal. My whole life I've called him by his first name, but he said if I called him Dad, then he would start calling me Click.

It felt like total blackmail, but I said ok, because I really didn't know what else to say.

He drove me back home to the shack and on the drive was asking me questions about how the name change process works. When we got into the driveway and I was going to get out, he said he had one more important thing to talk to me about. That sorta scared me. He said he wanted to make sure that I was being careful. I think I looked really confused because he said, "I mean taking precautions to not get pregnant." I know it's not nice, but seriously, I busted the fuck up laughing. He knows I'm always at QYRC and I never really came out and told him I was queer, or that it's the reason why I left mom's house and then my coach's, but fucking look at me!!!!

I said there was nothing to worry about. He looked confused. I told him that Hunter was trans, and that there was no way in hell he could get me pregnant. I had to sit in the car with him for another twenty minutes explaining what the hell all that meant. I think by the end of the conversation he understood.

The minute I got in the door I started laughing again. Hunter was watching a movie and looked pissed that I was being noisy. He asked how dinner was so I handed him the leftovers and told him about the hilarious shit with bio dad. I thought he was going to think it was funny, but instead he started yelling that I don't respect him or his gender, and if he was actually passing to someone that I should never ever out him. He punched a hole in the kitchen wall and then locked himself in the bathroom.

Date: April 3, 2003

When I got back from the grocery store with pasta and chips and a frozen pizza that I thought would make Daddy happy he seemed pissed, so I sat on the floor with the dogs and started wrestling with them because sometimes that makes Daddy smile. He said I shouldn't have taken so long, that we needed to get going. I didn't know we had anywhere to be today. Turns out after I left some of the guys called and said they needed shots and Hunter said I would do it. We put the food away and went over to the Safety Net which is

a big tranny fag house so I could shoot
guys up with hormones. I wasn't really in
the mood for it, but Hunter said just to
think of it as service.

Date: April 4, 2003
Security: Friends
Subject: SS#

Fuck yeah! I went to the Social Security office this morning with Hunter the Safety Net guys. I waved at the lady with the short red hair just like the Clit Shack boys told us to, and sat down to wait for our numbers to be called. Somehow she managed to get all of us. I told her we were there to change our gender and handed over our new state ID cards, the letter from the court with our name change and gender changed on our new Social Security cards!

This rocks! Now the only document of mine to say "F" is my birth certificate, and I don't give a fuck about that, cuz no one will ever see it. After we left the social security office, Travis and Hunter and I went and hung out down at the waterfront park. Travis had just shaved his hair into this hot mohawk and he was wearing these coveralls like mechanics have. It was really hot.

Date: April 7, 2003

Got word at QYRC that Saucer got off
probation and moved up to Vancouver to
live with Kristin and her parents. I guess
they came to say goodbye to Gus before

QYRC opened. Saucer says she can't be here anymore because there are too many memories of back in the day, shooting up with Scummy and everyone. I don't know where Billy and the ferrets are staying now. Anyway, I really wish Saucer and Kristin the best. Gus seemed almost glad that Saucer was moving. She and Piglet have really been in bad shape for months now and everyone's worried that they're going to be the next to have something happen.

Date: April 8, 2003

A letter from my mother came in the mail today. She said that she was uncomfortable with me being on hormones and wanted to know if anyone had touched me when I was a kid, and if I thought that was what's wrong with me. Fucking hell, how dumb does she think I am?! She fucking laid on the other side of the bed while my stepdad fucked me. She knows someone "touched me." But that isn't even the point. I'm not fucking trans because of that shit, and the last thing I'm going to do is talk about any of this with her. I haven't talked to her since the day in high school I walked out of her house. The part of the letter that really got me

```
pissed off, was that she even knew I was
on T in the first place! Total proof that
everything my grandma knows goes straight
to my mother. I hate this so much.
```

Date: April 10, 2003
Security: private
Subject: Cops

I had to talk to the fucking pigs last night. Growing up in the sticks, I actually used to admire them. As a little kid, I wanted to be a cop or a detective or something when I grew up. I think it was something about that "serve and protect" language that always spoke to me. Maybe that's why I like leather so damn much. Anyway, that was before I realized they didn't really do shit to protect the people that need it most. I mean, I remember when my mom called them cuz my stepdad threw her down the stairs, and they actually arrested her. She wasn't no angel and used to beat me real bad, but that time it was so clear she hadn't done shit. Then when I left home I tried to get them involved cuz she bruised me up really good and they just told me I should get over being gay. Fuckers.

I've always been sketched out about the neighbors. Everyone said I should stay the fuck away from them and just keep to myself. That's what Billy did when he was living here, but I figured I should at least try to make friends with the folks next door. They're always sitting outside while their dirty little kids ride big wheels up and down the driveway. The day I moved in I went to introduce myself as soon as Sunny drove away.

She was the only person I knew with a working car so we just made a bunch of trips over with bags and stuff shoved into the backseat. Hunter threw a fit about that, since it's his ex, but there wasn't any other option so he just had to get over it. The neighbors seemed nice enough, but also really uncomfortable. My hair was shaved into this sick mohawk and dyed bright blue. I'm sure that, along with the eight piercings in my face, didn't help anything.

It's been bad for a while, but got real scary last night. Hunter got chased from the bus. He barely made it into the house before the boys caught up with him. Cosmo and Orbit were barking, which I hoped would keep folks away. I peeked out the window and it looked like the guys had run off once they saw Hunter was inside. I made sure all the windows and the front and back door were locked. We don't have curtains or blinds or anything, just extra sheets and blankets hung with tacks. I kicked Hunter's cats out of the kitchen window where they like to sit so I could cover that too.

He was pretty shaken up. I was too, but I tried not to show it. We ate dinner, some pasta with dented-can discount pasta sauce on top. I probably should have heated up the sauce but I always figure if the noodles are hot, then the pasta sauce will warm up eventually. I had a bad feeling about everything and wanted to stay up, but Hunter was really tired and I didn't want him to know that I was freaking. I didn't even take the dogs out, figuring they had gone out late in the afternoon right before Hunter got back, and they could wait until it was light again.

The place is so small we couldn't really leave a light on and actually get it dark enough to sleep, so finally I turned off the light. I tried to stay awake but eventually just dozed off. I woke up to knocking on the windows and yelling too. Cosmo was growling and Orbit was glued to me. I don't know how many guys there were, but they circled the little house, banging on the windows and the walls, scaring the shit out of me. Hunter was awake too and not saying anything.

I had kept my binder on when I went to bed because he thinks I'm hotter that way and I was hoping he'd want to fuck me. I realized I'd left my jeans in the living room under the futon, so I crawled on my stomach out of the bedroom to avoid making shadows against the blankets. Cosmo was growling at the back door. Orbit followed me, but Hunter stayed in bed. I crawled back into the room and pulled a baseball bat out of the closet, then handed it to Hunter and pushed him at the backdoor. I whispered that he should stay right there in case they tried to come through it.

There wasn't much else good to use as a weapon so I picked up an old concrete garden gnome that I had pulled out of a dumpster near QYRC and held that near the front door. After about an hour it got quiet outside and the dogs stopped barking. At some point I fell asleep sitting on the living room floor with my back against the front door.

We didn't talk about it this morning. I think Hunter was too scared, and I wanted to pretend that it was all a nightmare. We were fucking tired all day and mostly just hung around the house, trying to get the antenna on the TV to pick up anything. Mostly it was just bad baby daddy, teen boot camp, surprise transsexuals daytime TV. The only time we went out was when Hunter needed to have some soda, and to quickly let the dogs piss in the backyard. There wasn't much food in the house, so we had more nasty pasta for dinner, tried unsuccessfully to get more reception on the TV, and eventually gave up and decided we should get some sleep. We didn't even get undressed, just pulled our boots off and crawled under the unzipped sleeping bag flung across the mattress.

I didn't think I was going to be able to sleep, but then I woke up to the banging again. Cosmo had jumped off the bed and was growling in a way I've never heard out of him. The house was surrounded by guys pounding on the walls and windows so hard I thought they might shatter. Hunter bolted out of bed and grabbed the baseball bat. I reached for the gnome, and realized what a stupid faggot idea of a weapon that was.

I didn't really know what to do. Then, I heard some of the guys talking about grabbing some gasoline from the neighbor's garage and torching the place. Hunter and I looked at each other. We were both against calling the cops under any circumstances, but even I was scared. I didn't know how many men were outside, but it was more than I could fight, that's for sure.

I picked up the phone and called the cops. I said I was gay, and that my house was surrounded for the second night in a row. I said I thought they were going to try to burn us out of it. I asked them to please hurry. It only took about ten minutes for the cops to show up. They whole time I tried to listen to the voices outside. I knew the place would catch like paper if they doused it in gas. I made Hunter shove the cats in his backpack so we could get the whole pack outside safely. When I heard the sirens the voices got quieter and I could hear them take off running and then a door slammed. They were camped out with the goddamn next-door neighbor. Problem with getting harassed by assholes who are your neighbors is all they have to do is go home and you can't prove a damn thing.

Hunter and I talked to the cops for about twenty minutes. They pretended to be sympathetic for a little while. Actually took a statement about what happened, which surprised me. Then, I asked what we should do if they came back. The cops just laughed at me. They said we should get a plant for the porch in case the folks thought the house was empty and were just causing trouble. I thought better of asking if they were fucking stupid. These guys knew we were in the house, which was the whole fucking point.

I told the cops that I knew the guys had run into the house next door. They said they hadn't witnessed that themselves so they couldn't go wake up random people in the middle of the night just because I had a theory about where these supposed attempted burglars were. Then they said folks like us really shouldn't be out in these parts, that we should expect this kind of treatment and that it might be best to talk to our landlord and just get out of the lease. I should have known better.

When the cops left we locked the door and tried to go back to bed. I took the bat with us. Hunter kept asking what I was going to do, but I didn't really have any answers. I guess I'm going to have to fucking move again.

Date: April 13, 2003
Security: Friends
Subject: Public

I don't really like this new apartment, but I didn't have much choice, after the crap with the cops I had to get out of the shack. Hunter wasn't much help. I've never lived in a place so clean before, and honestly I'm a little confused why they even decided to let us rent from them! It's this new building over on Sandy, it's totally ugly and looks like a hospital, but the building is secure and it's close to downtown so we shouldn't have trouble with the neighbors like we did out in the shack.

A bunch of folks I had called didn't pick up and I had to leave voicemail messages, but the folks at this building did. They had a one bedroom that we could afford and since the management office was on site (which I don't really like) they said we could come look at it. I put a hat over my funny hair, and I made Hunter put on a clean shirt which pissed him off cuz he just wanted to keep watching his movie. They said the place is dog friendly so I brought Orbit and put a little jacket on him. We told them we had another dog, and just decided not to mention the cats since we couldn't afford that many pet deposits.

The apartment was way too nice and clean. I know there's no way it will look like this when we leave, but they offered it to us on the spot. There was some sorta lease signing special where we got free rent the first month so long as we signed a year lease. Hunter freaked out at that. We've only been together a couple months. I told the management people to give us a second and when they walked out of the room I dropped to my knees. "Daddy, don't worry, I'll take care of it. If you decide you don't want me, I'll get us out of the lease. I just want us to be safe and we can't stay at the shack anymore."

He walked to the door and told the management agent that we'd take the apartment. I know I shouldn't, but I like that it's a year lease. I know nothing's guaranteed, but it seems like I can at least hope that it means I know I'll be taken care of for a little longer. We signed the lease and gave them the three hundred dollars security deposit and they gave us the key. If it hadn't been for that free rent we would have been fucked. I only had enough for the security because rent on the shack was due this week and I hadn't paid it yet. After all the crap, I'm not going to.

Hunter seemed to get happier about shit once he had a key to the new apartment. We went back to the shack, and I ordered pizza to surprise him, and we started throwing everything in trash bags. When the pizza came, Hunter called around to see if anyone could borrow a car to drive us to the new place. The pack and one of his buddies from the small town he's from who had a truck showed up around 11pm. It took two trips, but we got everything to the apartment. The cats are freaked out and not moving off the top of the kitchen cabinets but the dogs are loving it here already, because there are tons of dogs in the building. Hunter told me not to get too friendly with any of the neighbors. He said that's what got us in trouble with the shack.

The one cool thing about this place is that it has free internet so I can plug in my old computer that I've been carting around to all these different places, and actually get online! Right now I'm just fucking around on the internet and Hunter is watching a movie.

Mood: Tired

Music: screaming from Hunter's movie

Date: April 15, 2003
Security: Friends
Subject: Wedding

Just found out Buck's getting married! He and Luke haven't even been together that long, but I guess things have been pretty good. I think it's really funny that they're getting married, since Buck's always been really against all that kind of assimilationist shit.

He met me at the park tonight to break the news about the wedding. I think he thought I was going to be really judgmental. When he first told me, I thought he meant they were going to get civil unioned, but then he explained their plan. Luke just got all his ID switched to male and Buck is planning on doing it really soon, but right now, according to the state of Oregon they are a straight couple. So when they went to get their marriage license this morning, even though Buck has a beard starting to grow, there wasn't a damn thing the clerk could do! It's kinda hot that they are getting to fuck the system! I haven't been seeing or hearing much from Buck since he and Luke got together, and I'm a little worried that this is going to mean we see each other even less, but I know he and his Daddy have to work on building their relationship.

Granddaughter ~~Natalie Styles~~ Zander ~~Nate~~ Click
Birthday: May 16, 1984

~~3258 St. Jude St. Clackamas, Oregon~~
~~c/o Cindi 13352 rural road 5 Oregon City, Oregon~~
~~c/o Frank 1345 highway 8 Molalla, Oregon~~
~~2344 9th ave, basement SE Portland, Oregon~~
~~c/o James 2345 Heart St. Jacksonville, Florida~~
~~944 apt 60 35th ave Jacksonville, Florida~~
~~c/o Mr Jahn 2415 Beach Drive Jacksonville Fla~~
~~c/o Buck 1469 apt 5 NW Portland, Oregon~~
~~133 Hawthorne Blvd apt 3 Portland, Oregon~~
~~67 East 75th St Portland, Oregon~~
3875 NE Sandy Blvd 4N Portland, Oregon

Date: April 17, 2003

Last night Hunter and I hung out with Travis. He lives at The Safe House. It's a cool place and a bunch of old QYRC kids have lived there in the past. The house rules say you have to be in recovery and be serious about it to stay there. The idea is that they all help each other stay clean. Travis came up here from SF sometime last year. He's shy but really cute. He's a visual artist and does these intense collages full of blood and fish and clock parts. He's not on T yet, but has been off speed for about a year.

The three of us were hanging out downtown in waterfront park for a long time, but then it got dark and some cops started hassling us about park curfew so we went back to Hunter and my apartment to watch a movie. I'd had Orbit with us down at the park but I knew Cosmo couldn't stay alone for much longer. It was cute to watch Travis with the dogs. He has a bunch of pet rats that he brought up from SF with him, but he misses the dog he had growing up before he ran away. I must have dozed off during the movie. When I woke up I was alone on the living room

floor with the dogs pressed against me.
The movie had ended and the TV was all
black and white buzzing static.

I couldn't find Hunter and Travis anywhere.
I guess maybe they heard me walking
around or something, because the front
door opened and they came in. Hunter said
they hadn't wanted to wake me up with
their talking so they went to sit in the
building hallway.

Date: April 20, 2003
Security: Friends
Subject: Canada

Hunter and I are heading up to Canada tomorrow night after the
spoken word show at The Hotel. I hope the car makes it there
and back! We're crashing at this sweet punk house that folks at
the Safety Net connected us with. We're heading up to check
out the community and stuff because Hunter wants to move
and we gotta figure out what kinda work we can get under the
radar.

We'll be back in Portland sometime next week.

Date: April 23, 2003

Going to Canada was such a bad idea.
We didn't leave the show until almost
10pm. At least the dogs were already with

us, so we could just leave town. Right
when we hit the freeway the car started
making some crazy noises and then steam
was coming outta the hood. Hunter jumped
out and popped the hood. I don't think
he really knew what he was looking for.
I asked if we were still gonna be able to
go to Vancouver. He told me to shut the
fuck up.

Thankfully some dyke driving by stopped.
She said we needed more radiator fluid or
something and that there was a gas station
up the road. Hunter left in her truck and
I stayed behind with the dogs. They were
back pretty quickly and she stayed to
help with the car. She was really hot and
had on these coveralls like my grandpa
wears. She told us that she's a mechanic
and works at a garage over in SE.

"You gals be safe," she called when she
slammed the hood and was walking back to
her truck.

Hunter yelled, "FUCK YOU!" at her. I knew
he was mad that she thought he was a dyke.
I tried to mouth, "I'm sorry" through the
windshield but she'd already peeled out
into traffic.

Hunter and I didn't talk much until after Olympia and then it was just because he was falling asleep and ordered me to keep the radio on, and to talk to him. I think I slept through Seattle. We made good time and hit the border about 4am. We were the only folks crossing then, and the border cops gave us a hard time. They wanted to know why we were visiting Canada and why we were crossing the border in the middle of the night. We ended up just saying that we were there to visit friends, which caused a whole different set of problems because they wanted names and addresses.

Augustus had put us in touch with his friend, Hatchet, who lives at this punk house called the Hiding Hole, and has been living up in Canada illegally for years now. I didn't have a last name for Hatchet, and I didn't know if that was his government name, and I didn't even know where the house was. The border patrol was pissed. Augustus had just given us the phone number and told me Hatchet would be expecting our call, but not to call until after 3pm because he works overnight at a strip club. The cop asked for pay stubs or some proof of employment, but we couldn't give her that either. She said they were concerned that we didn't have substantial

ties to the United States. I told them we
had two cats and an apartment and would
definitely be coming back.

They let us through at about 5am. Hunter
was exhausted. We drove a little while and
it looked like we were in some suburbs or
something. We pulled off the expressway
and drove around some neighborhoods until
we found a high school. We figured that
being near a school, folks might not be
so weird about a parked car. The car is
just a shitty little two door, but you
can lay the back seat down. We did that
so we could at least stick our feet into
the truck. I didn't even bother to take
my boots off, and we kept our binders on
in case anyone came to hassle us. It was
really crowded and Hunter wouldn't stop
talking about how fucking stupid it was
that I made him bring the dogs. It was so
crowded the dogs were sleeping on top of
us, so I just buried my face in Cosmo's
back and pretended to be asleep already.
I didn't have anyone I trusted to leave
the dogs with, and I was worried that
Hunter would decide it was so good in
Canada that we wouldn't come back at all
and I couldn't risk losing the pups.

We slept for a couple of hours but then the dogs started getting restless. I took them to run in the high school field so Hunter could sleep a little more. All Cosmo wanted was to play ball. Orbit was just running around but started barking when I went and peed in some bushes. Hunter was still sleeping when I opened the door and crawled back into the car with the dogs. I'd seen some folks working in their yards and glaring at our car. I was worried they might call the cops, so I told Hunter that we needed to get going.

Before we left Portland we printed a map of Vancouver off the internet. We got lost a couple of times, but made it to Commercial Drive. Someone at QYRC had told us that it was the gayborhood and definitely where we should go when we got into town. Portland doesn't really have a gayborhood, so even though I haven't been real sure about this whole move to Canada thing, this was something I was excited to see. I hate straight people, and if I could live in a neighborhood where it was just us that might be pretty cool. When we parked, Hunter wanted to leave the dogs in the car, but it was way too hot.

The gayborhood wasn't anywhere near as cool as I thought it was going to be. It's mostly just lesbians with yoga mats and strollers, and every block was a fancy gym, and through the big glass windows I could see all these dudes working out. I didn't see any punks anywhere. Hunter went into a grocery store and came out with a bag of chips to eat while we wondered around. I kept checking my watch, hoping it would hurry up and be 3pm so we could get directions to figure out how to get to the Hiding Hole. Hunter just kept getting pissed off that we didn't have enough money to buy shirts and other crap that he wanted.

I found a payphone at 3 and called Hatchet. He sounded really groggy, I must have woken him up. At first he didn't even seem to recognize me. I told him that Augustus had said we could crash in our car in front of The Hiding Hole and use their bathroom and stuff. Hatchet was quiet for a second and then he said that a bunch of anarchist circus kids came in from Toronto, and there wasn't room for us. I was afraid to tell Hunter. I knew he was going to blame me. I called Augustus, trying to see if he knew anyone else in Vancouver, but he didn't. He said he was sorry that shit hadn't worked out so good up here this trip. Hunter took the news better than I thought he would. He said that Vancouver was no place for queer punks like us, and that we should just go back to Portland.

We sprang for veggie burgers at a restaurant with sidewalk seating so I could keep the dogs with us. There was a line to get back across the border. Hunter was worried that the car was going to overheat. When we finally got to the front of the line, they took our ID's and were gone for a long while. When the border guards came back, they told us we needed to pull into the parking lot and get out of the car. When Hunter closed the window he asked if I thought they would start shooting if he just gunned it straight ahead instead of parking. I asked if there was anything in the car that I didn't know about, and he didn't answer.

They took us into an office and said they had to search the car and talk to us separately. I was really freaking out. The border cop at least let me keep the dogs. I zipped Orbit up into my hoodie and had Cosmo sit next to me while the investigator asked me questions about who I was and why we were in the country.

I think they thought I was maybe an identity thief or something. They kept saying I didn't look like a man and I kept trying to explain what transgender means. I thought a lot about the education trainings Buck and Jacob and everyone back at QYRC do all the time. I tried to remember to breathe, and to stay calm. The border cops wanted to know why we stayed in the country less than twenty-three hours, and if we had any drugs. I told them no, but was freaking out. We haven't had the car very long and it's really likely that Hunter's stepdad used drugs in it before he sold it to us.

Finally they let me back into the waiting lobby. I could see through the windows investigators looking through the car and our backpacks sitting open on the curb. Hunter was sitting and waiting. Cosmo ran up to him but Hunter wouldn't even pet him. I sat down and tried to talk to Hunter but he just told me to shut up. After another fifteen minutes or so, one of the officers came in and said we could go. I loaded the dogs back into the car and Hunter peeled out over the border and into Washington. He had the radio up real loud and I was worried it was going to hurt the dogs' ears, but was afraid to say something and make him more angry.

I started talking about how scared I'd been when they separated us and asked Hunter what they had said to him but he just said this whole thing was my fault. I didn't even want to come to Canada. I pulled at my lip ring with my teeth really hard to try to keep from crying.

Date: April 31, 2003
Security: Friends
Subject: Back in PDX

Hunter and I got back into Portland early this morning. Trip was ok, but we definitely don't like Canada so we're gonna be staying put.

Date: May 4, 2003
Security: Public
Subject: Owwwww

Ugh! My nose hurts really bad. I got my septum pierced last Thursday. Hank, the tattoo aritst/body piercer, told me to keep it clean, and I did. I even made a special trip to the store to get anti-bacterial soap to shove up my nose. It had been helping pretty well I think, but then on Saturday, Daddy got drunk and told me that I needed to suck his little dick. I couldn't tell him no, so soon my face was all up in his junk. Now my piercing's all infected and it hurts! I should probably go talk to Hank, but I know he will be hella pissed at me for not following his orders.

Date: May 8, 2003
Security: Friends
Subject: Dog People

The only queer folks in the building that I can spot are Lisa and Jenny. They are these really weird yuppie lesbians. Jenny is some sort of shoe designer, I think, and Lisa stays home to care for Phoenix, their golden retriever. We don't know each other well other than Cosmo and Phoenix play a lot in the field behind the building. Anyway, they invited us to come over for Phoenix's second adoption day party today. Hunter refused to go so it was just me, Orbit, and Cosmo. I made some vegan dog cookies as a gift and had an ok time. I hate how much after all this time I still really like being around dog people.

It was weird, though, to realize that they are queer because they sure don't act like it. They're kinda like any other yuppie I know, talking about where they go out to eat, and how they will decorate the apartment, and their plan to have babies in a couple of years and get married, that kinda shit. They got Phoenix a special doggie cake from some bakery downtown and had invited a lot of dogs from the building and some of their other lesbian friends. I didn't stay very long. Hunter was alone in the apartment with the cats and doesn't like it when I stay out for too long.

Date: May 11, 2003

Hunter sat me down tonight and said we needed to have a serious conversation. He said that he couldn't do this anymore, that he wanted to be with me, but that he wanted to fuck other people too, not just crush on them like he'd been doing with Sarah at the Clit Shack a little while ago. I asked if this was about Travis. He said he needed to fuck him. I started to cry. I don't know if I want to be poly or not. I used to fuck around a lot, but he's my Daddy and I'm scared. He got really pissed that I was crying and said I could either be ok with it, or he would leave.

I guess we're poly now.

Date: May 16, 2003
Security: Friends
Subject: Happy Birthday to me!

Turned 19 today!

Date: May 16, 2003

Buck's busy with planning the wedding, so I'm sure that's why he forgot to return my calls about maybe getting together for my birthday. I thought maybe Hunter and I could go do something like hangout with the dogs at a park or something, but he said he had plans to hang out at the Safety Net. He said I could come with him, so I did. The house was working on building even bigger cages for all the rats. Travis' rats keep having more and more litters and no one can part with them unless another punk house takes them, so now they have like ten rats. They keep dumpstering more cages and putting them together to give the little guys more room. We were there for a while and I kept waiting for Hunter to suggest we leave and go do something fun for my birthday but he didn't. I'm not sure he even remembered.

Date: May 18, 2003

I can't believe that Buck's married and collared now! I'm happy for him but I'm also really worried that I'm not going to see him as much. I almost didn't make it to the wedding today. Hunter was obviously supposed to go with me, and this morning, when I started getting ready, all of a sudden he said he wasn't coming.

He's been telling me since we got together that he thinks Buck's a bad influence on me. Hunter always says he's not one of those tops who think everyone owes him something and should serve him. But he does expect a base level of respect, and he doesn't feel like Buck shows him that. He gets really moody when I talk too much about Buck, and says he thinks that Buck puts bad ideas in my head about my Daddy.

This morning when Hunter first said he wasn't going to go to the wedding I thought it was just his normal moodiness and he'd get over it and in the end decide he needed to come to chaperone me. I did laundry so my work pants are clean. I put my binder through the dryer, which isn't very good for it, but shrinks it a little so it's extra tight for today, and I splurged and bought a new pack of black undershirts. I even cleaned and polished my boots, and Orbit's collar. Hunter thought I was making way too big of a deal about this, but the way I see it, it's not every day your big brother gets married! I would have done Hunter's boots too, but he said no.

When it was time to leave, Hunter still wasn't dressed. He said that his ulcer was acting up and that he was too sick to go. I didn't even know he had an ulcer. He said it would be best if I stayed home today and took care of him. I told him I would try to hurry back, but I really couldn't skip the ceremony. He said if I was a good boy I would stay. That made me really mad because I try so hard to be a good boy, but Buck's my family! Walking out the door and standing at the bus stop was one of the hardest things I've ever had to do. I hate disappointing my Daddy.

The wedding was in Aurora and Big Billy's house, which was a little awkward for me. They fucked Billy up real bad when Grace dumped him, and he had to get out of their house. They stopped doing the 101 Leather workshops at QYRC then too because Billy's on steering committee and I'm sure they knew they wouldn't be welcome back in the space.

Luke is leather family with Aurora, from back when they were both street punks down in San Francisco. Eight years ago Luke was Aurora's Master. They came up to Portland and Aurora hooked up with Big Billy and became hys little girl and the three of them were this big kinky triad for a while until it all just kinda slowly fell apart. They aren't together but are still close. The last time we hung out, Buck told me how excited he was that Aurora and Big Billy had offered for the ceremony to be at their house. He said it felt important because it was a symbol of becoming part of this big family like the one he'd always wanted. I wanted to ask Buck if it meant that they were going to be my family now too, but I was afraid he'd say no, so I didn't ask.

The ceremony itself was nice. There were about thirty of us down in the basement dungeon. It was mostly folks that I think must be friends with Luke, because I didn't really know them. Buck's ex girlfriend was there, which weirded me out a little. Buck said that his breakup with her went really well. She knew that she couldn't give him the kind of life he needed in terms of leather and stuff, but I was still surprised she came. I haven't seen her since I stayed with them in the fall when I had to come back to Portland after James. I went up to say hi so she didn't think I was ignoring her. Buck and Luke looked so hot. They were wearing fresh black work pants with red button down shirts tucked in. Luke wore black leather suspenders (a present that we all watched Big Billy give him right before the ceremony started) and they both had crisp hunter green hankies in their back pockets.

They said a few words about commitment and care taking, but the main part of the ceremony was the cutting. There was a table laid out at the front of the basement with candles all over it and two sets of black latex gloves and a scalpel. We all watched as they took turns removing their dress shirts, pushed up the sleeves of their undershirts and cut a spiral into each other's bicep. It was so hot. I've never been cut before, but it's something I've always wanted.

After they bandaged each other up, the ceremony was over and everyone just started hanging out. There were vegan cupcakes and chips and all kinds of good junk food. I was feeling kinda weird being there without Hunter, and worried that he was going to be mad when I got home. It was hard, too, because I didn't really know anyone and Buck was obviously busy so I couldn't talk to him.

I left Orbit down in the dungeon and went to the bathroom. It sounds stupid, but I cried. I don't even know why. I'm so happy for Buck, it's fucked up that at his wedding I was feeling so upset. When I came out, Big Billy was waiting outside the door. I was trying to apologize for having taken so long, but I just kept stuttering. I guess splashing water on my face didn't do much to hide that I'd been crying. I was so embarrassed and turned bright red. Hy didn't say anything, just clapped me on the back real hard and held my shoulder blade in hys hand. I closed my eyes and leaned back into hys grip, feeling my breathing quiet. I whispered, "Thank you," then ran downstairs to get Orbit.

Buck didn't seem to notice I left so early. I didn't really want to leave right then, but I knew the longer I was gone, the angrier Hunter would be. When Orbit and I got back, Hunter wasn't around. Cosmo was bouncing off the walls, which meant Hunter hadn't taken him out to play ball, and I couldn't find a note. I took the dogs out to the park for a while, and when we got back Hunter was still gone. I was a little worried that something had happened with his ulcer and he had to go

to the hospital, so I called the Safety
Net to see if anyone there knew what was
going on.

One of their house guests picked up the
phone, and said that Hunter had been there
but that he left with Travis a while ago
to go hang out downtown. Hunter finally
came back smelling like rat piss, which
of course confirmed that he'd been with
Travis. Travis lets the rats sleep with
him and always has at least one in his
sweatshirt and they end up peeing on him
and he doesn't have a good sense of smell
so he doesn't realize how bad he stinks.
I asked how he was feeling and he said
much better. He didn't ask me about how
the wedding was.

Date: May 20, 2003
Security: Private
Subject: untitled

Had to go do shots at the Safe House tonight. The guys
there were late on getting it because they all kept trying to
do it themselves, but couldn't. Finally, they called me and said
everyone in the house really needed their shots like now. It was
already after midnight but I didn't want to say no. The busses
were barely running at that point, so I walked over. I brought
both the dogs with me since Hunter was in a bad mood. It took
me over an hour to get there. I did everyone's shots right in a

row on the living room rug. It was free time for the rats so there were rats crawling all over everyone and I had to keep pushing them off whatever ass I was about to stick a needle in. Thank goodness Cosmo and Orbit are used to the rats. They were really good about ignoring them. I thought we might hang out for a little while afterwards, but the guys said they were tired, so I just walked back to the apartment.

Hunter was asleep when I got back. I guess he decided to jack off while I was away because the TV was still playing this VHS of fag porn he got for five dollars last week when one of the video places had a big clearance sale. I pulled off my pants and crawled into bed with him and I kept my binder on because he likes it better that way and scooted right up against him. I thought he was sleeping, but his hand was still stroking his cock. I moved my hand to touch him, but he shoved me away. He didn't stop me when I got out of bed and came out here into the living room, he just turned up the volume on the TV.

Date: May 23, 2003

Buck called me today and said we needed to talk privately. Hunter was in the shower so I said now was ok. I brought the phone into the bedroom and closed the door. He said that he knew I left the wedding early, and he thought it was weird that Hunter hadn't come at all. He was worried about me. I told him Hunter was sick and couldn't come and I had to leave because I was worried about how Hunter was feeling. I hoped we were going to keep talking but then he said his Daddy said he needed to get off the phone.

Date: May 29, 2003

Big Billy came over after the open mic tonight. Hy had asked if Hunter and I wanted a ride back to our place and we said sure. When we got to the apartment I asked if hy wanted to come in and hang out for a little while. Hunter actually likes Big Billy which surprises me, since usually he doesn't like anyone who's got more leather experience than he does. Especially if it's someone that I became friends with first. I still feel a little weird hanging out with Big Billy because of my old loyalties to Billy. Billy and I don't really talk anymore after he moved out, and Big Billy is family with Buck now, so I think it's ok for us to be friends.

Hunter suggested we watch some dumb horror movie he had borrowed. I don't think Big Billy really wanted to, but hy said ok. We had some chips and soda so I brought that over for everyone and then sat on the floor at Hunter's feet. I really hate

those sorts of movies so I kept talking
and trying to distract Hunter by poking
him in the knee with my finger. I wanted
him to turn the movie off so we could all
talk or go do something.

"See what a disrespectful boy I have?"
he said to Big Billy. I know I got all
red and embarrassed. Big Billy didn't say
anything but took one of Hunter's nasty
dirty socks that was lying on the floor
right by the futon and shoved it into my
mouth. I was shocked and kinda scared. I'd
never played with Big Billy and I really
didn't see that coming. Hunter gave Big
Billy a high five and started laughing.
I bit into the sock to try to keep from
puking or crying or both.

The dogs could tell I was upset. Orbit
crawled into my lap and Cosmo sat between
me and Hunter until he shooed them away.
"You don't even deserve the floor," Big
Billy said as hy stood up. Hy grabbed my
arm and pulled me up onto the futon.

"Lay down," Hunter commanded. Then they
both sat on me and one of them reminded me
not to let the sock slip. Hunter was on my
thighs and Big Billy on my back. It hurt
worse than binding with duct tape, and

I liked that part. I was crying and they just ignored me until the movie was over and Big Billy said it was time for hym to be getting home. Hunter told me that I needed to pretend I was a good boy and escort Big Billy down to his truck, and that I was to do so with the sock still in my mouth. I'm not into humiliation play, and I knew that there was no way I could avoid running into at least one of the neighbors in the hallway. I wanted to beg for forgiveness, but I couldn't take the sock out of my mouth and it's not like I have a safe word or anything anymore, so I just had to do it.

Date: June 1, 2003

He broke up with me. I still don't think that's sunk in.

The absolute worst thing you can do is listen to advice from the person who just broke up with you. I think I've known for longer than I want to admit that things have been over between Hunter and me, but maybe that's more about saving face than being honest. I was in a rage by the time he actually did the breaking up. I mean not in a screaming rage, and I'd already cried myself out in the hours and hours that he didn't come home. But I was pissed at 10 am, sixteen and a half hours after he had left to go on a date with Travis, when he finally got the balls to come home and tell me that after eight whole months he was done with me.

I sat on the living room floor while he went into what had been our bedroom and started shoving clothes, all of which I had bought, and most of which were actually mine, into his backpack. I tried to get him to talk. If we were not going to be lovers, I figured we should at least be friends.

Who am I kidding,? I was begging Daddy to take me back, asking what I could do and he was totally uninterested. I think the only reason he actually bothered to physically break up with me was because I'd been calling the Safety Net repeatedly since his date with Travis should have been over. One of their other roommates had sleepily picked up the phone at 4am when I'd called looking for him and said the car was parked outside and it looked like they were in it. I'd proceeded to call back every hour after that, until Hunter finally showed up at our apartment. This was their first real date. The first

time that he and Travis had gone out
alone, and I was so nervous beforehand.
I kept thinking about James, and that
made Hunter mad. He said it wasn't fair
for him to have to pay for someone else's
sins. He was right of course. Maybe it's
my fault. If I'd trusted him more maybe
he wouldn't have done this to me.

Hunter started shoving VHS tapes into a
paper bag that we'd gotten at the bulk
grocery when we'd gone on a huge grocery-
shopping trip earlier in the week the day
his food stamps came in. I watched to make
sure he didn't take anything I actually
cared about, like some of the lesbian folk
albums I got from James. I kept trying to
just get Hunter to talk to me. I was asking
him what I could have done differently,
and what I could do to get him back. He
told me that he'd been talking with folks
at the Safety Net all night, and they had
decided that I was codependent, and that
maybe I should start going to meetings.
I was pissed but didn't show it until
he walked out the door with a promise
of being back later in the week to get
his cats and pick up his twin mattress
that we'd pushed together with my twin
mattress to make this DIY king sized bed.
He didn't even say goodbye to Cosmo and

Orbit. Right when he was at the door, he asked for his cuff back. I didn't want to give it to him. That seems like the sort of thing you should save, but I was so tired and I didn't want to make him angrier, so I handed it over.

I started pacing the apartment. What fucking bullshit! The person who started using meth with his mother at twelve years old, who gets drunk all the time, and who smokes pot and who knows what else when he thinks I'm not paying attention seriously just told me, the only person in our circle of friends who has never been drunk and never been high, that I have unresolved addiction issues and that I need to get myself to a meeting!

I ate some crappy hummus and started cleaning out the refrigerator. Last month at a party at The Hotel, Hunter and I met this kickass animal rights activist who's been train hopping around the country. After hanging out with her we decided to go vegan. Hunter was already starting to cave but I've mostly been sticking with it. Well, except for that night he made hamburger pasta. I decided after Hunter left that I was in a space of extreme emotional distress, and that if I didn't purge the house of his toxins I was going to relapse. So there I was on very little sleep Friday morning at 10:30am pitching hotdogs, frozen pizzas, and packaged lunchmeat into a grocery bag. I thought about taking the food to QYRC but they weren't open yet. I knew if I let it sit in my house I would end up having some meat fest feast for lunch, so instead I threw it in the trash. I felt guilty about that right after I did it. It went against everything I believe in, like how there were all these fucking starving kids and here I am with an apartment throwing out food because I couldn't handle my loser boyfriend finally breaking up with me. Maybe I did need to go to a meeting.

I turned on my computer, played it cool, and avoided making a melodramatic online diary update. Middle of the night, off the hook calling to The Safety Net was enough public embarrassment for one day. I started searching for codependent anonymous meetings. I knew that over on Burnside there was a place with different LGBT twelve-step meetings every day of the week. It took a while, but I finally found their listing.

Of course they didn't have another co-
dependent meeting for three days! I called
Buck, who I'd also woken up in the middle
of the night with my panicked phone calls
about Hunter's absence. I really wanted
him to come be with me so I wasn't all
alone, but his Daddy said he couldn't
go out. I told Buck about my inability
to go to a meeting for three days, how
I wasn't sure I was co-dependent, but how
I was panicking about what to do in the
seventy-two hours before I could go sit
in a room with other heartbroken people
and talk about our problems.

His best advice, based on having gone to
al-anon in Philly after breaking up with
some girl he met at the bar, was that a
meeting is a meeting, and if I needed a
meeting then I should just go to whatever
twelve-step program I could find to get me
through. This seemed like strange though
believable advice, so as we got off the
phone I went to the listing of meetings
that day. I immediately ruled out all the
alcoholic meetings. My mother drinks and
that shit freaks me out. I didn't think
I could spend an hour in a room with drunks,
even ones who weren't drinking. I decided
that the closest, least triggering thing
I could attend would be a meeting for

sexaholics, which coincidentally met in about four hours at the center only blocks from my building.

I walked down the hall to Lisa and Jenny's and told them about the breakup, but then asked their advice on what to wear to my first twelve-step meeting. They are good suburban lesbians in sweater vests and khaki pants who'd found themselves dropped into the middle of Portland, and my tranny boi punk rock problems left them clueless. The good thing was Lisa and Jenny agreed to watch Orbit and Cosmo when I went out to the meeting. The dogs have been pretty freaked out since Hunter went on his date last night. I guess they can sense how upset I am. I went back to my apartment to find something attractive out of the small pile of clothes Hunter had bothered to leave me.

Even though I showed up at the meeting early the room was already filling up. Pretty immediately I knew I was in the wrong place, but I was already there so I figured I should stay. Besides, if I walked out it would totally look I wasn't ready to face my problems, which wasn't the issue at all, it's just that I was quickly realizing that maybe

I didn't have such a problem. Anyway, in the time between finding the meeting online and showing up I'd sorta forgot it wasn't an LGBT codependents meeting, which in my imagination would be filled with benign though obsessive forty year old lesbians struggling to figure out how to handle their partner walking out and leaving them to raise the a dozen cats on their own.

The room was filled with middle-aged gay men who were practically licking their lips over me until I pulled of my sweatshirt. Oh yeah, Hunter "accidentally" took my binder along with his when he packed his stuff up this morning. So I spent the next hour sitting in a room with non-trans men talking about the dangerous and risky sex they partook in because they couldn't control themselves.

When my turn to talk came I started explaining how I was in the wrong meeting, but then everyone was giving these knowing nods like they were all silently communicating to one another that I wasn't ready to face my issues, which wasn't the situation at all. Finally I gave them the abbreviated whole damn story. They looked at me completely stunned. The facilitator asked for clarification about gender, not understanding that I was a boy talking about my boyfriend and then it was time for the meeting to end.

I made my escape quickly. I did not want to be trapped in conversation with any of those men for a moment longer, and I wanted to get back with the dogs. I started walking home and thinking about how much had changed in twenty-four hours.

I guess I'm an orphan now.

Date: June 6, 2003

I can't believe Hunter. I know that I shouldn't trust him, but he was my Daddy. He called last night asking if would be able to come over today to get his cats. I guess he's found a place to stay, and I've never really been too bonded with the cats, but still I thought I was going to have more time to say goodbye. I think his new place is in Travis' room at the Safety Net, which I also think is fucked up.

When Hunter called, he asked if I would leave the dogs at the apartment and go out while he picked up the cats. That made me

nervous because I barely left him alone
with the dogs when we were together. He
said that he wanted the chance to properly
say goodbye because he wouldn't be their
Daddy anymore. That really fucked me up,
and I said ok. We agreed that he'd be
over at eleven, so I went downtown to
hang at the bookstore. On my way back
to the apartment I walked through the
tennis courts by the light rail tracks
and collected all the lost tennis balls
as a present for Cosmo and Orbit. When
I got back to the apartment and put my
key in the door it was weird how quiet
it was and then when I opened the door
I knew something was wrong. There's never
been a time that Orbit and Cosmo haven't
met me at the door.

They were gone.

I started crying and freaking out.
I looked everywhere, in the closets and
in the bathroom just in case, and for a
second I thought maybe Hunter had taken
the dogs out for a walk, but the cats
and all their stuff I'd packed up this
morning weren't there. I knew they were
gone. Hunter knows the only thing that
really matters to me in the whole world
is my dogs. I called the Safety Net but

nobody picked up. It was the only place I could think of where Hunter might have taken them.

I almost went and talked to the lesbo neighbors but I knew they would tell me to call the cops and that's about the last thing that would help. I tried to call Buck, but he couldn't come to the phone. Finally I settled on calling the Safety Net over and over again until finally, a couple hours later, Travis picked up the phone. I tried to stay calm but I know I was hysterical. I asked what the fuck he'd done with my dogs.

Travis told me I needed to calm down. I told him I needed my dogs. He said that Hunter had missed them and wanted to take them for a visit. He said they were out back right now playing and that Hunter would bring them back in the morning. He just wanted to have a night with them. I said no, that none of this was part of the deal, and that the dogs had to come home right then.

Travis said he'd talk to Hunter, but that he knew Hunter wasn't going to like that. I was freaking out so bad for the five minutes before I called back. Travis picked up and said I'd get the dogs back today. The next hour felt like it was never going to end, but finally Travis opened the door and Orbit and Cosmo came running in. I probably should have thanked him for returning my dogs but I was so mad all I wanted to do was get Hunter's keys from him and get him out of my house. Hunter didn't even have the balls to come inside with Travis.

Once Travis left and I had inspected Orbit and Cosmo to make sure they were ok, I took them on a really long walk in the park and showed them all the tennis balls I found. I never ever thought I'd say this, but I can't trust Hunter at all. I never thought he would hurt me like this.

Date: June 7, 2003

Buck's Daddy hasn't been allowing him to go out much, especially if it means hanging out with me. I don't know why. We haven't been able to see each other since Hunter dumped me, but we were able to talk once. Buck's started to help me realize that Hunter really was an asshole freeloader pretty much the whole time we'd been together. The big issue with us breaking up is that I'm not going to be able to do my shot on time if he's not my Daddy. Hunter and I are two of the only people able to give injections. I'd sorta just been ignoring that, but I really needed my shot today, so this afternoon I started calling all of the pack. I'm doing shots for about fourteen guys right now, so I figured one of them would be able to stick a needle in my ass just this once.

I didn't bother talking to the answering machine at the Clit Shack because no one ever checks the messages. How they aren't out of tape on the machine I have no idea. I left messages with roommates or houseguests at a bunch of other houses, but doubted I would end up hearing anything back. I managed to get the Safety Net to pick up, but the guys there confirmed what I already knew. There is no way any anyone was going to do my shot since they're all sober and holding needles is way too triggering for them, not to mention Hunter is there.

He said I was really insensitive for even calling since it could put any of them in jeopardy of a relapse just by thinking about needles. Being XXX, I really don't get how getting a needle pushed into your ass every week is not triggering, but someone calling to ask if you can do the same for them is. As it's been explained to me again and again, there are some things that I will just never understand. Whatever. Augustus, who lives at the Safety Net, did say that I should call Sarah. She got kicked out of the Safety Net when she relapsed. That happens a lot, people relapse or break the house's sober rules and then end up at The Hotel or Clit Shack. Sarah's been staying at the Clit Shack for a while and I guess has done shots for guys who are really desperate and it doesn't fuck her up too much.

I found Sarah's number in a pile of notes and newspaper clippings Hunter had left on the kitchen counter. Sarah's housemate said she'd already left for work but gave me the number of the video rental place out on 82nd and said she should be there in about thirty minutes. Thirty-three minutes later I called the video store and asked for Sarah. We haven't really hung out since the day Bush declared war, and even then we never knew each other very well. She's the ex of our super sexy tattoo artist, and really the only reason we ever hung out was because Hunter wanted to fuck her. I told Sarah that Hunter and I had broken up, which of course she already knew. She said she was sorry and sounded all sympathetic, which made me feel all defensive because he was a real asshole but I tried not to think of that because I desperately needed her help. When I explained to Sarah that I needed my shot really badly and that no one else could do it, she agreed that if I made her dinner and let her crash at my place she'd ride her bike over at 1am when she got off work.

I was convinced Sarah was going to flake on me, but then I realized she wanted to spend the night and thought I might get lucky. I called back later in the night to make sure she remembered. She sounded annoyed so I stopped checking in. At 1:45 she buzzed the apartment and lugged her mini bike up the stairs and through the hallway. I'd made some spaghetti. Sarah lied and said that it tasted good. We sat on the floor and started eating, she was soaking wet because it had been raining so I grabbed Cosmo's blanket and she wrapped it around herself.

While we ate, we started talking about gender. Sarah is one of the only people I know who isn't on T. We started talking about what it was like for her to be friends with all these boys and then out of nowhere she asks me why I wanted to start T since I'd always been so genderqueer identified. I was surprised, like that's just something you don't really ask someone. I started telling her about how it felt right, and made my body match up with how I saw my gender as really fluid even though other people might not think so. She seemed interested and I thought that she was really hot. I kept staring at the tattoos on her hands as she fingered the fork, playing with the sorta soggy, sorta crunchy noodles on her plate.

I probably shouldn't have, but I told her about that old QYRC therapist and how I was really proud of myself for fucking with the system and getting a letter anyway, but Sarah didn't look that impressed. We threw the dishes on top of other dishes in my sink and I went into the bathroom to get the supplies. Sarah wanted to draw up the shot for me which I figured was fine since she was going to stick it in my ass. As usual I started getting all shaky.

I really hate needles and am always convinced it's going to rupture some vital organ and kill me on the spot, which doesn't make any sense since the shot goes into your butt, but when I'm freaking out I don't think very logically. I was being all stupid and running my mouth, talking about how I was still a dyke even though I took T, and how sometimes it was really frustrating to pass, and how I hadn't really thought about all that shit before I started. Sarah got all freaked out and put the capped syringe on the floor. I was lying there in front of her with my pants around my knees and started getting pissed. I mean all that shit is true, but mostly I was just freaking out about getting a needle shoved in my ass, and I fucking needed my shot and it was two in the morning, and there was no one else who would do it.

Sarah said we needed to process everything that I'd just told her. I said I couldn't process anything until I had my shot. She demanded I give her my vial of T for safekeeping until I felt more solidly about what I was doing. I told her she was nuts and that I knew she'd just sell it to someone else the minute she left my place. She got offended and acted like

I was calling her a drug dealer. All I wanted was my fucking shot. Finally at like four am she agreed to do it just this once, but said after that I had to find someone else to do it, because she just didn't feel right about the decisions that I was making.

Date: June 9, 2003

I met Pocket at the zine symposium last year. Problem was hy was married to some other tranny fag, and so we couldn't really do anything. I thought hy was really hot, though, and totally wanted hym to bend me over the copy machines. But as a rule I don't help people cheat. Besides, the hubby was always around. I didn't really understand why Pocket was so into him. He seemed pretty boring to me and didn't even make zines but just tagged along with Pocket for the symposium.

Last week Pocket posted on hys online diary that the marriage was over. It sucks a lot because they had just (like three weeks ago) gotten tattooed together. They got these little old fashioned spoons on their wrists. At least it's pretty easy to cover up with a watch or something. Anyway, when I read the post that they had broken up, I was super sympathetic about it. Then, last night Pocket called and said hy wanted to come down to Portland for the weekend and asked if hy could stay with me the first night.

Pocket is round and sorta femme boy faggoty in a really hot way. I told hym it was ok to come and hy bought a ticket for the bus leaving Seattle this afternoon. I didn't really have any plans for today, so I said I would go downtown and pick him up. The bus was supposed to get in about eight, but of course the stupid thing was hella late and we didn't get back to my place until midnight. Hy was so cute though, even cuter than I remembered. Hy wore these old fashioned trousers and an animal liberation t-shirt.

Neither of us had eaten, so I made some noodle packets. The "oriental" ones are vegan even if they are fucking racist. While I was cooking Pocket sat on the floor and played with the dogs. It was nice, sometimes folks think my little pack is too much, and get weirded out, especially if I'm talking about how awesome they are. I spent most of the day before Pocket arrived hanging out downtown with Buck. His Daddy was at work and said

Buck could go out. I miss him so much. I didn't tell Buck I had a booty call coming down from Seattle, cuz sometimes my brother is fucking conservative. He probably would have given me some lecture about how much casual sex I have, and if shit with Pocket actually had a potential to be something bigger. It doesn't.

The only good thing about the bus being late was that it meant I had time to rush back to my place and change the sheets and bring the dogs back so they didn't have to trail down to the bus station with me. Well, I only have one pair of sheets, and didn't have time to do laundry so I didn't really change them, but flipped the fitted sheet over so it's basically like having clean sheets. Pocket didn't seem to notice.

After we finished eating hy said hy was really tired. I told hym hy could have my bed and I could go sleep in the living room. I didn't want to assume we were going to fuck, or that hy was up for it tonight. Pocket started laughing at me and then we were making out. Hy pulled off hys binder and boxers right away and left me alone.

Pocket was really loud, like maybe the loudest person I've ever fucked before. I wonder if the neighbors are going to complain to the management company. There is no way anyone slept through this. I fucked hym for a while with my hand. Hy kept asking for more but couldn't quite take my fist, which I think pissed hym off. Hy kept referring to hymself in the third person, "Fuck Pocket harder," and "Touch Pocket's clitoral region," really weird shit like that! I ended up flipping hym over onto hys knees and fucking hym with my cock. It took hym a long time to cum. By the end, hy was screaming. Hy kept begging for more of me (still in the third person), and then right as hy came hy screamed, "THANK YOU SIR!!!!!!"

I'm a boy, I ain't anyone's Sir. Total boner killer.

Hy laid there for a really long time, and I thought maybe hy had fallen asleep, but then hy rolled over and started trying to touch me and asking if hy could clean my cock and that kind of shit. I told hym I was tired and rolled over. I really wanted to get fucked, but I couldn't take hym seriously after all that. Anyone who can get off on calling me "Sir" isn't going to fuck me how I need. Anyway, I waited a few minutes until I was pretty sure hy was asleep and then grabbed my journal and headed into the bathroom. It's cold in here and smells kinda bad cuz the sink stopped draining last week-I should probably buy some of that drain clean chemical shit.

Anyway, I'm just glad hy's leaving in the morning.

Date June 13, 2003
Security: Friends
Subject: !!!

The feminist bookstore collective said they had news for me when I went to deliver more copies of my new zines, "Life Doesn't Come With Training Wheels" and "I want to be a real boy…or do I." I am real proud of the cut and paste work on that one. I just brought zines in last week, and already they needed more. The collective representatives brought me into the back room which is pretty much just row after row of stacked books. Mostly it's books for the Women's Studies department at the local university. They order their course books from here, because the campus bookstore is patriarchal.

The collective wanted me to know that the woman who ran the monthly open mic had just quit. I guess she had only started a couple of months ago, but had gotten bored. Not only had she not been doing it for very long, but the numbers for the event had sucked, too, and the collective said that the store wanted it to go in a different and edgier, more queer direction. I wasn't quite sure what they were getting at until I was asked if I would be interested in taking on the monthly event.

I got all excited and started asking all kinds of questions about ways to I'd want change the event around. They said that I was in charge and could do whatever I wanted. I went back to the apartment and started planning and making flyers and decisions. Guitars will be banned from the open mic. I also decided that this isn't just going to be an open mic, it's going to be a queer open mic zine read where queer zines are finally going to be front and center in Portland. I went back to the feminist bookstore with the edges of my flyers still sticky from glue stick and sharpie bleeding through. They thought the posters were great and even gave me some cash out of the register to go across the street to the copy shop and make the first batch of copies to hang around town.

I told everyone about the zine read. A lot of the guys weren't sure how they felt about being involved in what they see as a women's space. The Hotel was pretty into it, but the guys at the Safety Net especially were really uncomfortable with it. Travis said he didn't even know if they would come to the event, let alone read. I reminded all of them that the feminist bookstore was a feminist space, and they had been trans inclusive forever so it's not like I was asking them to go to Michigan or some shit.

Besides, this was our night to take over, which meant I actually needed them to show up, ideally with stories and poems to share.

Tonight was the first reading and the pack totally came through for me, even Travis and everyone at the Safety Net. I read a poem I'd written about feeling misunderstood about my gender. It was a pretty obvious diss on Sarah after the shit she pulled about doing my shot. She didn't show up, but a bunch of her roommates from the Clit Shack were there, which was almost as good, cuz I know she heard about it when they got home. A bunch of people read shit. There were stories about being sober, and a poem about the love of a slave of his Master, which probably made the bookstore collective nervous, but whatever. There were just all kinds of stories and it was a really good night. The local gay paper even came and the editor said they might do a feature story about the event!

Date: June 15, 2003
Security: Friends
Subject: I hate her

I fucking hate my grandma. I don't honestly know why I even try. She called me last night asking if she could come see me today. She said she wanted to take me out to breakfast at the diner. I said ok because it wasn't worth dealing with her crying and shit if I said I was busy. I decided not to tell her that Hunter and I broke up because I didn't want to listen to her tell me again how she couldn't wait to see me settle down with a nice young man and be normal. We went to breakfast and while we were waiting for our pancakes to come she laid into me with this bullshit guilt trip about how I destroyed my mom's life and was ruining the family by refusing to talk to her. Typical.

Grandma and I have never even talked about what happened that night I ran away and went to the cops. That's how she likes it I guess. When I was growing up, she was my babysitter every day while my mom was at work. She never once asked about the bruises. We just didn't talk about what was happening. Leaving fucked all that up. Then she was all like, "you have to come live with me and grandpa," kinda shit. It was too late. I told her I could go wherever I wanted. She's tried everything to get me and my mom back together, even lying to me and saying we were gonna meet up and then having my fucking mother sitting there. Now, when we go out to restaurants and stuff, I always have to eyeball the place and make sure my mom isn't sitting a few tables away.

This morning at breakfast she seemed like she was going to start talking about what had happened back then. Well, that's that I thought she was going to do. Actually, she started asking if I'd be willing to have dinner with her and my mom. I said no. She said I couldn't avoid my mom forever. I said I could. She said that she knows that what I told the police isn't true. She said my mother told her I was lying to get attention. I told her I was finished eating. We drove back to my place and didn't talk at all.

I don't know why I even bother trying to keep any kind of relationship with her. Nothing will ever change.

Date: July 16, 2003

Sarah stopped returning my calls. I thought that whole "I won't do your shot" thing was going to just blow over, but it totally didn't. So now I need to figure out a more long-term solution. I called the Safety Net and Augustus was around. He and I aren't very close because he's Hunter's big brother now, although they aren't close like Buck and I are. He works with Sarah at the video rental place and has been clean for a couple of years but used to train hop all over the country living in squats.

He's got scars all over his face from piercings he used to have, and has a couple small stick and poke tattoos on his hands, but unless you get close to him he looks just like a normal guy. He even dresses preppy, but I guess he used to be really punk back in the day. After explaining to me again why no one in the house could do my shot, he finally said that he could probably manage to walk me through how to do a self-injection, as long as he didn't actually have to do it, and didn't watch me stick the needle in.

I don't know anyone who is able to do their own shots, so I felt pretty hard-core this morning when I went over to the Safety Net. It took forever because the #12 bus was late and then I had to wait like twenty minutes for the #6 bus to come. I finally showed up and Augustus was the only one home, except for the rats of course, well unless Hunter's cats were hiding out in someone's room.

The house just dumpstered a bunch of huge ferret cages from behind the pet store on Broadway, and then scored some really small chicken wire and turned an entire side of their living room into one big rat enclosure that you can almost crawl into. It's pretty intense, especially because the other side of the living room is always filled with bikes in various stages of completeness. When I got there I had to crawl over the bikes, and as I edged past the rat cage and into the kitchen seventeen pairs of eyes followed me. The worst thing is that they are

Travis' responsibility to keep clean and since he can't smell to well, everything really just smells like rat pee.

Augustus finished his toast by tossing it into the rat cage and we headed down into the basement where he sleeps. They just scored a washing machine off the internet so it was nosily clanking as we sat next to it on his bed. I'd never been down into Augustus's room before, it was dark and damp and the only window was made of frosted glass and was seven feet up against the ceiling- barely above ground level. Augustus explained that he'd learned how to do thigh shots from some kid he met train hopping in Montana, but the guy looked like he knew what he was talking about so it would be fine. He showed me how to plot the shot so I wouldn't hit any major nerves. I obviously already knew how to draw the shot. Then, the fucker left me. He was getting all jittery and triggered and said he had to get upstairs but to call him if I needed anything.

I sat there, on his dirty bed, dirty work pants and studded belt slouching around my knees and kicked some of his (I assume?) dirty boxers with my boots. Augustus's snake coiled and recoiled in her cage.

She hates the basement and how dark it is. She used to live in the living room before the construction of the rat colony. I could hear Augustus doing dishes, and then flopping loudly into a chair. I had to hurry. He was going to get pissed if I took too much longer. This was totally scary. My mind was swirling. I could hit an artery and die. I could get infected and need to have my leg chopped off. I could be unable to do it, and never get my shot again. I could fuck it up and inject right into a vein. Fuck. Fuck. Fuck. Fuck.

Finally I just closed my eyes, sunk the needle in, pushed down the plunger then removed it from my leg. I capped it and threw the dirty sharp into my messenger bag, making a mental note to head over to the syringe exchange and trade it in for a new needle when I went downtown later. I pulled up my pants and headed upstairs to find Augustus reading a zine at the kitchen table. "How'd it go?" he asked. I said that it was no big deal. I'm feeling pretty tough. I'm the only guy who can do his own shot.

Date: June 20, 2003

I never thought I'd want a cat. I really didn't even like Hunter's cats all that much, but Trash is such a cool kitten. I fell in love with him the first day that Piglet showed up with him at QYRC. I think it's because he's mostly like a dog and will follow you around and play fetch and stuff. Jacob called me this morning and it turns out that even though she took him when Piglet had to go to Detroit, she just got offered a room at a house down in the Mission so she's heading to SF next week and not sure when or if she'll be back. Billy's been staying in her room, but he's got his hands full with the ferrets. Jacob called me because she knew how much I loved Trash, and that I'm really good with animals. She probably also called me because she's got to leave really soon and knew I wouldn't say no.

I rode the bus across town today to pick him up. I brought Orbit because he and Trash always play at QYRC and I figured this might help Trash trust me. I don't know why I was so worried, this poor kitten has been passed around so much already he'll go with anyone who's nice to him. Jacob's stuff was almost all packed up. I'm not really sure where Billy and the ferrets will be going once Jacob leaves town. I almost offered to let him come stay with me again, but I knew I couldn't. We haven't talked much since he moved out of the shack when things were so bad with Hunter. Even though Hunter and I aren't together anymore that whole thing hurt so bad. I mean, Billy and I were tight, like almost family. I think Billy's hurt that I put up with so much shit from Hunter when he was my Daddy. We'd been so close before Hunter and I got together, always walking around in our matching boy scout shirts. I think he feels like I sided with my Daddy over the pack, and he's right. It's hard because I know he'd have done the same thing. It's what you have to do.

Trash was really good on the bus back to the basement. He and Cosmo had never met before, but I think Orbit helped get them all introduced and now the three of them pretty immediately started racing around the living room and playing. I had to go up to the grocery store to get a litter box and some cat food. I was a little worried about leaving them all together, but when I got back they were playing just like when I left.

Date: June 22, 2003
Security: Public
Subject: fucking gays!

So the gay paper came out today and just like they promised there was a feature story about the open mic. I took Cosmo and Orbit on the longest walk ever to get downtown to one of the drop boxes first thing this morning to pick it up. There was a teaser for the article on the front page, and then a big piece all about the bookstore and what the event was like. It was early, so no one was out of their squats or houses and downtown hanging out yet and it was just me and the dogs at the fountain near the bridge.

I was so excited when I sat down to read the article, but that changed pretty damn fast. They called me a girl. They used female pronouns, and put my name in quotes like it wasn't real. They messed up the pronouns for everyone. They called us all young women. I was freaking out, and worried that everyone was going to be mad at me since it's my event, and I had thought it was so cool that the paper was going to be there, and then this happened. Orbit was tired so I put him in my messenger bag with the crumpled up copy of the paper and Cosmo and I walked back over the bridge. I can't believe this happened, I feel like shit.

Date: June 24, 2003

Got home to a voicemail today. I'd been
hanging out with Travis when he went to
get his septum repierced. It was nice to
see him. We haven't hung out since he and
Hunter got together. It was hard though,
to see that he was wearing Hunter's cuff
on his wrist. It looked just like mine.
Travis first pierced his septum when he was
sixteen and living in his car, but then
when he tried some reconcile bullshit with
his parents, he agreed to take it out.
It's been a whole year since he talked
to them, so getting it pierced again was
to honor that. I'm glad he asked me to go
with him, because I know this is the sort
of thing that Hunter wouldn't understand.

I decided to get my conch pierced while
we were there. I'd been thinking of doing
something with my ears for a while.
I stretched up to 00 months ago and don't
really want to go bigger than that right
now. When Travis' nose was done, I told
Hank I wanted to do something with my ear
but I didn't know what. He thought a conch
piercing would be cool, and said that
he had just gotten some big eight gauge
needles in, so we could make it hard core.
I asked if he had a big enough hoop, and

he started laughing and said only femmes wore hoops through that piercing, and that I needed a barbell. I really wanted a hoop, but I sure as hell didn't want him to think I was a femme or anything gross like that.

I got all scared right before he pierced me. No one ever believes me because I've got so much metal in my face, but I'm actually really bad at getting pierced. I was shaking and nervous when he was getting the piercing lined up. Once he stuck the needle in I was good, though. I heard the cartilage in my ear crunch, which was pretty sweet, and then, just this really good burning as the jewelry was pushed through. Travis and I went and got some fries at the diner downtown and sea salt from the grocery store for keeping the piercings clean.

It was a really good day until I got back to the apartment. I was just about to take Cosmo and Orbit out for a walk when I noticed my answering machine blinking. It was my mom. I haven't seen her since I left her house but a few times a year she gets it in her head that if she calls I'll talk to her. She was slurring her words and not finishing her sentences. It was a really long message. She talked about how she had done the best she could, and that she didn't know why I was punishing her and that she prays every night that I'm going to come home and how in the meantime she sleeps with a body pillow that she pretends is me. I listened to the message all the way through three times, and then I deleted it and went outside. Cosmo and I played Frisbee until my arm hurt he couldn't run anymore. My piercing was throbbing.

Date: June 26, 2003

Sunny just called me crying. She and I haven't talked much recently. She's been kinda weird since Hunter and I broke up. I think she feels responsible, since she set us up. She said that things were really bad with her and Cody. His mom is at work and I guess he and Sunny were fighting and he got mad. She said he signed all kinds of mean things and then pushed her onto the bed. He grabbed the TTY machine and ripped the plug out and smashed the whole thing in the wall.

Sunny was calling me from her car down the block from his mom's place. She had their pit bull puppy with her and was really

```
upset. She said she couldn't decide if
she should wait until his mom came home
and then try to go back or if she should
leave. I told her to come over and that
she and the puppy could live here for
a little while, since with Hunter gone
I have way too much room.
```

Date: July 3, 2003
Security: Friends
Subject: Fuck

Got a call from the management company this morning. They said I needed to come down to the office to have a conversation. I knew something was wrong, but I had no idea what it might be, other than maybe they had noticed the third dog and the random person staying here. When I got to the office, they said there had been a bunch of complaints. They said the neighbors were upset because they could hear inappropriate noises like yelling and hitting coming from my apartment late at night. The management lady said that when the first few complaints came in they said I lived alone (I guess they saw when Hunter moved out) but there wasn't anything that they could do for me anymore and that they were gonna kick me out.

I was freaking out sitting there. The stupid lady with her bleached poofy hair and her fancy ass dress just looked at me like I was a piece of shit. She handed me a letter that said I have ten days to get out of here. I don't know what the fuck I'm going to do and Sunny's going to be so upset. I also don't know why the fuck I have to get out again. I'm guessing it's because of that night I was fucking Pocket. Or maybe shit from when Hunter was still here. Sunny and I sure haven't fucked so who the fuck knows? I guess why doesn't matter. What matters is that I have to go because these homophobic assholes can't handle me being here. I have no clue where I'm gonna go.

Date: July 5, 2003

Orbit and I had to go do my rounds of shots this morning at the Clit Shack and The Hotel. Sarah wasn't around at the Clit Shack. She's mostly been staying with some new girlfriend. I asked everyone else if she was going to leave her room cuz I still need somewhere to live but they said probably not.

One guy in the house who's new and up here from SF is really particular about the whole thing. He has to draw the shot himself, and then do some yoga crap to plot his own ass shot. All he needed me to do was stick the needle in. After his shot we went down to the kitchen. It was kinda messy but he made grilled tofu sandwiches and gave me one to share with Orbit on the way to the bus stop. He also had some sick earplugs in 00 he said I could have, which was pretty sweet since my ears are finally healed from getting real infected after that last stretch. The bus took a long time to come so I dipped them in my water bottle to get them cleaned up a little and sat on the curb trying to shove them through. My ears were burning real bad by the time the bus came, but I'd gotten the new plugs in.

Date: July 8, 2003
Security: Friends
Subject: Success!

Sunny and I found a sweet place to move that doesn't even care about all the dogs. It's a two bedroom basement apartment way out in North, past Lombard. It will take forever to get to on the bus, but the rent is cheap and we have our own entrance. There are two rooms with a bathroom between them, and a big living room with a strip of a kitchen. The folks who own the whole house live upstairs and seem cool enough. I think they think Sunny and I are some kinda weird lesbian couple, but who cares? We got the place and already have keys.

~~Granddaughter~~ ~~Natalie~~ ~~Styler~~ Zander ~~Nate~~ Click
Birthday: May 16, 1984

~~3258 St. Jude St. Clackamas, Oregon~~
~~c/o Cindi 1235 23 rural road 5 Oregon City, Oregon~~
~~c/o Frank 1345 highway 8 Molalla, Oregon~~
~~2344 9th ave, basement SE Portland, Oregon~~
~~c/o James 2345 Heart St. Jacksonville, Florida~~
~~974 apt 60 35th ave Jacksonville, Florida~~
~~c/o Mrs Jahn 2345 Beach Drive Jacksonville Flas~~
~~c/o Buck 1469 apt 5 NW Portland, Oregon~~
~~135 Hawthorne Blvd Apt 3 Portland, Oregon~~
~~67 East 75th St Portland, Oregon~~
~~3875 NE Sandy Blvd 4N Portland, Oregon~~
3298 North Yamhead Basement Portland Oregon

Date: July 9, 2003
Security: Friends
Subject: Gross

So I woke up this morning to hear Sunny moaning. I thought maybe she was jacking off or something but then when I was in the kitchen getting some cereal Cody walked out into the living room in his boxers and an a-shirt and fucking asked me if he could have some! I was so shocked he was in our house that I almost forgot how to sign. I haven't really been around QYRC much for a while because the GSA kids have kinda taken over. A lot of the gutter punks have been sticking to downtown and the houses and shit so my ASL is real rusty anyway. I shoved the cereal box across the counter because I didn't want to fight with him. He took the whole box back into Sunny's room and their puppy came and hung out with me and Cosmo and Orbit. It peed on the carpet and I should have made them clean it up, but I didn't want to deal with it.

WTF?! I can't believe she's giving him another chance.

Date: July 10, 2003

Fuck so I sorta knew this might happen because Cody has been here the last couple of days and Sunny has been avoiding me, but I thought she'd at least have the balls to tell me herself that she was leaving. Instead, I came back from making zine copies and found a note on the counter with her key sitting on top. I knew something was wrong even before I got into the apartment because I had Orbit in my messenger bag, but I could only hear Cosmo barking and not the puppy. Sunny never takes her anywhere unless I nag her to. In the note, Sunny said that Cody had apologized and she realized how much she really loved him, so she was gonna go back to his mom's place. The least she could have done was give me some damn notice.

Date: July 12, 2003
Security: Friends
Subject: wanna buy my biscuits?

I was walking with Orbit and Cosmo downtown this afternoon. Getting there with Cosmo is challenging because he's too big to sneak onto the bus, but for five dollars I just scored this sweet bike trailer made for toddlers at a garage sale down the street yesterday. I don't ride my bike much, but now that I can put both dogs in the trailer and get places I'll probably start biking more. I rode with them downtown and didn't die pulling them up the hill over the bridge. When we got there we played ball by the waterfront for a while until the cops came by and threatened to give me a ticket for Cosmo being off leash. Whatever. We walked back through the artist market and I saw a bunch of folks selling homemade dog cookies. I've been making these applesauce vegan dog cookies for a while now and they looked as good as the hippy sweet potato ones everyone seemed to be buying. I went by the main booth for the market and asked how to get started selling stuff. They gave me an application I have to fill it out and return with a sample of my product. Should be easy enough.

I think I'm going into business!

Date: July 18, 2003
Security: Public
Subject: Roommate Wanted!

Howdy, my name is Click and I'm a trans guy fag parent of three fuzzy kids—two dogs and a cat who is a little bit canine identified—with a room to rent. I live in a two-bedroom basement apartment in NE close to MLK and Lombard. I'm a zinester, straight edge (xxx) and sometimes vegan. I'm looking for a queer housemate who is preferably vegan or vegetarian, but if you eat meat just don't leave your meat grease on the stove over the weekend when you're gone :)

The basement is about 600 sq feet. The bedroom for rent is good sized, with a closet, a heater, and a phone jack. The apartment has a large carpeted living room with a gas wood stove for heat. The rent is $345 per month which includes ALL utilities and cable internet + cable TV. There is also a yard which is shared with the upstairs neighbors (the landlords).

Move in costs include last month's rent and a $50 cleaning fee. The room is available immediately for showing and for move in. Furry kids encouraged!

Date: July 21, 2003

I need a roommate really badly, and for whatever reason no one (with any money at all) seems to be moving this month. I've thought about just letting folks crash in the room because I also just hate being alone down here in the basement, but I really need the help with the rent. I thought about making a roommate wanted zine and leaving it all over town, but realized that would take too long, so I ended up just putting an ad online. It took me forever to figure out how to write the ad itself. I needed to make it clear just how serious I was about needing a roommate, but not sound too desperate. Most importantly they have to be cool with the trans thing. I'm still pissed about the way that Sunny left, but she was pretty nasty to live with. She never cleaned up after her puppy and ate tons of meat. When she and Cody got back together she even left a cup of bacon grease on top of the stove for days!

Date: July 23, 2003

I was hanging out with Buck this afternoon. Luke is away visiting his parents so Buck has permission to be more social. It was nice just to have some time with him. It feels like it's been forever. He wanted the dogs to go out with us, which was obviously fine by me. It felt so good to have our little pack back together. We wandered down to the train tracks and took turns climbing up onto the boxcars and throwing balls for the dogs. From the top of the train you can see all the way back to my house. I hate that the damn thing is pink, but love how that makes it easier to find from up there. I wanted to ask Buck if he was happy with Luke but that seemed rude. I know he must be, it's just hard to tell because we can't see each other as often as we used to, and I knew asking would make me sound like a whiny little kid.

On our way back to my place for dinner we found an awesome free box. Buck scored a baseball hat and I got a bunch of fabric. I've been trying to figure out how to package the dog biscuits I'm including with my application to the artist market and when I saw the fabric I had the idea of cutting it into bandanas! Buck suggested making a stencil that says "vegan dog" and spray painting that onto the fabric! My brother is brilliant! When we got back to my place Buck pulled out his knife and grabbed an old pizza box I'd left by the door and started working on the stencil for me while I put water on to boil for the pasta. After dinner I cut out a bunch of bandanas and we took them out onto the sidewalk with a can of spray paint I had left over from repainting a bookcase I dumpstered last month. The bandanas turned out hella sweet. Once they dried I tried them on Orbit and Cosmo. I think I'm going to go drop off my business application at the artist market tomorrow.

Date: July 26, 2003

Got a call from a dyke who I've never heard who wants to see the basement. I said she could come over that afternoon, but the second we got off the phone I realized it was bad idea. The landlords haven't taken the best care of the place and so every couple of weeks the sewer pipes get all clogged and back up all over the carpet in the living room. Of course this happened last night, and it was worse than usual and spread to the carpet in the bedrooms even. I stole the landlord's workshop vacuum out of the garage and tried to get some of the water up, but walking around was still kinda soggy. I opened windows, and lit a bunch of incense in every room, but she still wasn't impressed. She made some comment about it being dark and dirty. Whatever.

No one else called about the room, and I was starting to freak out. I was over at the Safety Net because we were supposed to be working on zines, but it was mostly just flirting with random folks. The guys from The Hotel came over because one of them had his bike tire pop up the road, and he wanted to try to put more air in it, and see if that would hold until he got home. I was complaining about my roommate problems when he said that he knew this guy Ethan who might be. Ethan's this tranny punk who's moving out here from Nebraska and needs a place to live. I said that sounded really sweet. Ethan has been on the road, so it took a while to figure out where he was and actually get in touch with him. It turns out he is totally stoked about the place, and decided to rent the room without even seeing it. I learned most of that through

Mickey who was able to get in touch with him a lot easier than I was. I still haven't talked to the guy.

July 30, 2003

Ethan called me this morning from a pay phone somewhere outside of San Francisco. He said he thought he would get into town in about three days. I told him I'd be around and to just come over and knock on one of the windows and I'd come up and let him in. He asked if the house had a name, and I said not really, at least not one that had stuck, but I was open to naming it. He suggested we call it the Cub Cave since we're both little guys on the prowl. I think that sounds really hot. He asked if I could do his shot when he got here cuz he was late.

Date: August 1, 2003

I completely embarrassed myself at QYRC tonight. I thought that a little humiliation would get me into Grace's bed, but it didn't. Now I look stupid and am pissed off. Ever since Billy and Grace broke up for real, Grace and Johnny have been cruising real damn hard. They show up at QYRC in their boots and jeans, bound down really tight under black t-shirts and always flagging black and hunter green. They don't even try to look butch, they just are. I know how to get laid when I want to, but I haven't found anyone who can really beat me up since Hunter left his boot prints all over my heart. Almost everyone is too damn nice, which defeats the whole point of playing with them in the first place. If I wanted someone to be nice to me I'd just pick up a girl at the bookstore.

I don't know exactly what's going on, but from what Johnny's let on, and then everyone else at QYRC says, Grace and Johnny are bringing folks back to where they're squatting, beating them, fucking them, and doing some heavy ass roleplay of some kind, all different kinds probably. They're always hunting for someone new. I'm not sure about everything they do, but it's some heavy kinky shit. When I say it like that it doesn't sound like that big of deal, but they are seriously hot, not to mention tough. They could fuck me up so good. When I play with someone who knows what they're doing, the world looks different. I come away from it all raw and oozing and fucked up. I feel better that way, all mixed up and bleary. Everyone says nothing's the same after the night

you spend there. The whole world looks
different. The sober kids say it's better
than any trip they've ever been on before
getting clean.

Usually, folks don't come back to QYRC
for a few days after getting brought
home by Grace and Johnny, and when they
do they either never talk to Johnny and
Grace again, or they follow them around
in really pathetic ways. We'll all be
hanging outside while folks smoke and
someone they took home once like a month
ago will just butt into our conversation
and ask if they can get them anything
at the corner store, or if they would
like some dinner. Pretty much the kid
will stand there and keep offering stupid
stuff. Sometimes Grace will take them up
on an offer, usually if she thinks she
can score a pack of smokes out of them
or some takeout from the Chinese place up
the street. When the poor sucker comes
back with the Styrofoam takeout Grace
will sometimes even let them curl up at
her boots, but then ignore them for the
rest of the night, and make a big show
out of picking up someone else.

I'll never forget the way that Grace treated
Billy. She fucked that boy up, but even
having watched all that go down doesn't
change how badly I want her. I think the
most unethical part of how Grace left him
was the way she took his fucking family.
Billy had been family with Aurora and
Big Billy since they found him trying to
sneak into dyke night at the Eagle. He
was like thirteen then, and he had only
been on the street a few months. They
took him home, named him, and started
to train him. Back then Billy thought he
was a top, but he loved that old guard
training too much and pretty soon they
realized what was up. I guess he became
the houseboi for a while. I didn't know
him then. He's told me stories about how
hard they were on him, but how good it
was. When Billy and Grace got together
they fucking loved her, said she was real
good for him. Problem was, they started
liking her too much. Aurora and Big Billy
ended up liking Grace more than they
loved Billy. He says it's cuz she's a
top and they wanted to cultivate more of
that in the community. I don't know about
all that, I just know they put him on the
streets when Grace dumped him for Johnny.
Billy won't even talk about it anymore.
One night back when we were still living

together, he said losing them was worse
than his mom and stepdad kicking him out.
We don't see much of each other now,
but I hear Billy's flagging left. I don't
know if he'll ever go as deep as he did
with Grace ever again after the way she
treated him.

Johnny is staying at this fourth floor
apartment half a block from my basement.
So when I take the dogs out late at night
I can look up and see shit through the
windows. It's kinda embarrassing to admit
that every night I watch her window.
I mean I can't see anything real good,
mostly just movement. I want to be up
there so damn bad. Folks who go to the
fourth floor don't come back the same.
I don't know what happens, but it's like
they've seen god or a ghost or some shit.
Grace really knows what she's doing. She
was down in San Francisco for a while and
that's where she got jumped into leather.
She's been teaching Johnny everything she
got schooled in while she was there.

I've just been hinting that I want them
to take me down, but most nights someone
at QYRC is already licking their boots
by the time I get the nerve up to start
flirting. When I go to QYRC I always make

sure I'm flagging black, right. If it's a quiet night, I'll talk to Johnny and Grace about how hard it can be to find folks who are serious about this stuff. They never get the hint, or maybe they do, and don't want me. I'm not sure. Last night, while the staff and volunteers were distracted, Grace and Johnny took this boi into the bathroom to play. I tried to focus on stuffing condoms and lube into little baggies for safer sex kits, but I just couldn't. It's been so long since I got really fucked up. By the end Hunter wouldn't even touch me so it's been a while since someone's played with me. I need it so bad. I just couldn't handle the thought of someone else getting what I needed. I remember Billy trying one time to teach me how to beg respectfully, where you don't come across sounding whiny and needy. He said Aurora had been working on teaching him that so that they could be proud when they took him to public events. I don't really remember how the hell you're supposed to actually pull that off.

I haven't played with anyone since Hunter left. Some nights I feel like I can't breathe. I mean, I can get lots of ass, but it's different. That's mostly me

running fucks, and besides this kinda
shit isn't even about fucking. I'd be
all over Grace fucking me, she's like
everything I've ever wanted in a butch.
Johnny I don't care as much about, she's
not really hard enough for me. More than
I want Grace to fuck me, though, I want
her to chew on me for a while, and spit
me out.

Tonight I just couldn't fucking take it
anymore. I wanted it so damn badly. Grace
and Johnny came in together, as usual.
For the first little bit they stayed
mostly to the pool table. Pool is like
the one fucking thing at QYRC I've never
figured out how to do well, so I stay away.
I figured making a fool out of myself with
a big stick and some balls was not going
to help. I waited until they needed a
smoke break, and Orbit and I followed
them outside.

Piglet was out there smoking. I had a
little bouncy ball from a vending machine
in my pocket and threw it for Orbit for
a couple of minutes. Piglet was about
done with his cigarette when we came out
so pretty quickly went back inside. He'd
started playing with Orbit and asked if
he could take him in. Normally I don't

really like Orbit to be too far away from me, but I said ok. It was just the three of us sitting on the picnic table in the smoking area. Grace and Johnny were on the table part with their boots on the bench. I sat on the bench. I couldn't believe it, they were actually flirting back with me! Johnny started teasing me about how much I could take, and if my eyes were too big for my own good, that sorta shit. I was fucking loving it. Pretty soon they finished their cigarettes and went back inside. They were paying attention to me. I thought my plan was going to work. I was real glad I'd put on mostly-clean boxers before heading over.

When we got near the kitchen, I thought maybe they were going to get distracted. See, Gus had brought in their food processor and was teaching about half of us youth how to make hummus from scratch. I didn't give a shit about the hummus and I didn't think Grace did either, but Johnny has a granola side and I was worried she would be tempted. I did the only reasonable thing I could think to do. I dropped to my knees. Right there outside the kitchen in front of the memorial wall, I just dropped on that concrete. My knees are sorta fucked up from running around with dogs in high school, and my work pants don't give all that much cushion, but I didn't give a shit. I wanted them so bad, and I wanted them to know it. Poor Gus, no one was paying attention to the chickpeas anymore.

I thought Johnny and Grace would be surprised to see me on my knees. Maybe Johnny was, but Grace just had this grin that I couldn't read. "Boy," she said, "what do you think you're doing?"

I tried to remember all that shit Billy had been trying to teach me about begging without whining, but my brain just wasn't working right. I started stumbling and stuttering and the worst part was that Grace just stood there, looking down at me, waiting.

"Sir, please, I'd like for you...well, you and Johnny...to take me."

I could hear Gus talking about settings on the food processor, and the cost effectiveness of not buying the little tubs of stuff at the grocery store, and how everyone could work together to make their own food. I tried to tune them out. I concentrated on keeping my eyes on the

gouged toe of Grace's boot. I stiffened,
but then forced myself to relax when
I felt her hand on my head. She left it
there for what seemed like a long time.
I hoped that everyone in the kitchen was
paying attention to Gus, but I knew this
was more interesting.

"Boy, get up. I'm not taking you home."

That's when the tears started and goddamn
when that happened all I wanted to do was
disappear. I bit on my snakebites really
hard with my teeth, and then the barbell
in my tongue to try to pull myself together
but it didn't work. I wanted to run, but
couldn't. I forced my eyes up.

"I can't," Grace said. "You're too sweet
of a boy. I just can't destroy you."

I felt like she'd kicked me in the
stomach. That's what I wanted her to be
doing, not standing there talking about
how fucking sweet I was! I started trying
to argue, saying that I knew what I was
getting into, that I was ok with whatever
happened, that I could take anything she
wanted to throw at me. I knew everyone
was staring now, and I was for sure not
remembering any of that not-desperate

begging that Billy had taught me. I was snotty and crying, but also pissed. I saw her hand move and I thought I'd won. I thought she was going to slap me. Her hand came back down softly and she ruffled my hair, and just fucking walked away.

I kneeled there for a while, trying to figure out what the fuck just happened. No one came to check on me, and I was so embarrassed I didn't want to talk to anyone anyway. When I got up I thought about joining in the hummus making, but realized I needed to just go. I called Orbit, it was weird actually that he hadn't been with me during all that, but I guess everyone was feeding him pita that was supposed to be for the hummus. He came right when I called and jumped up my knees into my arms and started licking the tears. I didn't look to see who was out in the smoking area. I just slipped Orbit into my messenger bag and took off fast down Belmont. I didn't know where I was going. I didn't want to go home alone. Instead I headed down here to the waterfront to write for a while on one of the benches. I put my sweatshirt around Orbit in my messenger bag so he could sleep. The cops just came just now to chase me out for park curfew.

Date: August 2, 2003

It ended up taking Ethan longer than he thought to get here from SF but he arrived tonight. I still don't really know much about him, other than that he collects comic books and action figures. The coolest thing about Ethan is that he has his own business. He pays his rent by making one-inch buttons for bands. When he got here I was shocked by how hot he was. He's a redhead with snakebite piercings and dresses way more skater than punk, with baggy shorts and big t-shirts. I wish that someone had told me how hot he was! Housemate 101 says you can't sleep with your roommate, but I'd be lying if I said I didn't have a hard-on for this guy. I did his shot and then had to rub his ass to make the T go all the way in. I don't know if that really is medically true or not, but it's how we do it. Seriously, I was so turned on, but then he started talking about his ex-girlfriend. I guess he's totally a femme's man, and wants nothing to do with faggotry, which is too bad.

Date: August 3, 2003

I was asleep when the phone rang. I brought some random cute guy home last night and spent the night fucking instead of sleeping. I think he's from SF or something, I don't even know his name. I kicked him out early this morning because the dogs seemed really weirded out by having him around. Today I spent the whole day hanging flyers for the zine read in different coffee shops and all the independent bookstores. Tomorrow I'm supposed to stuff envelopes with information about the safe schools campaign over at the Oregon LGBT Rights office, so I decided not to go hang out with the pack at The Hotel and crashed early. I was just dozing off when the phone rang. I figured it was one of the guys calling trying to get me to come over and do their shot so I let the machine grab it. There was no way in hell I was getting out of bed. But then I heard Travis' voice, which didn't make much sense, because he still hasn't started T.

The answering machine is in the living room, so I couldn't hear what he was saying very clearly but he kept talking for a damn long time, which made me think

something important was up. Finally,
I dragged myself out of bed. I was just in
briefs and an undershirt so I was freaking
out that Ethan would come into the living
room and give me shit. He always sleeps
in his binder and never takes his packer
off. He says a real man would never be
caught without it. He learned that lesson
the hard way at some truck stop on his
drive out here from Nebraska a couple of
days before he got to San Francisco.

I was at The Hotel earlier and everyone
was talking about how Hank had to go to
the hospital. I guess he thought he was
having a heart attack or some shit. Turns
out, he broke a fucking rib from binding
too tight and too long. No one had ever
seen him without his binder, not even any
of his girlfriends. The ER doctor said he
couldn't bind for at least three months.
Everyone said he put his binder back on
before he even left the hospital.

Travis was still chattering on the
answering machine when I hit the talk
button and the tape stopped. I guess
I sounded groggy or something because
he asked if he woke me up. I said yes,
but he didn't apologize. I don't think
he was really paying attention. He was

freaking out, tweaking most likely. He said he needed to come over, that it was important. We hung-up and I went to put my binder and the rest of my clothes on.

I couldn't believe he got here so damn fast. I was barely cinching my belt when I heard knocking on the window. The dogs started barking and I went up the back stairs to let him in. Travis must have jumped on his bike and coasted down the hill from the Safety Net. I figured since someone jacked the lights off it the other day he would be walking. He was all jittery and wouldn't calm down until I assured him that Ethan was either not home yet, or passed out drunk and not going to hear anything.

Travis said that he had a problem, and that I was the only one who could help. Then he pulled out a wad of cash. That freaked me out a little bit. No one's really got much money, so for a second I thought he robbed a bank, which would explain how freaked out he seemed. He started explaining extra fast. See, he's been escorting for a while now and I guess after he pays rent and gets more art supplies the rest of the cash gets shoved into his underwear drawer. He'd been talking about saving up for surgery, but I hadn't thought he was actually doing it, cuz he's always talking shit and most of it doesn't turn out to be true.

Then he told me about how someone bought him some shots at the bar last night and then he remembered how good it felt to be high, and there was all that money sitting there, and he and Hunter had a little relapse. He explained that he wasn't safe around the money anymore. and that no one we knew would be either. He was shaking pretty bad at this point. He was probably still a little doped up, though thinking shockingly clearly about all this given the circumstances. He said that because I'm XXX I'm the only one who is safe. He said that he needed me to take the money, hide it, keep it safe, and not let him have it, no matter what. Travis said he'd been talking to a doctor in SF and planned to have surgery in eight months. He had to put a certified check in the mail with half the amount in four months, and then deliver the rest of it the day before surgery. Even with what he'd blown last night he said he could still make it if he gave up the idea of riding on a bus and just train hopped instead. He said the only way he would make it is if I agreed to hold the cash.

We went outside and fished around in the recycling bin for a little while before coming up with a not too nasty or crushed frozen pizza box. We went back downstairs and into my bedroom. I think he was still freaking out that Ethan was going to appear and catch us. Travis shoved all the cash inside the box and then we put the whole thing in the back of the freezer. I stacked a bunch of shit in front of it to keep it hidden. He seemed to have calmed down a little bit, and said he had to get going. I guess he'll be coming back on Monday after he gets paid to deposit more cash into the freezer. I asked if Hunter knew he was here. Travis said it had been his idea. He said that Hunter told him I wouldn't let him down.

Date: August 4, 2003
Security: Friends
Subject: cookies!

The dogs and I biked over to the vegan grocery store this afternoon to get fake cheese. The hippy girl who was working came outside to play with the dogs, and she asked what I've been up to. I told her about the dog cookie business. When she found out they were vegan she got really excited and asked if I wanted to sell them on commission at the grocery store. She said they're always looking for more vegan pet stuff, and mine are locally made which is even better. I showed her some of the cookies that I had in my backpack and she said they looked really cool. She showed me where she can put together a display and everything! On my way out she gave me a free pack of vegan gummy bears!

I told her I'd be back tomorrow with cookies for them to sell. I was gonna go to QYRC tonight but I need to hurry and get baking or I'll run out of time!

Date: August 6, 2003
Security: Friends
Subject: Needle Exchange

I had to go downtown today to the needle exchange at the homeless medical clinic. The sharps container that's been living in the bathroom since Hunter started T has been full for a while now. I've been storing mine and everyone else's needles in a plastic bag. It didn't bother me too much, but I know if anyone saw it, they would get really triggered, and if the landlords came in I could get in big trouble cuz they would assume it was from drugs. I had a huge box full of sharps in my bag, and was scared I'd get stopped by a cop or some shit on my way there.

There was a line at the needles exchange and I had to sit in the waiting room for a long time waiting for them to call me. The kid next to me was nodding off but everyone else was really noisy. When they finally called my name, I had to answer a bunch of questions about how I fuck, and what sort of drugs I use. I tried to just tell them I was XXX and the needles are from my hormones, but they said it was policy to ask me every fucking question.

I felt really weird about the whole thing. I know it's fucked up, but I was worried that everyone sitting there thought I was a drug addict. I know that shouldn't matter but fucking hell, I'm XXX. At least all the used needles are out of my house so no one can get mad at me now, and on my way home I got a bigger sharps container so I shouldn't have to go back for a long time.

Date: August 9, 2003

I first met Sean when I was brand new to Portland, he and I were both at some tacky benefit that the gay male singers were throwing for QYRC and its rural outreach program. I was supposed to talk about how the rural program saved my life, and how rich yuppie gays should give money, so that more crusty kids like me cannot hang ourselves in barns, or jump in front of trains. Talking at these kinds of things has always felt different than

the community education trainings. Those
at least are about educating fucked up
homophobes. The benefits are about making
rich fucking gay people give money so
they can feel better about themselves and
feel lucky that they aren't me. I hate
that. I don't want anyone feeling sorry
for me.

Don't get me wrong. The rural outreach is
a good program. I don't know where I'd
be if I hadn't found it. Still, it feels
weird to stand up in front of people and
talk about my fucked up life so that
they will give money. Right away Sean and
I had started talking. We were some of
the only youth left after everyone else
bailed and headed down to the waterfront,
and we were totally chowing down on all
the catered food. After that night we've
always talked at QYRC but didn't hang out
a whole bunch, what with the whole dyke/
FTM and faggot divide.

The fags own the stage and spend all
night dancing and we never leave the pool
table and smoking area. Sometimes we
come together in the kitchen for dinner,
but the conversations are usually pretty
divided. We always have each other's
back, though. I guess that's why Sean

called me. He'd been missing for a while. I wasn't too worried because he always disappears a lot, pretty much whenever he finds a boyfriend who can keep him hooked up. I didn't even remember that he had my number and when I picked up the phone and he said it was Sean it took a minute for me to realize who it was on the other end.

Sean said he'd gone to his brother's house in Idaho but things weren't working out so well and he was really sick. He said he hadn't been taking his meds and had been in the hospital a couple of times. The doctors out there said he didn't have much time. He told me he wanted to die in Portland, but he can't afford to get back. Gus talks about how everyone they knew died of the plague. Gus says it was like blinking and having the whole community gone. Sean is the first person I met who is sick, I remember he told me he had it at that benefit the first day we met. Now it seems like about every fag I know who isn't trans has HIV.

Date: August 11, 2003
Security: Friends
Subject: Who's going?

Who's going to the benefit at the Clit Shack tonight? I can't even remember who it's for. I think that kid who just got up here from New Orleans, but we haven't actually met yet. I just got asked to perform a poem between the bands.

Date: August 13, 2003
Security: Friends
Subject: DIY for life

The artist market turned me down for a booth! When I talked to the lady at the information booth before submitting my packet it sounded like this whole review thing was more of just a process to be followed than an actual review. They sell all kinds of crazy stuff there like menstrual pads made from recycled fabric, and kombucha starters, not to mention the bunches of dog treat vendors! The rejection letter came in the mail today while Riley was over to use my computer and to hang out. He's a sweet kid, but really quiet. Before he left home his parents convinced him that he's got all kinds of mental health issues and fucked him up on a million heavy psych meds. He's mostly off them now, but sometimes really struggles to concentrate on any one thing. The letter said that my product wasn't "professional" and that they were concerned about the "environmental impact" of my using spray paint on the bandanas. The guys at The Hotel think I'm being discriminated against and that we should protest the market. I don't think I even care enough.

Date: August 15, 2003
Security: Friends
Subject: Ouch

It was really hard to do my shot tonight. I almost chickened out completely and didn't do it, but I knew that would fuck everything up so I manned up and stuck the needle in. I've figured out that if I use the anchor tattoo on my thigh as a guide it makes it easier. I just have to wrap my hand around the anchor and stick the needle in by the lower right point. Only problem is I've turned my right leg into a total pincushion where I'm going through pretty much nothing but scar tissue now every time I do a shot.

Date: August 16, 2003
Security: Public
Subject: Fuck

Anyone have any money they want to donate to get Sean back to PDX? He's stuck in some hick town in Idaho and needs to get home. I just called Gus, and they said QYRC can't pay for it. Anyone have anything? I called the bus company and it will cost about forty bucks.

Date: August 18, 2003

No one had any money to give to get Sean back to Portland and Gus said there wasn't anything they could do to help. Sean said that he remembered something about me having a bank account, and asked if I be willing to help him out just enough to get a bus ticket into town. He said he'd pay me back as soon as he could start working again. He sounded so little and scared on the other end of the phone. I thought about how I'd feel if I was trapped out where I grew up and couldn't get back here. I thought about how it must feel to be that sick, to have your body turning against itself.

I wired him the money and said he could stay with me as long as he needed. I probably should have asked Ethan about it, but he's kinda been a disappointment. He's not around much and when he is, I think he's drunk or high because he turns the music on really loud and doesn't come out of his room.

Sean bought a bus ticket for that night. The bus broke down and took three days to get through the Columbia gorge. I kept calling the bus company and asking when Sean's bus was going to arrive, and they said they didn't know and that there had been a lot of delays. I figured he was blowing boys in the rest stops for food, but was still worried he wasn't getting enough to eat. Finally, when I called the bus again yesterday afternoon they said the bus had started moving but they didn't know when exactly it would get into town.

I gave up and just went downtown to hang out in the cold for a couple of hours to wait. I left Orbit home with Cosmo.

Sean looked so tired climbing off that bus, all sunk-in and fragile. I was worried he wouldn't be able to get back to my place, but he said he felt better just being in Portland. I made macaroni and cheese (that vegan thing is so over) and let him take a long bath. Ethan was staying at some girl's house so I thought about letting Sean crash in his bed, but figured with my luck Ethan would come home and get pissed. I set Sean up on the couch in the living room. This morning I forgot he was there and turned on the light. It was really early, like nine o'clock, but I just couldn't sleep. I hadn't meant to wake Sean up.

I poured us both some cereal, but then found a layer of green mold on top of the soymilk. I told him dinner would be better. I planned to spend the day hanging flyers for the zine read around town, and asked Sean if he wanted to go with me. I sorta didn't want to leave him alone in my place, because even though he said he was clean I wasn't sure I believe him and I could take the dogs with me, but

I don't trust him with Trash kitty. Sean didn't want to go with me, but said he had to find some new body jewelry before a couple of his piercings closed over. I asked if he was going to try to see his caseworker about food stamps, and getting an appointment with his old doctor. He said he'd try.

I loaned Sean bus fare and waited until he was on the #6. Then I walked up to the Safety Net to tell folks about everything that was going on. I tried to get them to come with me to hang flyers, but they wouldn't. They also said they wouldn't help Sean because they didn't think he was actually clean. I hit the coffee shop up on Alberta and the diner where the Clit Shack kids wash dishes in the early morning. Then I headed downtown and dropped flyers at the zine shop where they don't really like me. I was supposed to volunteer there but forgot to go to one of my shifts. Well, I didn't really forget. Riley had spent the night and we didn't get a lot of sleep and I got up in time to make it down to the shop but then I saw him curled up in my bed with his mohawk flopped over and leaving little green stains on my pillow and I couldn't help but get back into bed with him. The owner got pissed and yelled at my answering machine. I never called her back, so now every time I go in it's really awkward.

On the way back to the basement from flyering, I stopped at the ninety-nine cent grocery. They have all kinds of packaged foods just a little beyond their expiration date and food that is a little bit damaged. I grabbed some old pasta and dented tomato sauce and then scored a couple frozen pizzas. After the craptastic breakfast, I couldn't wait to show Sean a real meal. I was so excited about the food I scored that I didn't want to bother with the #6 bus which I knew wasn't gonna be coming for another fifteen minutes.

Normally I don't walk down MLK, cuz there are a couple of blocks with these tire recycling spots and mechanic shops and it's kinda deserted except for the pit bulls they keep chained up and I always get tempted to try to break them out or something but that's just stupid. I figured that Sean would be hanging out on the front steps waiting for me, but he wasn't. I thought maybe the busses must be running late. I put the groceries away and took the dogs out to the park.

When we got back he still wasn't around so I put water on to boil and started pre-heating the oven so that we could have a big dinner when he got here. Then I noticed the blinking light on my answering machine.

I pushed play. It was Sean. He said he'd found body jewelry downtown, but then gone into the bar. He started dancing there on a fake ID when he was like fifteen or something. He said they said he could start dancing again tonight if he needed the money. He said that while he was waiting for his shift to start he ran into this guy who he used to know. They had coffee and the guy had asked him out, and he said yes. Sean said the guy was hot, which probably meant he had cash, or drugs, or both and was probably sitting right there. Sean said he was going to stay with the guy for a while but that he'd run into me at QYRC when he could.

Date: August 17, 2003
Security: Private
Subject: Virgin?!

I went to QYRC to officially resign from the steering committee before heading to the feminist bookstore for the open mic. There's not really a good reason, I guess I just feel weird there now, after everything with Grace didn't happen. Chris and Riley said they wanted to come to the open mic. Riley and I have been flirting every time we run into each other or hang out. He's living at this big punk house of unschoolers. It's not all queer which is kinda weird. Flirting with him is weird, too, because he's such a baby. Seriously, he just turned eighteen, but he's been on his own since he was like sixteen, so that makes things a little better. Chris is still living with her mom. She makes me feel old, because I remember when she first came up to QYRC. She's not a GSA kid, she's more part of the next generation of crusty kids I think.

Chris asked if it would be ok to spend the night at my place after the open mic because the busses would stop running back to her town. I said she could, so long as she called her mom and told her where we were going. Her mom said ok so we left QYRC and headed over to the bookstore. On the way there Riley grabbed my hand and whispered that he wanted to spend the night too. I figured Chris could crash on the broken futon in the living room and Riley would just have to stay in my bed.

The event was hella good. They both read, and the audience was packed. The only problem was that by the time we started heading back to the basement, we were past youth curfew. It's this dumb Portland law where technically kids under eighteen have to be inside before midnight. I haven't had to worry about it for a long time since I'm over eighteen and so's most everyone else. But with Chris I was a little nervous that something would go wrong.

We took the side streets, but I saw a cop car and started freaking out. There's no way looking like I do the cops were gonna believe this kid had a right to be out with me. Luckily we got back ok. We were all hungry so I made pasta, and then said I was tired. I gave Chris one of the dog blankets and an old sleeping bag that Sunny left behind and she made a little bed for herself. Riley followed me into my room. The main problem with him is that he's terrified of dogs. I think he's slowly warming up to Cosmo and Orbit but it's hard for him.

I closed the door and pushed him up against it. We made out standing there for a while before I pulled him to the bed. I was nice and asked the dogs to get off. We were making out really heavily and then I moved my hand toward his thigh when he stopped me and said there was something he needed to tell me. He said he was a virgin, and just wanted me to know. I didn't know what to think. I've never been with a virgin before in my whole life and we were like three seconds away from fucking and he was cute so I just went for it.

In that moment I was thinking about the first girl I ever fucked. She's this strung-out artist. Not all that cute. I mean, she was just barely butch, but she was into me, and back then that's about all it took. I was still couch surfing way out in the country right after my coach kicked me out. I was so fucked up back then, I didn't know how to live without my dogs and was so desperate for any dyke to want me. I faked coming so she would stop. I'd been so fucking excited to finally sleep with a girl, and then it was so bad I just wanted it to be over so I could go find someone who could fuck me the way I needed. I wanted Riley to have a better experience. I started stroking his cock with a couple fingers slipping slowly into his boy-hole and he came hella fast before falling asleep curled up against me.

This morning he was clingy. I'm worried about having fucked him like that, now. What if he falls in love with me or something? He's a cute kid, but I don't want that from him.

Date: August 20, 2003

Dean called me today and asked if I wanted to go to a play party tonight. I guess he found a flyer for this thing downtown. Cover is like five dollars, which I thought was stupid, but I said I'd go with him. We got all dressed up in clean pants and white t-shirts. I ditched the binder and went for duct tape to get extra flat and I put my hunter green hanky in my back pocket, right side, obviously.

The play party was happening in a bar and all the way there I was worried that they were gonna card us. We watched from down the block for a little while and it didn't look like folks were being asked for ID so we walked up. The butch taking money gave us this really dirty look and said we couldn't come in. I assumed they knew I wasn't old enough and was about to take off running down the block, but Dean started to argue. He asked why they wouldn't let us in. She said we weren't wearing enough leather, and that they have a strict dress code for these kind of events. Dean pulled his pants up to show his boots, but she just laughed. She said for us to come back when we were dressed appropriate and knew how to take care of our leather. Fucking elitist pricks. I don't want to go to their stupid party anyway.

Date: August 24, 2004

I slept with a girl last night. It was weird, but kinda fun. I don't know what's up with Riley and me, which made things complicated. Phoenix and I were at this top surgery party at The Hotel and we were flirting hard and I wanted to take her home, but I realized I didn't know if Riley and I were together-together, and if so, are we poly?

Phoenix and I had been flirting in the kitchen so I went into the living room and used the phone to call the unschooled house. They told me that Riley wasn't home, but was staying with other unschoolers out at the beach. Thankfully they recognized me and gave me the number to that house. I felt bad about calling him out there for this, but I didn't want to cheat. When he came to the phone I think he thought that someone had died or something cuz I'd tracked him down all the way out there. I told Riley that I was at a party, and that there was a girl I wanted to fuck and then asked if we were poly.

I guess this is the shit you're supposed to get all figured out first, but he seemed ok. He said as far as he's concerned we're just friends and I can do whatever I want. I went back into the kitchen and leaned Phoenix up against the counter and started kissing her really hard. She's this fat activist who does radical cheerleading and is super femme. She's got hair all the way to her shoulders and is covered in tattoos of rainbows and naked women and has this hot piercing right on the little flap of skin inside her mouth on the gum line. I've never seen anything like it before, but it's fun to play with it with my tongue. She's kinda old, like twenty-five or something, and is close with Hank from the tattoo shop. They used to squat together about seven years ago when they both first hit the streets. I've never really even been friends with a femme before, let alone slept with one.

Date: August 27, 2003
Security: Public
Subject: Fuck Vegans

The last word was so good tonight! All the guys from The Hotel and the Safety Net read, and then afterwards we went to the all night diner downtown for cheese fries. It's times like this I'm really glad I didn't keep with that whole vegan thing.

Date: August 30, 2003
Security: Friends
Subject: Date

This guy named Kaden asked me out on a date tonight. He was all straight and formal about it. I don't think anyone has ever called and asked if they could take me on a date before. It was weird. I don't even know him very well. I think he's mostly dates girls, but started T and suddenly decided to fag and ask me out. I think he's old friends with Buck so I tried to call him to get some dirt, but he hasn't called me back. I think his Daddy isn't letting him talk to me.

Date: September 1, 2003
Security: Private
Subject: Fag

Phoenix didn't have to be at her job until late so she came and got me. We swung through the taco drive through, and I wanted party potatoes, but didn't get anything because I was convinced they weren't really vegetarian even though the Safety Net says they are fine. Another rule of living there is that you have to be vegan. Anyway, she got some five layer meaty burrito thing. I can't believe I'm fucking this girl, let alone a girl who eats meat.

When we hooked up last week after the surgery benefit at The Hotel I made her brush her teeth before I'd let her kiss me, but I gave up on that this week. Phoenix is pretty much the only person I know who lives on her own. She scored this crazy little one bedroom just a few blocks from Alberta. I'm not really sure how she got it, but it's a pretty cool place, or it would be if she ever cleaned it up.

Since I first hooked up with her I've been wishing that I were more service oriented, and then I'd pretend to be her houseboy and do something nice like surprise her by cleaning. Sometimes I sit in my basement and think about sneaking into her apartment collecting all of her panties and dresses and taking them down the street to the laundromat and watching the stains dissolve as they swirled through the rinse cycle, but I'd probably shrink something. And then I think maybe I'll just collect all the dishes from under her bed and across the counter and do those. I tried to do that on Wednesday. I was going to do the dishes, but she started grabbing my ass and before I could even turn off the faucet we were stumbling back over piles of clothes and ricocheting off walls and onto her unmade bed.

Phoenix has the dirtiest apartment I've ever been in, and if you've seen the cave I call home you'd know that's saying something. It doesn't help that she's a chain smoker so the whole place, which is really just a little studio room, is covered with the residue of her cigarettes. Pretty much everyone smokes, but not inside. Phoenix doesn't have roommates so she can get by with that, and of course I can't even appreciate not having to go outside in the rain to light up, being XXX and all.

Phoenix didn't have to be at work until late so we went to her place. We were going to have a marathon viewing of some early 90s teen TV show. Phoenix has a credit card and bought the whole first and only season off the internet, but by the time we got to her place she could only find the DVDs, and not her laptop. She was convinced it was somewhere under her clothes so we rooted around on the floor for a while, stepping gingerly, afraid of crushing the thing in our search. I tried to get Orbit in on the search so he was digging around for the videos too. I was a little scared about that, because Phoenix had adopted two of the most recent rat babies from the Safety Net and then had let them free roam her apartment like they do at the house and one of them hadn't come back, or had gotten lost somewhere.

I was worried that Orbit was going to find it and it would be dead. After a while Phoenix got bored with the searching, and flopped onto her bed. She reached over and turned on her stereo. We've been fucking all this week, so the radio was already tuned to country music. Phoenix thinks it's hot that I look all punk but still like country, or she thinks I'm hot and just ignores my music. I'm not really sure which. So the music is playing and Phoenix finishes her post-unsuccessful-laptop-hunt cigarette and I lean over and start kissing her.

Phoenix is the first person I've ever slept with who likes to have her chest touched. I mean, Phoenix is the first femme I've been with, so that probably has something to do with it. When we're making out I always have to remind myself to not keep my hands clear of her breasts. The first time we fucked I never even took her shirt off, she called me a fag and started crying and saying I didn't really want to sleep with girls. So now I've got to remember, because I don't really know what to do when she cries and it's not that I don't like her boobs, it's just I don't really know what to do with them.

When Phoenix called me that afternoon and asked if I wanted to come watch videos I knew that at some point we'd end up fucking so I figured I should be prepared. Phoenix likes to read really sexy zines that involve butches fucking femmes in bathroom stalls, all San Francisco style, which makes sense cuz she's from there and she's always telling all of us boys that guys in the bay know how to treat a femme.

She's pretty convinced I don't really listen when she tells me all this stuff, but I do. To prove it I went over to her place packing. In my breakup with Hunter I lost all the good silicone cocks but I still have my purple one that I bought when I was with James. Technically I guess he bought it. Daddy had this rule that the person you bought the cock with was the only one who could ever be fucked by it, so they got it when you broke up. I followed his rule for a while, but that gets expensive. I figure if you're using a condom it doesn't really matter. Anyway, the purple one fits just right into my Y-front briefs and in my work pants you can't tell I'm packing unless you're up close and personal.

Phoenix has a sixth sense for this stuff, and totally knew I was packing before we even started making out, so after a while she reached over and unzipped my fly. We were still kissing, and I was working on not forgetting to play with her tits, when she pulled my cock out of my pants, pulled our lips apart and grinned at me. She started jerking me off while she reached over to her nightstand and fumbled for her lipstick. This might be the main difference between fucking boys and fucking Phoenix. She has to make sure her lipstick is fresh before sucking me off. It was sorta hot. Pretty soon she had her freshly reddened lips around my purple cock and her fingers up my boy-hole and then real rodeo country music came on the radio and I was seriously rocking. I kept trying to look in her eyes but I couldn't concentrate, all I could do was play with her hair. Then, she stopped right as I was about to cum and turned off the radio. At first I thought she maybe just didn't like the song. I pulled myself together a little bit and was like, "Baby, are you ok?" trying to get my brain working clearly again and ignore how hard I was. Phoenix started laughing and was said, "You are just such a boy. Like a boy, boy. I don't know what to do with you sometimes but giving you head with country music playing is too weird. It's like being back in high school."

Date: September 3, 2003

Hunter asked me if I could make the next open mic be a benefit for his surgery. No, that's not true, he had Travis ask me. I guess he's trying to go down to some doctor in Texas cuz he's cheaper than the good doc in SF. Hunter has some of the money but has quite a ways to go. He knows that my event has been going well and wanted to see if I'd help him, since he'd been my Daddy. I told Travis I was going to have to think about it. I don't really want to throw a benefit for Hunter after all the shit he pulled, but at the same time I'm worried if I say no people are going to get mad, and will think I'm being immature and holding a grudge against him, or that I'm a bad boy or something. I really see this event as service to the community, and if that's true then of course I should be doing the event. I wish I knew what to do.

Date: September 5, 2003
Security: Friends
Subject: single

So I dumped Kaden. I mean I don't even know if you'd call it that when we only we went on a couple of awkward dates. Things with him had been ok but it was also boring. He mostly just wanted to kiss and got uncomfortable if I ever tried anything with him. He said he was used to femmes who just lay there. Last night before we broke up I started telling him about being Daddy/boy with Hunter and James and how that's really was what I was looking for. He got all freaked out. He started telling me how sick and perverted I was. He said that because I'm a survivor I shouldn't be playing fucked up games like that and that I needed to see a therapist really badly. I told him to get the fuck out of my house.

Date: September 6, 2003

OMG Ethan seriously hasn't done his dishes in two weeks. I found some shoved under the bathroom sink, it's really nasty. I tried to talk to him about it tonight but he was drunk and said he would do

them later. I ended up going all through
our basement, except his room, and threw
all the dishes in the sink and fucking
washed them myself.

Date: September 7, 2003

I called Buck because I just couldn't
decide what was the right thing to do
about Hunter's request. I guess I sounded
pretty upset because Luke put Buck on the
phone fast. I hate the part of their power
dynamic where Luke screens all the calls
coming in. I told Buck about how Travis
had come up to me down at Waterfront and
said he needed to talk to me boy to boy
and ask me a favor for his Daddy. I told
Buck about how confused I've been, about
how I want to do good service to the
community, but how angry I am that Hunter
would even ask me to do this.

Buck got really mad. He said that Hunter
was a fucked up Daddy and that at this
point I didn't owe him any service at
all. He told me I should tell Travis and
Buck where to shove it and if anyone gave
me any crap about it, they would have
to answer to him personally. When I got
off the phone with him I called Travis
and told him that I decided it wasn't

appropriate for the event to do a surgery benefit there. He seemed pissed and said he thought I would say that. He asked if I'd be willing to help organize the benefit at another venue. I said probably not.

Date: September 9, 2003

I'm trying to be cool about Hunter and Travis being together. I mean what choice do I have? I know that if I freak out about it and make a big deal about how Hunter lied to me that everyone at the Safety Net will turn on me and side with Travis because they're roommates. It sucks.

Last night I was out with everyone at this sweet spoken word show in the basement at The Hotel. It was a good night because for the first time since Hunter and I split I felt like the pack was all back together, like we'd figured out our stuff, and everyone knew that Hunter and I could be mature about our relationship not working and everything. I had Orbit with me and I knew he needed to pee so I went upstairs to let him run around in the backyard with the house pit bulls that Ava and some of her animal rights buddies kidnapped from a dog fighting ring down in North Portland.

It was a really nice night. Ava and I were just chilling on the old trampoline someone dumpstered forever ago. We bounced for a little while and then laid down on our bellies watching the dogs run around. I rolled over until we were touching. She's not normally my type. Honestly I don't even know how she identifies, just that she's queer, and uses female pronouns. She's got wild blue dreads but is super skinny. She's always wearing this jacket covered in patches from animal sanctuaries and she's hitchhiked with her dog, Road, all over the country. Road and Orbit and other housedogs were playing chase under the trampoline and around the side of the house. I could feel Ava's breathing and I let my finger trace the thick black bands tattooed on her arm covering the raised little cutting scars. Ava threw her cigarette into the garden and we started kissing. I've always been XXX, so I know I should hate kissing smokers, but there's something so so good about a fresh cigarette kiss.

We heard Ship yelling at the door trying to find Ava cuz the show got too loud and the neighbors were threatening to call the cops. Ava groaned, kissed me one last time and started jogging towards the house. I let Orbit play for a little longer before picking him up and heading back downstairs. It was dark and some poet from Olympia was onstage. I was trying to find somewhere to sit but it was really crowded. I put Orbit in my messenger bag and stood on a crate in the back of the room so I could see.

Right up by the pallet board stage Hunter was sitting in a chair and Travis was kneeling right at his feet with two of the rats curled up in the hood of his sweatshirt with their little faces pressed against his ears. I really thought I was going to puke or punch the wall. Orbit could tell I was upset and started whining. I climbed down from the crate, let him out of my bag and went up the stars and out the front door. It was late so the bus was only running every twenty minutes. Orbit and I started walking home. I feel bad I didn't say goodbye to anyone, but I was just so angry! At first I thought I was mad at Hunter for leaving me, or at Travis for flaunting to my face

Sassafras Lowrey 309

that he has my Daddy, but by the time
Orbit and I got back home, I realized
more than anything I'm mad at myself for
still wanting him.

Date: September 12, 2003
Security: Friends
Subject: WOW!!!!

The feminist bookstore collective called me today and asked
if I could come down to the shop. I was already dressed so
I just had to get my boots on. I didn't bother to spike my hair,
just threw on this new baseball cap I dumpstered and used my
"gender trash" stencil on it. I put Cosmo and Orbit in the bike
trailer and headed for the shop. They're really cool about me
having both the dogs there because one of the main collective
people is obsessed with dogs and brings hers into the shop
every day.

I was sorta worried that they were gonna say there was a
problem with my event, so I wanted the dogs with me in case
I got upset. The shop was empty when I got there, so I hopped
up on the counter to sit while we talked. Orbit and Cosmo
went racing around looking for their buddy. The collective
told me that they had just finished reviewing "Your world can't
fucking kill me," my latest zine that they have been selling for a
while. The bookstore lesbian said the collective had come to a
consensus last night at their meeting, they want to give me an
award!!!!!!!!!

The only other time in my life I've ever won anything was when I was doing dog sports. The dogs and I won all kinds of ribbons and stuff and we even got a special award from our local team for commitment and perseverance. Once I lost the dogs it never even occurred to me that I'd ever win anything again. Every year, the feminist bookstore has this yuppie dinner to honor emerging writers in the city. I've never gone, obviously, because tickets are stupid expensive.

I sorta just sat there on the counter, stunned. The event is in a couple of weeks. I need to figure out who to drag with me as a date. I know it's gonna be hella boring, but I obviously can't say no.

Date: September 18, 2003

Holy crap! Jullian, that hot kid who train hopped here from Nebraska to see Ethan, totally hooked up with me last night! I'm pretty sure he was drunk, which sucks, but he was hot so it was ok. It all happened cuz we were bored and decided we should make a porn zine. That didn't really end up happening, though, cuz part way through we got distracted. First, Ethan had to go get a disposable camera from the drugstore, and then when he was gone we went through his closet. He had this sick guerrilla costume from back when he was a girl and lived in this dyke activist punk house in San Diego. This was an authentic Guerrilla Grrrl suit from protests and shit! Jullian's cock is really big and black so we cut a hole in the front of the suit and stuck it in. When Ethan got back he had Phoenix with him, which was kinda awkward.

At first Lace, the femme Jullian is traveling with, was gonna be the one to suck him off, but she got all freaked out so I said I would do it. The camera only had twenty-four pictures. Ethan blew those really fast and was bored. I guess Lace and Phoenix were too, cuz at some point the three of them left my room where we were filming. Jullian fucked me hard, he even slapped me a little, but he wasn't really taking charge, which was crummy cuz he'd been talking earlier about what a big Top he was. Whatever. The guerrilla suit was off by then and we could hear Lace and Phoenix moaning in Ethan's room.

The only thing that sucked was right after I came, Jullian pulled his pants back over his boxers, and went out to sleep on the living room floor with Lace, leaving me all sweaty and naked and alone in my bed. I was just about to fall asleep when Phoenix came in. She was trying to pull her hair back into pigtails and the slip she had been wearing as a dress was falling off her. She sat on the edge of my bed so I kicked the dogs off. She said she hoped that her getting fucked by Ethan wasn't too awkward for me. I told her it was fine, not like we're actually together or anything. She said that it had been a long time since she'd been with someone who wasn't a fag. She said she thought she was falling in love with Ethan and that it would be best if she and I didn't see each other anymore. I told her that made sense.

Date: September 20 , 2003

Dean and I were talking tonight at QYRC. I haven't seen him around much since that play party. I thought he was back with his grandma, but it turns out he hopped a train down to SF and actually just got back into town. He started telling me about this sick squat he's got going with some buddies of his. They're calling it the Crystal Palace on account of well….. y'know. It's this crazy abandoned hotel place up near the big research hospital. QYRC was pretty boring with none of the pack around, just a bunch of GSA kids complaining about their homework and talking about prom. Gus looked way irritated about it. I don't even know why I come anymore. Dean cuffed the back of my neck with his hand and asked if I wanted to get out of there and go check out his place. It wasn't really a question.

I was wearing my navy blue sweatshirt with the big XXX on the back so I knew that at least no one would offer me anything. We took the #15 downtown then waited for the #54. It took almost thirty minutes for it to show. We were alone at the bus stop so I dropped to my knees while we waited. Dean kept running his fingers through my mohawk and every so often yanking my head around by it. I was so glad I hadn't waxed my hair this morning or brought Orbit with me to QYRC.

We had to walk a while when we got off the bus. Fancy ass neighborhood. I think my bio dad lives up here somewhere but I'm not sure. He likes all our communication to be through his office, so I've never even had his home address. Whatever. Anyway, so we finally get to this apartment building that looks all bombed out. Seriously, every window was broken out, and all the walls covered with graffiti. Dean pushed open

the door to one of the first apartments
and we went in. Some kids sat nodding
off against the door of the next unit.
Inside was nasty. There were fast food
wrappers everywhere and towers of beer
cans. When we got to Dean's room things
were a little better. He didn't have much
in there other than a ratty mattress and
some books. We chilled there for a while,
talking about QYRC and how his buddies
had found this place and asked if he
wanted to come stay with them.

It was getting dark so he pulled a
flashlight out of his messenger bag and
set it on its end to try to light the room
a little bit. Gutterpunk mood lighting!
They're all squatting, so no electricity.
We started kissing and kinda wrestling
around a little bit on the mattress, then
he stood up and walked across the room
towards the closet. He was mostly in
shadows now because the flashlight didn't
reach that far, but I saw him motion me
over as he opened the door.

It was empty inside except for the bar
that he put my hands on. There were
cuffs already attached to the bar that
he buckled onto my wrists. I kicked some
beer cans out of the way with my boots.

I was facing away from him now, towards the wall covered in cobwebs and dust. I closed my eyes. I could feel his hands on me, sliding under my sweatshirt and down into my boxers and then, he started punching. I felt myself fall away as his fists landed on my back. It was so good. None of that flashy bullshit like we saw from the door at that play party we couldn't get into. I kinda hung against the bar as he beat me down.

He finished just as I felt my eyes burning. Another hit and I would have started crying. He let me down from the closet and dragged me over to the bed where he unzipped the fly of his jeans and had me suck him off. He was so hard. He pulled my head up by my hair and slapped my face to get me to open my eyes. "I heard about what happened with Grace at QYRC," he said.

I got really embarrassed and couldn't even talk.

"I could give you what you need," he whispered into my ear. "I could be your Daddy, but don't answer me now, just think about it." Then he said it was time to go, cuz kids would be coming back

```
tweaking soon and he knew I couldn't be
around that shit. He walked me back to
the bus stop but didn't wait with me.
```

Date: September 21, 2003
Security: Friends
Subject: Are you my Daddy?

I had such good scene with Dean last night. I can't stop thinking about it/him. When I was leaving he said he knew what I was looking for, and that it was something he could give me. After Hunter, it's been so hard to really think about having a Daddy again, and believe that anyone will really follow through.

I've got this great history of having a Daddy get sick of me, bored with me. I've never been enough for anyone. That's what I want more than anything, just to be enough for someone. Mostly, it just scares me how much I know I want and need to be someone's boy, and to have them want to keep me.

Date: September 23, 2003
Security: Friends
Subject: got it!

I called Hank really late tonight. I'd been trying to get the nerve to do it all day. It was raining and already sorta late, but the shop was still open and he told me he had an appointment cancel and he had time to talk. I'd been asking everyone at the Safety Net how he was gonna react. I wanted to get a trans sign just under the stars on my right forearm. I told Hank that everyone said he wouldn't do it, but I really wanted it. I was sitting on my bed and decided that if he said no, I was going to say I would just go to another artist. I didn't think he was gonna believe that, but I didn't have to find out because he said clearly our friends didn't know him very well.

Hank told me if I could get there in thirty minutes he would do the tattoo tonight. I got there with five minutes to spare, even with having to take the dogs out before I left and needing to find an ATM. Hank had already drawn up the sickest trans sign I've ever seen. It looked like the graffiti on the wall in the park. On the phone he'd made me describe the symbol to him, saying he couldn't quite remember how it looked. Fucking liar.

Hank had to smoke before he could do the tattoo so he and I went outside. Like pretty much everyone else I know, Hank is sober. He just hit three years. The thing I love about him is that he really respects how XXX I am. While we were outside, some drunk girls from the bar down the street walked into the shop and started looking at flash. He had to go in and tell them if they had any questions to come out and talk to him. He handed me his cigarette when he went in, and when he came back he looked really upset.

He apologized for being so disrespectful, saying he hadn't been thinking and how much he admires that I'm XXX. Hank 's really hot, but unfortunately unlike everyone else in this town, he's straight. I don't have a fucking chance. When we got started I couldn't stop staring at the tattoos on Hank's hands as he gripped my forearm and concentrated on the thin skin over my wrist. There wasn't anyone else in the shop so he had control of the stereo. We switched it over from metal to the country station. That's the other thing I love about Hank, he fucking loves country music as much as I do. We both grew up outside of the city and are sorta good ol' boys at heart in a way that none of the rest of our friends really understand.

Date: September 23, 2003

Before he had started inking me, Hank said he needed to talk to me privately. I followed him into the back. He told me under no circumstances would the tattoo be black like all the rest of my work. He said I needed to be able to cover it one day. Then he had started rolling up his jeans. Hank is one of those people who you don't see skin on, other than his arms and hands. On his calf was a lesbian symbol that had been stick and poked into a one-woman-one-trans sign. He said he didn't want me to hate how I'd altered my body, and rolled his pants back down. I said I knew that I wouldn't, but I wanted the tattoo so I said fine to it being mostly color with just a black outline. He said I'd thank him later.

Once we started, he kept telling me to relax my fingers, but the way we were positioned my hand was only about an inch from his chest. I was so nervous. I didn't want to accidentally touch him. I just kept thinking about what was right beneath his t-shirt. Hank thinks our fancy undershirt binders aren't good enough. He also thinks that ace bandages are too messy to work with, and leave lines under his shirts.

Hank binds only with duct-tape, seven days a week, fourteen hours a day, and he's been doing it for over five years now. He doesn't have much skin left on his chest. Mostly he's adhering duct-tape to open sores and acting like it doesn't hurt when he picks things up or lifts himself into his truck. He showed me the scars and sores once, a couple of months ago when the shop was empty. The whole time he was tattooing me, I focused on making sure my fingers didn't uncurl and accidentally touch his chest.

Date: September 27, 2003
Security: Friends
Subject: Awards Dinner

Buck agreed to come with me to the IOW awards dinner tonight. I had tickets for a date and myself and I couldn't think of anyone I'd rather have with me than my big brother. I was surprised he came though, since his Daddy basically doesn't even let him talk to me anymore. I had to leave a bunch of messages before Buck finally was able to call me back and say he could come. We got all dressed up. Buck loaned me one of his button downs to wear with my work pants. I was the only zinester being honored. Everyone else has written an actual book. It was hella weird sitting there at this fancy dinner with the authors and their dates, eating eggplant and watching while people read from their books. The audience seemed ok with what I read. I did the one piece all about how I'm still hella genderqueer even if I'm shooting T. They clapped a lot, but I don't know if they really understood.

After the dinner Buck and I got outta there pretty fast. The event was full of yuppie lesbians who kept wanting to talk to me and ask questions about what I meant when I said I was still a dyke but that I was a guy too. Gender fluidity makes Buck really uncomfortable and I was worried he was going to go off. It was pretty cool, though, to get to stand on a real stage and have the bookstore be honoring me.

Date: September 30, 2003
Security: Public
Subject: Dean?

Has anyone seen Dean around? He wasn't at the fountain downtown today when we'd planned to meet up.

Date: October 1, 2003

I had to go to the emergency room last night. I'd slept all day and then woke up about ten and started pissing blood. I've been pumping my little dick with a cut off syringe, so I was worried I'd maybe really hurt myself without meaning to. I was freaking out and wanted my brother but his Daddy wouldn't let him come to the phone, so I called the Safety Net. Travis was the only one home. Stuff with him is so fucking weird, but I couldn't think of anyone else to call, so I told him what was going on. He said I had to go to the emergency room. As a kid I never went to the doctor, so hospitals and shit really freak me out.

I asked if he would go with me and he said yes, which sorta surprised me. I had to walk up to the Safety Net cuz the bus wasn't running and then after I rested for a few minutes we walked together over to the hospital. I wanted to sneak Orbit in, in my messenger bag but Travis had told me to leave the dogs before I even got off the phone with him. I had to walk slowly, cuz even walking hurt real bad, and I kept feeling like I had to pee, which was the last thing I wanted to do.

When we got to the ER they had me fill out a ton of paperwork, name and medical history and that kinda shit. I crossed out "sex" on the stupid form and wrote "gender" then wrote "male." Travis said he didn't know if that was a good idea, but ever since my name and gender got legally changed by the homeless health clinic I've been pretty militant about correcting folks about what words they should be using. Besides, my legal gender is changed on my ID so it would be a lie to put anything else. We got stuck for two hours in the waiting room before the nurse brought us into the back. They weren't going to let Travis come with me, but I freaked out at the nurse, and they decided to let him come with me.

I refused to put on the paper robe that the nurse left so the doctor was already a little pissed off when he walked into the room and saw me sitting there in my boots, work pants and hoodie. He made

Travis get off the little stool next to the bed and move over to the chair where we had thrown our messenger bags. The doctor asked about my symptoms, which was irritating because I already had to fill out all the forms and talk to the nurse about them. I started to mouth off but Travis gave me a look and I started talking nice. The doctor said to put on the gown by the time he got back.

Travis asked if he should leave the room too. I told him it didn't matter. I pulled off my pants and boxers but left my binder, hoodie and boots on. I'd just sat back down on the hospital table with the paper dress wrapped around my waist when the doctor came back into the room. I don't think he liked how many clothes I was wearing, but whatever. He pulled the paper away and gasped. I guess I'm passing better than I thought. He got really nasty after that. I had to go pee in a cup and then he insisted on doing a full examination.

I refused to take my boots off so I stuck them in the stirrups next to his head. He got really rough up in my shit and while his hand was in me I thought about how if it got any worse I could kick him in the face. Travis just sat in the little chair, staring at me. After Dr. Mean pulled his goddamn hand out of me he said everything seemed fine and I was wasting his time. He told us to wait in the room. I got dressed and Travis asked if I was ok. I said sure. It took about thirty minutes for the stupid nurse to come back. She said I had a bladder infection and had to take a bunch of pills. We left the ER and I ripped the plastic identification band off my arm and chucked it into the street. Travis said I shouldn't litter. I ignored him.

It hurt to walk, but no way in hell was I going to pay for a cab. We walked to the twenty-four hour pharmacy and waited around while they filled my prescription. The pharmacy is right by the Safety Net and I kept hoping Travis would say I could sleep there, but he didn't. I couldn't really have anyway, cuz the critters were alone and probably wondering what happened to me. When I got my meds Travis gave me a hug and went home. It took me another thirty minutes to get back to my place, because I kept needing to stop and rest. I don't even remember taking the meds or getting into bed, but this morning I woke up with the dogs and Trash all curled up against me and I feel a whole lot better. I wish I had a Daddy to take care of me, though.

Date: October 3, 2003

Rumor is that Dean took off. Sounds like he didn't just crash at the Crystal Palace because it was a sweet squat, but because he's a damn speed freak. Today I found out he left word for me with Gus at QYRC that he had to go back to San Francisco and that he was sorry. Sorry. Seems like everyone is always fucking sorry.

I think I knew all along that this wouldn't work out the way Dean told me it could. It sounds horrible, but I liked the idea of what I wanted him to be better than I liked him, I guess. I just really wanted him to be my Daddy.

Date: October 4, 2003
Security: Friends
Subject: Faggotry

I took this kid Sydney home last night. He's really short with this shaggy hair, not on T yet and a way bigger fag than anyone I know. He wears all kinds of body glitter and pink shirts and shit. He's probably only using me to get closer to the rest of the pack, but he's cute so I'm going with it.

Date: October 5, 2003

Sydney came to the zine read, and that weird reading I did at a local college for the yuppie kids and then to the Clit Shack house show. Sydney is new to PDX-he's from somewhere in California, LA I think. He's really into zines, and he's really into bois, and evidently he's really into me. I didn't even remember his name, but he sure knew mine. It turns out that he not only has been coming to all of the readings I've done or been part of for the last month or so, but he also has all of my zines, even that really old one that I never sold at the bookstore, just down at the street market under the bridge. It's a little creepy, but he's sorta cute and it's flattering that he's so obsessed with me. I had no idea he'd been coming to all the events until his roommate finally made him come up to me and introduce himself. He started talking about how he thought my writing was so deep and brave, and how he was working on a zine, and maybe I'd like to take a look at it sometime.

It was such an obvious pickup line but he was cute and I haven't really been seeing anyone since Dean and I'm still

pretty busted up about that. None of
the pack likes Sydney. Travis said it
was because we didn't know him and that
made it a little weird. He said that he
thought Sydney was only interested in the
starfucking. I told Travis that I would
be careful and was just having a little
bit of fun. I was kinda excited that
I had risen to a level of zinester fame
where anyone would see me as someone to
starfuck.

I gave Sydney my number and told him to
call me, which of course he did when
he woke up slightly hungover. Sydney
drinks, which is a major downside of
hooking up with him. He tells me it is
just recreational, and he understood that
under no circumstances was he allowed
to drink around me. We made plans to
meet up last night over on Hawthorne and
look at books. We were meeting up pretty
late so I was fairly sure he'd be coming
home with me. I was going to change the
sheets but realized the only other pair
I had were dirtier than the ones on the
bed. I'd switched to black sheets because
I thought they looked sexier, problem was
they showed all the cum. I realized I'd
only be able to bring him into my bed in
the dark.

Of course he came home with me, but he started annoying me right away. Travis was right, he was bordering on creepy stalker. Not only had he read all my zines, but he'd evidently memorized them too. He started walking around the basement pointing out different things that were referenced in one zine or another, like the moldy spot in the carpet from where the living room keeps flooding.

Worst of all was that when I came out of the bathroom I found him actually petting my typewriter and talking to Orbit and Cosmo like he fucking knew them! It was so gross and so transparent. I almost told him to leave but I wanted to get laid so I let him spend the night. The sex was all right, but then when I'd rolled over and was about to fall asleep, he asked if I'd tell him a story.

"What do you mean?" I asked. I was so freaked out when he responded that it would be so cool to hear me tell one of the stories in the zine, it would be like his own private reading. I told him I was really tired but maybe in the morning.

I got a call really early this morning from Travis. Sydney was still in my bed. He wanted to follow me to The Hotel, but I told him no way. Well, before he knew he wanted to come with me, he wanted to know what The Hotel is. I had to explain that it isn't like a hotel where you rent rooms or vacation or something, but this really rad punk house in NE. Everyone just calls it that because of how many people have been in and out of it over the years. The Hotel is the oldest house in the city. I think queer folks have been living in it in one form or another for like ten years now.

Travis said The Hotel called the Safety Net and said everyone needed to find a way to get over there really quickly, because the hot water heater in the basement burst and was flooding everything. Obviously everyone rents the house but it's been a punk house for so long no one's even sure who's actually on the lease anymore, they just send money orders every month from someone different. Even though no one knows who's technically on the lease, everyone knows what wasn't supposed to happen to the house. See, when the owner rented it to some now aging punk who hasn't lived there in decade, he was

really specific about what he didn't want
to see happen to his house. Folks weren't
allowed to paint, put up walls, have dogs,
or do anything to the carpet. Problem was
that folks had done all those things and
more.

The Hotel really is a crazy house. Someone
pulled up all the carpet and resurfaced
the hardwood floors underneath. Well, they
had started to. The living room where
dance parties happen has been resurfaced,
but the kitchen and all the bedrooms
are still pretty rough. All the walls
are bright colors and there are so many
added rooms. The attic, which used to
be unfinished at one point, now has four
extra bedrooms, and the basement has been
turned into an art room, band practice
space, and another two bedrooms, all of
which started filling up with water this
morning.

There was no way that the landlord could
be called. Everyone always wants to live
there because it's super famous. When
poets from San Francisco and New Mexico
are in town it's where they stay and
there will almost always be private shows
in the basement and the only way to get
invited is if you know someone who lives

there. Pretty much everyone was already
at the house by the time I'd avoided
giving Sydney a private reading, gotten
him out of my house, taken Cosmo out and
gotten Orbit and I onto the two busses up
Alberta.

All four of The Hotel dogs, giant pits
who'd been kidnapped by the animal
liberation kids from local dog fighting
rings, were lounging in the middle of
the living room when I walked in and put
Orbit down to play. Someone had managed
to get the water to stop pouring into the
basement so now they just needed to find a
new water heater. Some folks headed out
to the recycling center to try to find a
working one, so I just sat around for a
while talking to folks downstairs.

There had been a whole lot of water, but
mostly it was the band room that got
wet and none of the instruments had been
down there. Folks were guessing it would
take the pallet board stage a week or so
to dry out, but at least it didn't get
into the silk-screening room. They finally
came back with a salvaged water heater
they thought would work. While a crew of
folks got it installed, I went up to the
kitchen to help Ship, who's from Alaska

but has been staying in one of the little attic rooms, to make tofu scramble for everyone. She was standing in the kitchen in heels and an old slip with her bright blue hair up in two messy buns. I feel like in the last couple of months femmes have started to invade.

Date: October 7, 2003

Ship came over today. I don't know her too well, but we've hung out at house shows and stuff. My number's on the kitchen wall at The Hostel where she lives, so while I was a little weirded out she called, it's not like I was confused how she got my number or anything. She asked if I wanted to hang out later and I said sure. She biked over and we were reading zines for a while and talking about Pride and how it's totally messed up the way everyone's bending over for these beer companies that run the whole thing. Ship told me about a group of radical queers who are organizing an anti-corporate pride and how they are looking for folks to get involved. It sounds pretty cool. They're planning on disrupting the parade itself. I can't risk getting arrested

and being away from the dogs, so I told
Ship I couldn't get too involved in the
organizing.

My futon broke a while ago so now it's
just the mattress on the floor propped
up against the wall in the living room.
Ship was sitting really close to me, and
I realized that she was hitting on me!
I guess word has started traveling that
I hooked up with a femme once. Ship's
got good politics and wasn't dressed too
girly, baggy jeans and an a-shirt with a
pushup bra underneath, so I leaned over
and started kissing her. She crawled up
into my lap and straddled me. I'd packed
before she came over, just in case, and she
was grinding against me really sweetly.

I let her take my cock out of my jeans
and squeezed her ass while she started to
ride me. She came pretty fast. I didn't,
but that's ok. We looked at zines for a
while longer but then I needed to take
Cosmo out to the park. I asked if she
wanted to come with us, but she said she
needed to get going.

Date: October 11, 2003
Security: Friends
Subject: T

I had to go up to the pharmacy to get more T today. It's such a pain in the ass but I know I shouldn't complain. All the guys on the online message groups talk about getting hassled at the pharmacy and their T having to be special ordered so they are always missing shots. At least here in Portland there are so many trans guys this one pharmacy has just started making T themselves. It sounds sketchy but it's really not. It's this weird place, though, way up in this real ritzy neighborhood. I wonder what the folks that normally go there must think of all the crusty, short, round guys that come in all the time!

The crummy thing is that there is only one bus you can take, and it only runs every forty-five minutes. Today the worst thing was walking out of the pharmacy I actually watched the damn bus speed down the hill back towards downtown. I tried to run and chase it, but they didn't stop. I didn't feel like going back into the pharmacy and getting stared at by the yuppie folks shopping there, so I just started wandering around the neighborhood.

I know that my bio dad lives around here somewhere. It's so weird whenever I realize that I actually don't know where the guy lives, since all our communication comes through his office. I don't know why I've never just come out and asked for his address, I guess I'm afraid he'd tell me no, or that he'd think

I want more from him than I do. I just kinda wandered around for a while looking at the different houses and wondering if one of them could be his, until it was time to catch the bus. When I got back downtown I walked over to Buck's work. I haven't seen him around much lately since he's been so busy with his Daddy, but we were at least able to talk for a few minutes before his manager came out and started giving me dirty looks.

Date: October 13, 2003

I don't know what's wrong with me. I almost couldn't do my shot tonight. Even with the trick of just staring at my anchor tattoo didn't work. I was sweating and freaking out. I kept thinking about that night, right after Hunter and I broke up, when Sarah came over and threatened to take my T when I told her I wasn't really male identified. I almost wish she would have taken it that night, and then none of this would be my fault.

Date: October 17, 2003
Security: Friends
Subject: I hate femmes

Ethan told two femmes from Olympia that they could come and stay with us. I think he thought they were both going to be all over him and he could have threesomes for a week. I don't think that really is happening. Actually I'm pretty sure they are fucking each other. The most annoying thing is that they have been leaving their shit everywhere. They're in Portland to be part of a big drag show. So not only do they have all their regular clothes, but they also have all of their performance costumes. The girls are rehearsing all the time and leaving fucking glitter on absolutely everything. I even found glitter on my typewriter and my bed and on Cosmo's tennis ball!

I'm not really all that big a fan of burlesque on a good day. I don't know why, I've just never found it all that interesting. Probably because in general I don't really like girls. But anyway, they are doing a joint performance to some really obnoxious song that's been all over the radio this year. I only listen to country music, and the occasional dyke folk singer, and somehow even I knew this song. They also really like to party. Pretty much every one of Ethan's friends likes to party and so they are getting wasted after rehearing in the living room and then not waking up until the afternoon. They never start rehearsing before ten o'clock at night, so ever since they got here I've had to fall asleep with all the critters locked into my room and listening to that stupid song play on repeat.

Date: October 19, 2003

The Hotel called today and asked if I had plans for tonight. I didn't, so I asked what they had in mind. One of the guys there washes dishes at a diner a few days a week and I guess when he was there during the breakfast rush this morning,

some dude came in and put up flyers for
this new open mic happening out at a
coffee shop on Sandy. It's not one of the
coffee shops I've ever been to, and I've
never heard of the folks running the open
mic, but it sounded pretty cool and it's
not like I had anything better to do.

I didn't have any more copies of my zine,
so I decided to go by the office store
before meeting up with the house. I thought
about pulling the scam of running one
hundred copies and telling them it was an
accident and you meant to hit ten. That
usually works for the other zinesters,
but you can only get by with it once or
twice at a shop before they catch on to
you. I'm always afraid to pull shit like
that. I made all my copies, stapled the
zines together using their crappy stapler
since I didn't think I had time to get
back home before we met up, and handed
the casher some wadded up bills.

When I got downtown I took Orbit out of
my messenger bag to let him run around
until we saw Griffin and the rest of the
guys. Griffin's been clean for five years
now, longer than anyone else. He got
clean at twelve when his parents sent him
to rehab before he ran away, but he still

hangs out with the street kids who use.
Once we all met up we had to wait like
fifteen minutes for the right bus to come.
Griffin told me he'd seen Dean tweaking
with the other kids. Whatever. I started
getting really fucking nervous. Normally
I only read at my open mic, which isn't
as scary. It's different cuz I run the
space and it's at the feminist bookstore
and it's all crusty ass queer punk kids.

I was going to read this piece mostly
about how I think gender is a lot more
complicated than a lot of folks make it,
even more complicated than the pack says
it is. It talks about how I don't want
to change that shit, how I don't want
to be a man, how I want to be something
outside the binary, and all about actually
injecting testosterone. It's a piece from
my recent zine. I've even had a couple of
kids send me the concealed cash through
the mail from other states to buy it,
which makes me feel pretty good.

The piece I wanted to read is kinda graphic
about the needle going in and the blood.
I figured I'd read it at this new place
since I don't know who's going to be in
the audience, and so I can't be accused of
hangs out with the street kids who use.

Once we all met up we had to wait like fifteen minutes for the right bus to come. Griffin told me he'd seen Dean tweaking with the other kids. Whatever. I started getting really fucking nervous. Normally I only read at my open mic, which isn't as scary. It's different cuz I run the space and it's at the feminist bookstore and it's all crusty ass queer punk kids.

I was going to read this piece mostly about how I think gender is a lot more complicated than a lot of folks make it, even more complicated than the pack says it is. It talks about how I don't want to change that shit, how I don't want to be a man, how I want to be something outside the binary, and all about actually injecting testosterone. It's a piece from my recent zine. I've even had a couple of kids send me the concealed cash through the mail from other states to buy it, which makes me feel pretty good.

The piece I wanted to read is kinda graphic about the needle going in and the blood. I figured I'd read it at this new place since I don't know who's going to be in the audience, and so I can't be accused of intentionally triggering folks. We got to the coffee shop about ten minutes before the open mic was supposed to start and got our names on the list of readers. It was long! At my open mic, some nights I'm having to practically tell people I'll bring them home with me if they just get their asses up and read. It was weird too, because everyone was so fucking clean. They were all wearing black jeans and t-shirts that looked like they were brand new. They were all at least five or ten years older than us. I knew right away we were in the wrong place and I wanted to leave, but our names were already on the list and it would have looked like we were chickenshits if we actually just walked out.

The event started on time, which was really weird too. We didn't have time to do much but sign up and find a small table to camp out on in the back. I didn't see anyone else with zines, so I was pretty sure that all the time and cash I spent at the copy shop earlier was a total waste. I kept looking at the guys trying to figure out what they were thinking. At one point I asked if they wanted to leave.

I was playing it all cool like I was checking in and taking care of the house. I totally wanted them to say yes so it could be their fault that we walked out. Everyone said they wanted to stay. The people started reading and it was the worst shit I'd ever heard. None of it was real. Most of it wasn't even about people. It was all these heavy metaphors about nature and the river and peace and harmony and shit. I guess they were reading real poetry, but I sure didn't understand most of that crap. It reminded me of being in high school. Every time the poetry unit would come up everyone would groan, but for some damn reason it was always the teacher's favorite thing and they would spend weeks just standing there reading shit that not one of us understood.

It was my turn finally. When the guy read my name off the signup sheet he looked all confused like he didn't realize Click was an actual name or something. These were totally not my kind of people. They told me I had five minutes, which was just enough time to read this one piece I'd been planning on and then plug my zine at the end. People sorta clapped for me, but you could tell they were damn uncomfortable about what I read. Some girl read a poem about flowers and endangered butterflies right after me.

I wanted to just cut out of there right after Griffin finished reading a new and intense piece about how he knew that getting clean had saved his life, but he still wanted to get high every day. We decided we should be polite and stay until the end. I'd put my zines out on the little table, hoping someone would buy, no one did. When it ended and I was shoving everything into my backpack, this old dude in his fifties and balding came up to us. I guess he's a regular at the event or something. He said it was so nice to see people like us participating and staying out of trouble. I ain't never going back to that open mic ever again.

Date: October 21, 2003

I didn't bind when I went out to the grocery store to get chips and pasta. I know I should have, and I was really scared I was going to see one of the pack. They would never have let me live it down. I was tired so I threw on my sweatshirt and went for it. I've never really gotten the whole fucking obsession

with flat binding. James taught me how to
bind, and I'd never done it before I was
his boy.

In high school I wore sports bras and
was really uncomfortable with my tits,
but that was different. Daddy took me to
the drugstore and bought be an elastic
back brace, just like his. Back in his
bedroom he showed me how to push down and
separate my chest instead of flattening.
He said it was better for the tissue and
would make top surgery easier when I got
it later. I said I didn't want surgery.
He said I would, one day. Then, he helped
me to button up one of his old work shirts
and placed his palms on my new pecs and
pushed me down onto my knees in front of
his cock.

I've been growing a lot more facial hair
recently so I figured that made up for not
binding as much. I get really uneasy when
people think I'm like a regular man. The
dude who rang me out at the store called
me "miss" and I didn't even care enough
to correct him. I don't know what the
fuck that means. I had to put my real
binder on later, though, because Travis
called. He said he needed the cash out
of my freezer. I didn't want to give it

to him, but he said that he was ready
to send all of it down to the surgeon.
I don't know if I believe him or not.

Date: October 23, 2003
Security: Friends
Subject: babies!!!

Another litter of rats was born at the Safety Net last night. I was hanging out and then we all looked over because there was a bunch of noise in the rat colony and I couldn't believe that one of the rats was giving birth!!! Travis, who knows all the rats, wasn't home, so no one was sure if it was Sprinkles or Tofu or Smut who was the one giving birth. I don't think they knew any of them were pregnant again. I almost thought it was a sign that I should adopt a rat, but I've got my hands full over at my place without adding a little rodent. I think that Ship is going to take a couple. She was over there too and really in love with them.

Date: October 25, 2003

I went to complain to the upstairs
neighbors, aka, the folks that own this
place. The past few days the sewage lines
have been backing up into the basement
worse than usual. Usually it only happens
about once a week, but it's been an
everyday thing for a while now. I don't
really care for me, but I figure it can't
be good for Trash and the dogs! At least
the dogs and I are out a lot, but poor

Trash is stuck in the basement. I made him a cool cat tree with some pallets and carpet scraps I dumpstered.

The landlords wouldn't even talk to me about the soggy sewage carpet because they're mad at Ethan. They've been pissed ever since the femmes were down here, because their rehearsing woke them up. I tried to just say he had his girlfriend in town, but they weren't buying it. I guess they aren't as clueless as I thought. They said they've been watching all the different kids come in and out for the past couple of months. They told me I needed to evict Ethan or they would kick us all out.

This is so not cool. I know that the minute I tell Ethan he has to leave, he's gonna call everyone and tell them I'm a total square. I just left Ethan a note saying we need to have a house meeting tonight. We've never had one of those before, but it sounds like the sort of thing you're supposed to have if you're gonna kick out your roommate.

Date October 26, 2003

Ethan just knocked on my door and asked what's up with this house meeting shit. He seemed pretty awake and mostly sober, so I decided it was as good of time as any to spring the news on him. I thought he was going to be upset, but he was stoked. I guess he and Phoenix have been talking about him moving into her place. He said he'd be out by the end of the week.

Date: October 29, 2003
Security: Friends
Subject: I hate teenagers

Tonight I was walking down by the train tracks. The dogs had been alone most of the day, which I don't like to do, so I took them down to the park and played Frisbee with Cosmo for a long time. When we were coming back to the basement this group of fucking teenagers started to chase me. I had to pick Orbit up so that we could run faster. They were calling me a faggot and I barely got in with the door closed and locked. They stood there banging on it for a while before the upstairs neighbors got home. I think their car pulling into the driveway scared the idiots away. I just hope they don't come back, especially with Ethan already gone it's just me and the animals here.

Date: November 1, 2003
Security: Friends
Subject: Paradox

I keep trying to get everyone to use the right pronouns (ze/hir) for me and to understand that I'm not a fucking man. I don't know why it's so hard for everyone to understand. I'm so sick of having to explain that I'm more complicated than I look. Today I got the word 'PARADOX' tattooed right across my damn chest. For the next month I'm not going to be able to wear anything other than sports bras and a-shirts under my overalls and I'm looking forward to this tattoo being the first thing everyone sees.

Date: October 10, 2003

Last night was Griffin's top surgery benefit at The Hotel. Everyone was there, buying nasty beer and listening to some band from Olympia that had agreed to come down and play the benefit. Even though he lives at the Safety Net the benefit had to be at The Hotel because you can really only make money off of watery beer and that's not allowed in the house over there. Phoenix baked a cake that looked like tits and then Griffin got to do the honor of slicing it up with a big knife. We all paid a buck a slice. It wasn't very good.

The thing that pissed me off the most is that everyone kept making a big deal about me having this tattoo and not being able to bind. Everyone kept saying that I must feel really dysphoric and then they started talking about when was I going to have my top surgery and did I need help fundraising? It was just fucking assumed that of course this is what I'm going to do. At first I was telling people I didn't know, or whenever I could get the cash together, but by the end of the party I was just pissed and yelled in Griffin's face that I never was going to have the surgery. He asked if I was drunk, which made me even madder, because he knows I'm XXX and when I said that he said maybe it was time I left. I walked all the way home instead of waiting for the bus.

Date: October 11, 2003

Just earlier this week Sydney asked if I would be monogamous with him, which isn't something I'm normally into, but since I haven't been hooking up with anyone else for a little while, I figured why not? We were supposed to hook up tonight. He was going to come over after he got done bagging at the grocery store around ten and then spend the night. He called me at seven when he was on his dinner break and said we needed to talk. I was working on finishing up the last part of my zine and was just about to take the dogs out on a walk to the train tracks, so I asked if we could just talk when he came over. He said it was important we talk now. Turns out, he'd been on stockroom duty and ended up making out with this fag who works in the back. He said he was sorry.

Sydney is a different kind of guy. He didn't used to be a lesbian. On the phone he said he couldn't help himself. He said this guy was just there, and they had been sneaking beers out of the cooler and it just sorta happened. He started crying and I wanted to hang up on him and just be with the dogs. At least they never fuck me over like this. He said he was really sorry, but couldn't see me anymore. He started going on and on about how this whole tranny fag thing wasn't working out for him. He said he needed real men, real dick. I hung up.

The dogs and I took off to the park. I put Orbit in my messenger bag so we could walk faster but let him down when we got there. The three of us slid through the fence and walked along the train tracks for a while. I thought about the kids at The Hotel who travel all across the country by hopping into abandoned boxcars. I wanted to run away but didn't know how you figure out which way the train is going.

With my luck, I'd be trying to go to San Francisco and end up on the wrong train, stuck in Wyoming. I climbed up the ladder on the side of one of the parked boxcars so I could see the bridges stitching east and west Portland together. When I was a kid, my mom always told me bridges were dangerous because there could be an earthquake or a terrorist attack, and you could get stuck on one side and never be able to go home. Cosmo and Orbit had their front paws up on the first rung of the ladder and were barking for me to come down. I was supposed to do my shot tonight, but standing there I decided I didn't want to. I hadn't even realized I was thinking about quitting.

I climbed down from the train and we walked a little further down the tracks before crawling back through the fence. It was starting to get dark. I didn't want to be in the park much later and risk running into those boys again. When

I got home there was a message on the machine from Travis. Word travels fast and he already knew that things between Sydney and I were over, and wanted to check in on me.

When I called him back he started talking about how there were way better men out there for me. Then, he reminded me it was time to do my shot. We'd started this system of reminding each other of shot days, sorta like a phone tree, cuz otherwise one of us would forget and then get all moody and stuff. I said I wasn't doing my shot. At first he thought I mean that I hadn't gotten the prescription filled yet, and said to come over and borrow a shot out of his vial. I told him I had plenty of T, I just didn't think I wanted to do it anymore.

He didn't yell, but just started talking and not letting me cut in to explain myself. He said that he'd always had doubts about me. He said Hunter had been telling everyone that I wasn't really trans and I'd just been appropriating their experience. Travis said he'd been defending me, but that now it was clear that I was more disturbed than everyone thought. I tried to explain that T didn't

feel right but that didn't change who
I was. I got a trans sign tattooed on
my arm, for fuck's sake. This is my
community. I gave up everything for this.

I realized he wasn't listening when the
receiver started buzzing. He'd hung up on
me. It was late and I hadn't eaten all
day, but I wasn't hungry anymore. I fed
the dogs and went into the bathroom and
turned the taps on full blast, deciding
that maybe a bath would make me feel
better. I got into the tub and let the
hot water rush over me, closing my eyes
so I didn't have to see myself reflected
in the mirror. The phone rang. For a
second I hoped that I'd dreamed up the
call with Travis and jumped out of the
tub, slipping on the grimy linoleum,
and managing to pick up just before the
answering machine. It was Buck.

His Daddy hardly ever lets him talk to
me, so I was really excited to hear his
voice. I love him more than anyone. He's
the first person I ever met who was also
kicked out. Without him I don't know that
I would ever have found the rest of the
pack. I asked what was up, and he said
that he had just gotten off the phone

with Travis and was worried. He wanted to know if what he'd heard was true, that I was really quitting T.

I sat down on the floor not even caring that I was still naked and dripping wet from the bath. I told him that I was pretty sure I didn't want to do my shot anymore, and quickly followed it up with how I'd always be trans, this just wasn't my path. I tried to laugh it off and said that he knew I was genderqueer, and it wasn't that big of a deal.

He said it was a huge deal. He said that he didn't know me anymore. He said he couldn't trust me. He said that his Daddy was right, I was a bad influence, and that he didn't think we could be brothers anymore. I started crying, and was instantly embarrassed, but it didn't fucking matter because he'd already hung up. The phone didn't ring the rest of the night.

Acknowledgements:

I would like to offer my gratitude to the slumlords whose houses we rented, cheap copies, and long rainy Portland winters. To the punk bands and slam poets that toured to basement shows and other crusty venues and inspired us all. My thanks always to the gutterpunk leather kids of Portland, Oregon and Jacksonville, Florida that brought me out, especially Joey. To the daddies who left me broken and orphaned with boot shaped bruises across my heart. To the XXX kids and those who fought to grasp onto sobriety. For everyone who wrote the dangerous stories that fed me, and to those who lived lives so dangerous they could never put them to the page. A special thanks to Taylor K. for sending a nine-pound punk house time capsule right as I went into the final edits. Thank you for keeping the memories alive and being willing to spend years rubbing your scars against mine like the scratch of a match to ignite memory.

My sincere thanks to NYC subway delays, during which I wrote the majority of this novel in the Notes app on my iPhone, thus also thank you to Apple and the two MacBooks it took to get this book finished. Thanks to those brilliant tech people that created Scrivener, I can't imagine having organized and edited and reworked this novel without it.

Thank you to Alyshia Angel, Kay Barrett, Fureigh, Emily Millay Haddad, Sophia Lanza-Weil, Scott Turner Schofield, and Kit Yan for reading or giving feedback early drafts. My profound thanks to Elizabeth Anderson of Charis Books, Laura Antoniou, Bear Bergman, Ivan Coyote, Kimmie David of Bluestockings Books, Morty Diamond, Lee Harrington, William Johnson of Lambda Literary, Tom Leger, and Mamone of Riot Grrrl Ink for encouraging me to put this book out the right way, true to my DIY roots and not to let publishers tone down the leather and gender. To Mattilda who changed the ending. My thanks to the Sexual Minority Youth Resource Center of Portland Oregon, and the old days staff Zan, Tina and Melissa who gave us the space to grow ourselves up. Thank you to In Other Words Feminist Bookstore that gave me my first writing award, and everyone who sent trades and concealed cash through the United States Postal system for my early zines.

My gratitude to Linda for introducing me to all of my favorite authors and showing me that my stories deserved to be told. I wish you were here to see this book, To Kate Bornstein for getting me up onto the stage, for believing in me, and most of all for teaching me to harness the anger in my writing. To KD Diamond for combining my vague ideas with the hundreds of old pictures I sent and creating the most brilliant of covers. Thanks also to my big brother Matthew for loving me as your little brother no matter how many genders I've had, and encouraging me to write our story.

For Kestryl, my best friend, partner in life and art, who has showed me what a Daddy really is. Thank you for birthday cakes, teaching me to trust, and creating a world filled with magic where I could dream to create a book like this. Last but certainly not least, my humble thanks to Toni Amato of Write Here, Write Now. Uncle Toni, thank you for falling in love with Click, for encouraging me every step of the way, helping me to get my voice back, and editing every draft of this book from outline to the end. Without you Roving Pack would never have been born. Finders Keepers.

About the Author:

Sassafras Lowrey is an internationally award-winning storyteller, author, artist, and educator. Most recently ze received an Honorable Mention from the 2011 Astrea Lesbian Writers Fund. Sassafras is the editor of the two time American Library Association honored, and Lambda Literary Finalist Kicked Out anthology which brought together the voices of current and former homeless LGBTQ youth. Hir prose has been included in numerous anthologies and magazines. Sassafras regularly tours, lectures and facilitates LGBTQ storytelling workshops at colleges ,conference and community. Ze lives in Brooklyn with hir partner, dogs and kitties. To learn more about Sassafras and hir work, visit SassafrasLowrey.com

Lightning Source UK Ltd.
Milton Keynes UK
UKOW04f1831281217
315208UK00001B/68/P